# Half Windsor

Jaydon Azariah

PublishAmerica
Baltimore

First printing



ISBN: 1-4241-9734-1
PUBLISHED BY PUBLISHAMERICA, LLLP
www.publishamerica.com
Baltimore

To my beloved mother, Judy, and my dearest friend, Rachel, encouraging, and spurring me onward. I don't know that I could have finished this work without your persistence and patience. For all the words I know, I cannot describe how appreciative I am for your love.
J.A.

Thank you, Jesus! I shouldn't have been able to finish this book, but somehow, someway, You made sure I got it done. I trust you to be here for subsequent endeavors. Thanks to: my dad, Kenneth Bailey, for picking up the slack, and my mom, Judy Bailey, for cancelling that appointment so many years ago. I told you I'd make you proud. To Tiffany, Kenneth, Jermaine, Stephen, Karmen, Patricia, and Joshua for making me feel like I was always a cool brother, and always believing that I could do more than I ever thought I could. To my extended family, all the aunts and uncles, cousins and grandparents, blood-related or not, thanks to you all as well. M. Ross, thank you for all the insight, you helped more than you know. To R. Moss, thank you for pushing me and carrying me when I needed it. I told you I could write a book with only 100 words. To C. Crosswhite, M. Riep, and M. Thomason, thank you all for gracing my life with your presence. Mrs. Harlow, Mrs. McGeen, and Mr. Alander, thank you for teaching me how to write. To all the other people who I may have missed, I love you all. And to everyone who said I couldn't do it or that it couldn't be done, you gave me the courage to try. This is my first shot at this. I promise I'll get better. To you the reader, thank you for supporting my art. Without you, none of this is possible and I thank you sincerely.

# 1

I felt the condom break. That was exactly why I was abstinent, so I wouldn't have to worry about this sort of thing. The dread of eighteen years of abnegation started to set in. "Baby, is everything alright?" she moaned softly. By this point, I had already staggered into the bathroom. My head was spinning as the room kept getting smaller. They say that children are a gift from God, but as far as I'm concerned, all I want is the return policy. He can keep them. I don't want my own. At least I didn't want this woman to be their mother. The paranoia infused with despair washed over me. I felt my future slipping into the abyss between her divinely sculpted legs. No interviews on Oprah's couch, no developmental deal, no anything. Just suicide in Port Haven. Just a lonely, unfulfilled and otherwise boring life with some child that I didn't ask for on my back and in my wallet. I started to feel feverish as my face flushed.

"Jerry!" she yelled. Regret surged in, but by now it was too late. I couldn't believe this happened. Not only does she already have two kids, but she doesn't even remember my name. I had only known her for three months. Was there something in the nachos? The water? What's going on? My thoughts raced as the heat of shame began to overtake me. I started to feel woozy. The uncertainty in my knees was surpassed only by my light-headedness. As I fell to the ground, I heard her dialing 911. "Yeah, ya'll need ta hurry yup an' come through. My fiancée just fainted."

I groggily came to. Bianca was standing by my bed. She was infinitely supportive, and that was why I loved her. “Don’t scare me like that again!” she said in a nervous anger.

“Bianca? What are you doing here?” I mumbled. Before she could open her mouth to respond, the door opened.

“I called her. I told her you were helping me study for my anatomy final, and then you had an asthma attack.” It was Kymera. I couldn’t believe how treacherous she was. I wanted to say what really happened, but how could I without breaking Bianca’s heart? Even though it wasn’t my fault, she wouldn’t understand that.

”You are such a good friend!” Bianca exclaimed naively. I was getting sick. This woman was clearly a scam artist, and I, the only person who saw what was going on, was powerless to stop it. It was like watching a car wreck from the passenger seat. You know what’s going to happen; you just can’t do anything about it. She had only been in town three months, and already, the tranquility was being destroyed. Bianca’s phone rang.

“Don’t go anywhere, babe, I’m going to talk to mom really quick, okay?” she said, winking at me. She could make anything seem better. As soon as the door shut, Kymera was in my face.

“You gotta get well so you can sign that contract Saturday. We all want to see Port Haven’s favorite son do well, don’t we?” she said, rubbing her stomach.

“What are you talking about?” I asked. The fog was starting to lift and my mental strength was returning.

“Jerry, you didn’t really think I was that into you, did you? You are signing the creative production deal with Maclayne this week. I want my piece of the pie,” she said, reveling in her duplicity.

“My name is Jayson, you whore! You set me up! Piece of what pie?! There is only enough cake to feed me and my baby!” I yelled as the brightness of my future instantly darkened.

“No, no, no…you mean me and MY baby! As far as a set up, you bet I did. I didn’t know that the condom would break,” she said, feigning surprise in her voice. “…It was too easy. You were all over me, you animal. You couldn’t wait to get me into bed…” she said mockingly.

My anger began to consume me. I couldn't believe it. I never hurt anyone, what gave her a reason to come after me? I was genuinely trying to help a single mother study for an exam. I was simply trying to help her get a degree so she could make her life and her children's life better. Why would she go so far out of her way to destroy my world? Before I could ask, my fiancée walked back into the room.

"Your future mother-in-law says to get some rest. I'm going to call mom now," she said smiling at me. My agitation must have been visible, because she shifted her gaze to Kymera. "I think Jason needs to get some rest. You'll be at the signing ceremony on Saturday, right?" she asked.

"I'm pregnant with expectation, I wouldn't dare miss it," she said, grinning. Bianca walked her to the door, and gave her a hug.

"Thanks again, for saving his life. I don't know what I would do without him," she said softly.

"Girl, because he's important to you, he's important to me, n'yah mean? Girl if you eatin', I'm eatin' 'cause family takes care of itself, right?" Kymera said as she left. Bianca smiled at her again.

My mind raced. I had to tell her but how? Where to start? The truth, I would tell the truth.

"Were you able to get in touch with my mom?" I asked. I was stalling. I needed another moment to gain my composure, and to summon the strength to complete the task at hand.

"She didn't answer her phone, but I left her a message. Does she always turn her phone off at night?" Bianca inquired.

"You know my mom is always prone to doing something weird." I took a deep breath. This was going to be harder than I thought. I decided to just go for it. "Bianca, there's something you need to know…" I started.

"Jayson, don't worry about it. I know you love me.", what was normally an endearing statement only heightened the grief that I was feeling.

"Baby, that's not what I was going to say…Kymera didn't tell you the truth…" I stammered. Her eyes enlarged, the way they always did when she was eager to know something.

"What is there to lie about? Maybe your weight, Mr. Random Asthma Attack" she said as she playfully patted my stomach. "Even if she did have something to lie about, why would she? She has nothing to gain from that. You guys were studying, you had another attack, and she called the ambulance. Where's the lie in that? What, did my maid of honor slip you a roofie or something? Poor thing, the medicine is getting to you," she said, laughing sympathetically. Then almost if on cue, the IV in my arm started to take effect. I felt myself getting sick, and even though I tried my best to fight it, I felt like I was going lose to the battle, which in this case was synonymous with my lunch. Bianca left the room to get the nurse. The sheer magnitude of the situation in front of me made itself obvious, but I knew I had to tell Bianca, but I loved her entirely too much to risk losing her. If Kymera got to her before I did, I would lose the love of my life. I couldn't risk it.

The nurse came into the room, along with a janitor. They cleaned up my mess. As the nurse checked my vitals, Bianca came back in with a blanket, and a look that made me fall in love with her all over again. Our eyes met, and in that instant, I felt as though I could walk on water. I resolved to tell her in the morning. Anything that I said now would simply be dismissed on account of the medicine. Kymera would be exposed, even if it cost me everything.

I sat up, unable to sleep. I was having horrible hallucinations. One minute Kymera was by my bedside, grinning seductively at me. Then Father Potter was standing over me, pronouncing the last rites. I couldn't figure out what was real, and what wasn't. My mind had always been my greatest strength, and now it was proving to be my greatest liability.

The nurse, or at least the person I believed to be the nurse, came into the dimly lit room. The hallucinations were getting worse, because the person walking into the room looked like a gingerbread man. She rubbed my head and gave me a kiss on the cheek. I was still overcome with the burden that awaited me after dawn.

"Can I tell you something?" I asked, after looking over at where my fiancée lay to make sure she was still sleeping. The thin hospital blanket hadn't moved. "Sure!" the distorted voice said reassuringly. "You can tell me anything you feel like you need to get off of your chest."

Just as I was preparing to speak, my mother and Father Potter burst into the room.

"I came as soon as Bianca called me! Are you okay?!" my mom yelled, running to hug me.

"Yeah, mom, I'm fine…what are you doing here? I didn't expect you until the morning."

"Someone calls you saying your son's had a severe, life threatening asthma attack, and you aren't supposed to show up until the next day? What kind of mother do you think I am?" she almost sounded indignant.

"I wasn't talking about you. I was talking about him" I said motioning to Father Potter. He seemed caught off guard. It wasn't that I didn't want him there; I couldn't understand why he showed up with my mom instead of her showing up with Brock.

"My son, is there ever a point where having a servant of the Most High nearby is a bad idea?" he asked rhetorically. I couldn't argue with his logic. For a second there, I really did think this might be the end of the road for me. I couldn't lie, it was comforting to have him there, then again, it seemed like it was always good to have Father Potter around oneself. The nurse came into the room.

"Mr. Sullivant needs to get some rest," she said. My mother went over to give the still sleeping Bianca a kiss on the forehead, and blew me a kiss before she left the room. Father Potter bowed, slightly, his hands folded as though in prayer as he left the room. After checking on me for the last time, the nurse dimmed the lights and shut the door. As soon as the lock clicked, the full weight of my conundrum settled on me like a wet blanket. How was I going to tell her what happened? I mean it's not even like it was my fault, not something that I planned, I was taken advantage of, wasn't I? As emasculating as that must sound, that's the only way to accurately describe what happened to me. But how was I to explain that to Bianca? The only thing that I knew for certain was that I couldn't lose her, however based on what I was up against; I had no idea how I was going to keep her. I thought about the dream I had lived before tonight and dreaded the nightmare that I was going to wake up to. After what seemed like hours of self inflicted torture, I finally lapsed into a fitful repose.

# 2

"Mr. Washington, your grandmother is here, expedience please sir!" I called. A snarling thirteen year old slammed his locker shut, and then came in my direction, steadily attempting both hold his books and pull up his oversized jeans.

"Dawg, she ain't goin' nowhere," he growled in response.

"Bryan, we have been over this countless times. I am Mr. Sullivant. I am not your "dawg" nor am I anyone else's dog for that matter; Bryan, we have discussed this at length previously. Your grandmother may not currently be going anywhere, but judging by that gesture she's making, you may wish to make haste," I said correctively. He mumbled something inaudible as he walked past me "And don't show up here tomorrow unless you are wearing a belt!" I called out after him as he half ran, half walked to his grandmother's waiting minivan. The last child gone, I walked over to my desk and slumped down into my chair. The twelve hour days were beginning to take their toll. I stared at the mountain of paperwork that had yet to be filed. Tax forms, permission slips, church records, not to mention my own personal work that needed to be completed. It was going to be yet another long, lonely night. I started to pack up the most important papers, when I heard the door open slowly.

In stepped a woman that looked like the answer to every prayer I had ever prayed in my life. Every prayer and right down to the details. The fact that she showed up wearing a neatly pressed chocolate-colored business suit with a pink blouse underneath was in line with the same prayer. Perfect height, weight, even her hair length was exactly what I imagined when I was praying for the perfect woman.

"Hi! My name is Bianca, I'm the new administrator, is this the office?" the visitor asked. I felt myself about to choke on my words.

"Yes…um I mean no. I mean I can show you the way to the office, follow me," I sputtered. I led her through the halls until we got to Father Potter's office.

"Let me see if Father Potter is still here," I said as I moved towards the closed door.

"Oh, well I just spoke to him not ten minutes prior, and he assured me that he was still here," she coolly asserted.

"Oh…okay," I stammered. Then my poise, which had been mysteriously absent, flooded back to me.

"I'm sorry ma'am but I failed to introduce myself. My name is Jayson. Jayson Sullivant. Currently I am Father Potter's Administrative Assistant and Director of Community Outreach Initiatives, and you are?" I asked, attempting to get her name.

"Bianca Windsor. I don't have an official title yet, but for the mean time, here's my card," she said, extending the information to me. I extended my hand to shake hers as well as accept the document she was attempting to give me. As she clasped her hands in mine, our eyes met. It was one of those cliché, "magic moment" sort of things that people always talk about having. Just as I was losing myself in her big beautiful brown eyes, Father Potter materialized from beyond his locked door.

"Mind if I interrupt?" he asked.

"Not at all, Father," I replied. "Mrs. Windsor it was nice meeting you," I said, retreating back toward my classroom.

"That's Ms. Windsor, and it was nice meeting you as well," she said, smiling at me. I failed miserably at trying to suppress a smile.

"So you must be Ms. Windsor's great niece," Father Potter said to Bianca. Then turning to me, he said, "Jayson, be sure to have your mother give me a call either today or tomorrow. I tried to call her today, but no one is answering the telephone."

"I most certainly will," I replied. After packing up my things, I walked to the bus stop for the short ride to my mother's house, where I had parked my car. After about five minutes of waiting, a black Nissan Pathfinder pulled up beside me. "Mr. Sullivant?" the driver called. I looked over. It was Ms. Windsor.

"Yes?" I replied.

"Do you need a ride?" she asked, unconcerned with the traffic that she was effectively holding up. I didn't really need a ride, but it would have been stupid of me to pass it up coming from her. I climbed into the vehicle. She started driving slowly.

"So, where ya' headed?" she asked.

"Rock Canyon Drive" I replied.

"You're funny. You took that address of my card, didn't you?" she inquired incredulously.

"No, my mother lives on that street and that's where my car is parked," I replied.

"You're kidding! I'm renting a house on that street, and that's where I'm going to be for the next couple of months. No way!

"Uhh, apparently yes way," I replied dryly. She punched me playfully on the shoulder.

"Jayson, we are going to have a lot of fun. This could be the start of something beautiful," she said wistfully. I could only hope that she was right. We drove up the street until we reached my mother's house.

"Maybe we can work out some sort of car pool arrangement or something."

"Maybe, I work downtown during the day, but I'm sure we can think of something" I said.

"But you work out here at night right?" Bianca countered.

"Well, as of now, that decision is up to you. You're the boss, so I have to work from whatever position you put me in," I said innocently. As soon as the words were out of my mouth, I wished I could pull them back. Bianca smiled at me.

"Well for right now, I like the idea of having you behind me. A good leader is nothing with out a strong man behind her," she retorted as she smiled at me. It was just past innocuous, like there was something beneath it, but I was going to have to wait until later to find out just what that was exactly. Just as I was about to respond, I heard yelling followed by a loud crash from inside the house.

"Ms. Windsor—" I started.

"Bianca," she interrupted.

"Okay. Ms. Bianca, while I would love to stay and talk more, it sounds like my attention is required inside, so even though I would love to stay I have to go," I said while hastily gathering my effects.

"I understand. You should call me sometime…so we can set up some sort of car pool or something," she said as I climbed out of the gargantuan vehicle.

"Sure deal. I'll call you," I said, moving towards the house. She waved goodbye as she backed out of the driveway.

I fumbled with my keys as I heard yet another loud crash and more yelling. I finally got the door open. The scene in the front room was like something from a soap opera. Shards of glass littered the floor. I walked with a cautious expedience toward where I heard the commotion.

"How can you say you love me?!" my mother yelled as yet another plate flew across the living room, shattering against the wall. "No point in buying the cow if the milk is free huh?!" she yelled as yet another plate went flying. Brock could have only been narrowly avoiding impact. Even though his speed had diminished since his semi-pro playing days, his moves were still sound.

"Baby, what are you talking about? You know how I feel about you! I love you with all my heart!" Apparently the exercise was causing him to sober up quite a bit.

"Well then prove it! Let's set a wedding date!" Brock's face flushed. It was a scare tactic that my mom used, and it was devastatingly effective. Every time I had seen her use it, she wound up getting something out of Brock, or he made some concession for her. I wasn't really sure how it worked, but I knew the pattern was they fight, she threatens marriage, and he gives her whatever she wants. It was manipulative, but it worked. If there was anything I learned from my mother, it was the art of negotiating, and her first rule: you're likely to achieve your objective if the other party is under duress.

As bad as I felt for her, my mother was just as complicit in her own unhappiness as anyone else. I felt as though she could have helped her own situation if she had only made a conscious effort to do so. She had no real impetus to do so. She was living a pretty decent life as it was, so why mess that up? Brock's rigid definition of masculinity stipulated that he handle all the finances in the home. He seemed to feel as though that was doing enough right there. In fact, one of the things I heard him tell my mother more than anything was, "I show you how much I love you by going to work everyday," which was why they never got married.

My mom and Brock had been together for nearly seven years. He was playing minor league football, and tore his ACL. He needed somewhere to go for therapy, and my mom had just opened her shop. About a year later, his rehab was over, and the relationship had begun. They had been engaged for about three years now. My mom wanted a big showy wedding, Brock however, wanted no part of any such display. There had been two failed wedding attempts, each time Brock had called it off at the last minute. When my mom threatened to leave he simply offered an ornate gift of some sort to keep her around. It didn't make my mom look good, but who was I to judge? Besides, it didn't make me love her any less.

"Mom!" I called again.

"Jayson? I'm back here honey," she said, in a surprisingly calm voice. I made my way over the sea of broken plates. It looked like there was twenty dollars of plates on the floor. It doesn't sound like much until one considers that at most, my mother only paid fifty cents per plate at the craft store. As I went in Brock was hurriedly slipping out.

"Hey," I said to him as he passed me.

"Hey," he responded breathlessly. I had never seen someone look so excited to see me in my life.

"THIS ISN'T OVER!!" my mom yelled at Brock as the front door slammed shut. With glass shards crunching under my shoes, I made my way over to my mother and gave her a hug.

"Is everything alright? I asked her.

"Yeah, it will be. I just get tired of this halfway stuff, ya know? I deserve to be a wife, don't I?" she whined. I wasn't really sure if she was asking me or telling me.

"Either way it goes, you'll always be a phenomenal mom, regardless of what anyone says," I said, trying to find a positive point for her. As I took her hands in mine, I couldn't help but notice her engagement ring wasn't on. As big as it was, her without it was as noticeable as her without an arm and a leg, which was funny because that's about what it cost. I decided not to make a fuss about it.

"Awwww, I did raise you right. You staying for dinner or are you just getting your car?" she asked me.

"That depends on how late it is after I help you clean up this mess," I replied.

"Fair enough. I don't want to eat by myself. Brock won't be back until after the game goes off, probably down at the bar again. Oh well..." She opined. I honestly couldn't blame the guy, but I would almost always see things my mother's way. It wasn't so much that I was a momma's boy so much that it was she and I, we were a team. She had me at the ripe old age of fourteen. Here it all these years later and we were still running strong. It had been just she and I for the majority of that time. She didn't really start dating again until my junior year of high school. If there were other men, she never brought them around me. She was all I knew. All the manners, work ethic, every ounce of urbanity that was intrinsic to my personality was a function of something that I learned from her instruction. She had tried to mold me to be the best person possible.

After about twenty minutes of cleaning, the mess was manageable enough for my mother to handle with out my assistance. My mom had already started dinner before we started cleaning, but apparently she still needed a few items.

"Jay, I need you to go to the store and pick up some stuff to finish this off.," she requested, handing me a list with a few items scrawled on it. I always thought that if my mother hadn't had me, she should have been a doctor because if I hadn't been reading her writing for years, I was convinced that I wouldn't understand it. I guess having a certification in medical massage was as close as she felt she needed to get. I grabbed my keys and the list, and then made my way to my car.

I loved my car, a black, three year old Nissan 350Z. I got it from an auto auction last year for one third of the wholesale price. It was one of those love at first sight sort of things, and the first time I saw it, I knew I just couldn't leave it there. I put the manual transmission in gear, and raced off towards the store.

As I was gathering the last spices required for my mother's spaghetti, I noticed a woman down the aisle from me. I say noticed, when the phrase "was staring mindlessly at" or even "was drooling over" was probably more appropriate. Some women look just as good in a t-shirt and jeans as they do in a business suit, and from the view I had, I was sure she would look good wearing a habit. I strode towards her, not really sure of what I was going to say, but certain that I needed to say something. As I got closer, something about her seemed vaguely familiar. I got near enough to see that she was trying to decide on which brand of chocolate chip to use. My mouth started working before my brain did.

"You know if you put the chips in the microwave for ten seconds before you put them into your dough, they'll melt more evenly when you bake them" I said almost smoothly, considering how lame a line it was.

"So do you hit on all the girls in the spice aisle, or just the ones you work for?" the woman said as she turned to look me in the face. As luck would have it, it was Bianca. I was flabbergasted.

"Just the cute ones," I said, covering my surprise. She smiled.

"I thought that was you, but I wasn't sure. I see you've resorted to stalking me. You could have at least called me first," she joked. I blushed.

"I was having dinner with my mom, but I promise I was going to call you," I replied. It was true, I really had every intent of calling her, but I had only just gotten her number three hours prior.

"I know, I'm teasing you, lighten up, I can't fire you after hours," she said.

"You can't really fire a volunteer can you?" I asked. I worked for an advertising firm. I helped Father Potter just as a volunteer. I had no real business working in a parish. I wasn't even Catholic.

"Come again?" she asked, looking confused.

"That's just volunteer work. I'm a Junior Executive for Givend and Mosse Design," I said as we made our way to the checkout. She seemed moderately impressed.

"Why didn't you tell me that earlier? You passed up a chance to drop a name? I'm surprised. Most men would have a name like that tattooed on their tongue or something," she said.

"I'm not most men. Plus I can think of other things to do with the length of my tongue, not the least of which is scrawl "Givend and Mosse Design Junior Executive" on it. Besides, that's not what I want to do. I really want to write. That's just what I do when I'm not writing or performing," I said, trying to defer the newfound attention. We waited in line as the conversation continued.

"Perform what? Songs? Plays? Spoken Word?" she asked, seeming extremely interested.

"It's more spoken word than anything else, although I do try to write across all media. If it's literary art, I probably do it," I replied as I laid my items on the conveyor belt.

"That's cool. Are you any good?" she asked honestly. I hated questions like that, because I hate to brag about anything.

"I think so. I've had a couple pieces published, and I perform pretty regularly, so yeah, I think so," I answered as modestly as I could while swiping my Visa.

"Wow. I'd like to see that sometime," she said visibly intrigued. She paid for her items and then we walked slowly from the checkout to the parking lot. She stopped suddenly. "Shoot. My roommate isn't done at the mall yet. Well it was nice talking to you; I'm going to hang out here because my roommate has my truck," she said, sounding almost a little upset that the conversation had to end.

"If you'd like, I can drop you off. I still have to go back to my mother's house," I offered. She didn't hesitate.

"Let me call Quinn," she said. She followed me to my car while she dialed her roommate. I stopped in front of my car.

"I didn't figure you for the sports car type. I would have guessed you'd be driving a station wagon or something like that," Bianca jabbed.

"That is sooo cruel, a station wagon? You're just full of assumptions about me, huh?" I asked as I opened the door for her.

"Oh, quite the gentlemen aren't you?" she asked.

"My mother taught me well," I replied, shutting her door. I got in the car, stepped on the clutch, started the car, and we were on our way.

"Oooohhh, leather interior and it's a stick? I love it!" she said. "Okay, so why where are the bodies stashed at? You're married aren't you? Clearly you have to have a downside. Are you gay or something? This is just too good to be true," she blurted out. I laughed.

"I'm single, and straight. I got my feelings hurt pretty bad in college, and I decided that I'd devote myself to my work and helping the world and when it was time, she'd come along. The bodies however, are at the bottom of Lake Erie" I joked.

"College? How long ago was that for you? You don't seem that old," she asked.

"I graduated from Halos State two years ago. I'm twenty-four. I interned at Givend and Mosse, so when I got out, they wanted me on board. What about you, since we're asking so many questions?" I fired back.

"Ohkay, I'm twenty six, I have a Master's Degree in Education, specifically Administration—"

"So you want to be a principal? Are you serious?" I laughed.

"Yes, so what?!" she asked, with mock indignation.

"Nothing, I'm just saying, but to each his own, I guess. I'd try to get sent to your office every day," I answered playfully.

"Well I like working with kids. They deal with a lot and I like the thought that I might be helping them out," she said.

"Sounds pretty noble. So why work at the parish?" I asked. The connection wasn't immediately apparent to me.

"I need some sort of administrative experience, and my Great Aunt Ella said that the parish needed some help, so why not?" she explained.

"I see. That's admirable, the whole work your way up concept. A sister with a real work ethic, I love it. I guess I should be asking you where your bodies are. How is a woman like you single? Wait, you are single, right?" I asked, guardedly optimistic.

"I got tired of the frat boys and the wanna-be's. It's kind of the same thing you did, just devoted myself to my work and maybe he'll show up at my door when the time is right. In fact, you're here now," she said. I nearly choked on my own spit. She was cool and this was going unbelievably well, but I wasn't sure it was quite at that point just yet. She must have seen the effect her words had. "You need to lighten up a bit. I'm just messing with you. I was saying that you're here, at my door, as in this is my stop. You should really call me, because I would really love to go out with you. Soon," she said as she got out of the car.

"I will do just that," I said, smiling. I watched her walk into her house. It was half to make sure she got in okay and half because that was the best view I had seen in months. Corporate board offices typically offer little in the way of what I like to see. It's a boorish thing to say, but it's the truth. She waved as she walked into the house, and I pulled out of the driveway.

I raced up the street to my mother's house. What was ordinarily a twenty minute trip had taken nearly and hour to complete. As I pulled up, I noticed what I thought to be Father Potter's car on the street. I looked at my chronograph, which showed that it was about eight o'clock. I walked to the door, and after putting my key in the lock, I noticed that the chain on the door had been locked. Perplexed, I walked around and manually opened the garage door.

"Mom?!" I called. I could hear hushed voices coming from the back room. As I turned the corner I saw Father Potter in street clothes, sitting on the couch with my mom. The shock had to have been evident on my face. I knew that Brock and my mom were in counseling but for Father Potter to make a house call wasn't rare, but it was, as far as I knew, an unheard of occurrence for a simple counseling session. Father Potter in his typical fashion, sought to ease my relative discomfort before I had a chance to voice it.

"Hello son. I was just dropping of some literature for your parents to review. Also here are the activity plans for the shelter. While I trust Ms. Windsor's ability, you already know the ropes. You know the Fall Fundraiser is coming up soon, and we need a big turnout. I'm counting on you." I nodded in puzzled acceptance of my role. The Fall Fundraiser wasn't for another six months.

"I won't let you down Father," I replied.

"Good. Well I have to prepare a eulogy tonight, so I must make haste. May the peace of God be with you all." After the salutation, my mother walked him to the door, and let him out. She hesitated in turning around, probably because she could feel my eyes boring a hole in her back.

"What was that about mom?" I inquired.

"I'm tired of this nonsense. I'm leaving Brock, changing my name to Mary Margaret and joining a convent," she answered. I was unamused.

"Please be straight with me mom, what was that?" I replied dryly.

"It was exactly what it looked like—my marriage counselor brought over some literature and your mentor brought over some notes for a project that you are working on, notes that I suggest you review," she retorted as she turned to go up the stairs. The seething pot of questions that I had was beginning to boil over.

"Mom, what's going on? You don't seem very happy lately. I've never seen you and Brock fight like that before ever. Now you've got unusual guests at weird hours?" I asked. Her face flushed.

"What are you talking about?" she asked innocently.

"Why was Father Potter here so late?" I asked accusingly.

"Are you insinuating something between Father Potter and me? Jayson, that is ludicrous! Brock and I are working on our marriage. We are making progress and there's nothing more to discuss!" she said, seeming defensive.

"What marriage?! I never said anything about Brock. I simply asked what Father Potter was doing here. Are you sure there's nothing going on?" I asked again. My mother turned on the steps and sat down with her face in her hands.

"Okay Jason, you want the truth? Here it is: I'm in a marriage, no a relationship. A loveless relationship at that, and I can't stand it and I want, no I need more than that! All I really want is a little attention. At this point, I don't care where it comes from."

"But is this the best way to go about it?" I asked, sounding incredibly sympathetic for Brock. It's not that I cared about his feelings like that; I just wanted my mom to make a clean break.

"Jason, I have been engaged for three years. Not married, engaged. Don't you think I'm worth more than that?" She was crying at this point. I wasn't sure if she was still talking to me or imagining having this conversation with Brock.

"Mom, why don't you just tell him to leave?" I asked. I already knew the answer, but I wanted her to consider her options.

"You already know why I can't make him leave. We have a child together, and you need a father. I can't disrupt Sammie's life over this." I found myself at a loss for words. My mother's abnegation was admirable. Foolish, but admirable.

"Mom, I'm old enough to be a father, so I don't really need one at this point. You did a great job with me by yourself, so what makes you think you can't replicate that with Sammie? Are you ever going to make yourself happy? This man is single-handedly going to be your undoing!"

"No one ever asked me what I wanted; I've always tried to make the best decisions I could for you and now for your sister. Brock was the best alternative in a bad situation! What more do you want me to say Jason, huh? What more can I do?! My kids have a father, and there is a provider in my home. So what if I'm not one hundred percent happy all the time. Who ever is? Things are the way they are and there is nothing that you or I or anyone else can do about it, period!" she fired back. This issue was one of those ones that forced us out of the equals mentality and back into the mother-son roles that life had assigned us.

"Well, here's what you asked for. Where's Sammie at?" I asked, trying desperately to change the topic.

"She's over Jennifer's house," my mom answered. "Are you going to stay and eat?" she asked.

"Yes, ma'am," I replied. That was ingrained in me from the beginning of my conscious memory. Yes ma'am and no ma'am. Yes sir and no sir. I don't remember when it started; I just knew I did it.

I sat in the back room and waited until my mother brought dinner in to me. The two of us ate in silence. Not because of sullen feelings, but because when it was time to eat, it was time to eat. After I finished my meal, I gave my mother a kiss on the cheek, and headed to my car for the half hour drive to my apartment in the city.

# 3

I sat up. The clock on the wall showed that it was only a quarter past one. I looked over to where Bianca had been sleeping. I didn't see her. A seemingly clairvoyant voice from the opposite corner of the room spoke.

"I told her to go home. We've got a busy weekend ahead of us and she needs to be at full strength. Besides I don't think the things you are dealing with are things that she can help you with." It was Father Potter. "Do you want to talk about it?" he asked.

"Father, I don't know where to begin. I'm still not really sure what happened," I said.

"Allow me to help you. I know that you didn't have an asthmatic episode. That IV in your arm is Dantrolene, it's a treatment for ecstasy. I read your chart. With as many hospitals as I've been in over the years, I've learned a few things," he said insightfully.

"I just don't understand why she would do that to me. The money isn't important; it's the fact that she would jeopardize my happiness for her greed. It just doesn't make sense," I surmised.

"Doesn't it, though? Jayson, it's called greed, not compassion, not consideration, greed. People make this compromise all the time. Jeopardizing someone else's happiness for their own or asking someone to give up some component of their happiness for the benefit of someone else. That is the very nature of humanity. May I share a story with you?" he asked. I nodded in approval.

"I wasn't always going to be a priest. In fact, there was a point where becoming a Man of the Cloth was the furthest thing from my mind. My mother died when I was very young, and so it was only my father and I. He was a simple man, spent everyday of his adult life down in the coal mine. Sun up to sun down. He wanted a better life for my brother and I and more accurately, he wanted us to help others in a way that he felt he couldn't. My brother Charles and I both wanted to be in a band. It was my father's dream for us to become priests. Charles was having no part of the priesthood. Left as soon as he was sixteen. So that left just my father and I. He did everything that he could while I was growing up to get me to think about it. Time passed and while it had weighed on my mind, I had no reason to give up my world. While it displeased my father, I had everything that I wanted. I was dating a beautiful young woman who I loved dearly. We were young and in love and in fact, we were engaged. Things could not have been more beautiful. Then my father fell ill with cancer. Years in the mines had finally taken their toll. He pleaded with me to enter the priesthood. I didn't want to. Not even in the least bit. But with all the sacrifices he made for me, how could I tell him no? How could I tell her I was leaving our perfect world? I was torn. They were the most important people in my world, and I was going to devastate one of them."

"I see which choice you made, but how Father, how did you come to that conclusion?" I asked impatiently.

"That is the point I seek to explain to you now. I thought, perhaps foolishly, that if I went into the Priesthood, it might somehow give my father a renewed vigor. I chose his life over ours. A decision I wish I had reconsidered. I had already given my word to my father, and I felt somehow that my entering seminary was the reason for his cancer going into remission. She and I fought bitterly over the whole issue. The week before I was set to leave for seminary, we stopped talking altogether. Then after I had been gone about a month or so, I got two phone calls. My ex-fiancée was pregnant. Then one hour later, it was the hospital. My father was dead. Both on the third Saturday in

September, historically, the date of the Fall Fundraiser," he said solemnly. I sat transfixed. I thought I knew this man as well as humanly possible, and here was this whole chapter that I had no idea about. While I appreciated the story, I still wasn't any clearer on how to handle my situation. Sensing my confusion, Father Potter spoke again. "Jayson, the point that I'm trying to make is this: The only way to handle an issue of this magnitude, is simply to do it. Don't worry about the ramifications until they make themselves evident. You know how to tell her. It's simply the matter of do you want to deal with the consequences. You know she deserves the truth, regardless of how she elects to deal with it; all you can do is provide the truth, and hope she sees it for what it is. Don't lie to her, don't try and cover it up. Just talk to her plainly and I assure you, things will work out fine. Even if things don't go the way you plan, they always go the way they are supposed to go." I was inspired, even if still a little afraid. There was still one thing I wanted to know.

"So what happened to your fiancée?" I asked as he got up to leave.

"We stopped talking after a few months. I haven't spoken to her in years at this point."

"And the child?" I asked, pushing for as much information as I could get.

"I've never been introduced to my son as his father," he said, looking at the ground. "That's one of the things I'm most ashamed of in my life. But with all the accusations having been levied against the church, I didn't think it wise to make that sort of announcement. I put the energy that I would have spent on him into trying to guide you, so I guess in a way, he's you. All the fishing trips, the extra effort to make sure you reached all your goals. You may not have known your father, but I wanted you to never feel as though you didn't have one, much as I never felt I didn't have a son. In my mind you are at least as much a reflection of me as he could ever be," he said lovingly. It was a reassuring statement. He gathered his things and moved towards the door.

"Thank you for the counsel, Father," I said.

"Not a problem, son. Get some rest, and don't forget what I said," he admonished. The clock on the wall showed a quarter to two, and I started to feel sleepy again. Just as my eyes started to close, I thought I saw Bianca walk back into the room. Before I could figure it out, I was asleep.

# 4

I waited a full two days to call Bianca for the first time. It didn't really matter because I still saw her everyday at the Beacon, so any conversation we could have had at night we had in the twenty minute car ride from her house to the Beacon. Still there is a difference between office interaction and the after hours conversation. I had decided to invite her to Café Vive , a local coffee house, where I performed every other week or so. Since Friday was open mic night, I decided that we going to go on Friday. It just made it easy on me. That however, was twenty four hours away. I still had to get through today, a task that was proving much easier said than done. I was helping the children complete supplemental homework and I came across something that shocked me. Bryan Washington, by far the most notorious student, had aced the pre-algebra exam I had given a few days prior. At present he was busy trying to con some of the less observant children out of tomorrow's lunch money. He had so much talent, but so little direction.

"Mr. Washington, a word please!" I called. The smile on his face disappeared.

"Man what?!" he barked.

"Try "Yes Mr. Sullivant?" I spoke to you with respect, did I not? Will you afford me the same decency?" I asked. His eyes rolled heavenward.

"Yes Mr. Sullivant? How may I help you Mr. Sullivant? What is you on my balls for this time Mr. Sullivant?" he asked in a mock female voice. In the six months of our interactions, I had grown callous to his crassness.

"Testicles, Mr. Washington. The organs you are making reference to are called testicles. If you are going to be disrespectful, at least be accurate," I replied. If it took embarrassing myself to get through to him, that's what I was going to do. I could tell it worked because his face was as flushed as it could be. "I called you up here because you got the highest score on the pre-algebra test," I said as I handed him his perfect paper. He tried initially to suppress a smile, then gave the effort up and allowed himself to enjoy the moment. Then he stopped.

"You mean I did better than Jonathan?" he asked as he pointed to the routine high scorer.

"Yes, even better than Mr. Lee," I replied.

"Yeeeahh Boooiiee!! Dat boy got dem numbahs on lock, ya dig?" he said, jumping around excitedly. As much as I wanted to allow him his moment of rapture, I had to stop him.

"Mr. Washington! What is the class rule for celebrating?!" I asked. He instantly stopped jumping.

"Only losers are surprised when they win. Winners expect to win. It is not a surprise to us, so we smile and prepare to win again," he said dryly. I hated to do it, but I had to be uniform.

Six o'clock came, shortly after all the other children were gone. Bryan was still waiting on his ride at six fifteen. Bianca and I had driven separately today, because she had to take Quinn to the mall, which I suspect meant she was gathering clothes for tomorrow night. I walked to Bryan.

"Hey, where's your grandmother?" I asked.

"Granny's sick. She went to the hospital this morning. I'm waitin' on my sister's boyfriend, Lil' D'easy. He gon come scoop me," he said. The red flag in my head went up.

"Lit-tle Dee-Eazy?" I asked, enunciating every sound.

"Naw, Lil D'easy. His real name Da'Rell, bu e'ry since he got dat new burnah, cats been callin' him 'nat. He gotta Desert Eagle, n'amsayn? Dat' mean he got a D'easy. Mr. Sullivant, where is you from dude?" he asked incredulously. I was beside myself.

"You mean a Desert Eagle, as in the firearm?" I asked in disbelief. This child was flirting with disaster. This program was the only thing keeping him out of juvenile detention. I couldn't let that happen. He had far too much promise.

"I tell you what. I'll take you home," I said. I called Father Potter to inform him of the change and to have him call the Bryan's sister Brittany. Father Potter gave his word that he would handle the situation for me. I walked over to Bryan. "You ready man?" I asked.

"Fo sho, fo sho," he replied. I shot him a corrective glance.

"Yes, I am ready" he said preempting my vocalization. He followed me outside and began walking toward's Father Potter's restored 1975 Lincoln Continental.

"Yeah, see dis sum'in like what Andre and Vince be pushin, 'cept fa dat got a Bonneville," he said grabbing Father Potter's doorhandle. I wouldn't have been caught dead in Father Potter's car and I laughed quietly to myself as I hit the unlock button on my key fob. Bryan's jaw dropped.

"Dang!! Mr. Sullivant you is a D-Boy! This ride is sooo tight!!" he exclaimed. I decided to let him have that one.

"If d-boy stands for Design Junior Executive, then sure. This is all legal in here sir," I explained as we got in the car. Just before I started the engine, my phone rang. It was Brittany.

"Ay-yo, dis mistuh Sullivant?" the voice asked.

"Speaking," I replied.

"Ay, do you think he cud jus stay wit chu ta night? I'm finna go up to da haspitell an' chek on my granmahl," she asked. I didn't really know how to say no to this one, and considering everything I had to do, I needed to say no.

"Uh…uh…okay," I stammered.

"Thanks, bye" the phone went quiet before I could voice my objection. I looked over at Bryan, who seemed to know what exactly was going on.

"D'easy must be coming through tonight. Man it's cool Mr. Sullivant, I'll just walk home," he said dejectedly.

"No, it's fine. You're just going to have to go run some errands with me. Is that okay?" I asked him.

"Man, it's whatever," he replied as I put the car in gear.

I turned up the radio, which I had left on the oldies channel. I was willing to change to something that I thought was more his speed, until I saw him mouthing the words to Archie Bell and the Drells' "Tighten Up."

"What do you know about that?!" I asked. He smiled.

"Man, granny only bumps the oldies. All day e'eryday, that's all I know" he responded. I was surprised. You would have never guessed from his demeanor that was what he was listening to on a regular basis. I couldn't understand why no one had ever taken a look at the potential that this kid possessed. I was notorious for picking up pet causes. I was determined not to allow this child to fall through the cracks. I realized that I couldn't save them all, but I could at least save this one.

"Are you hungry at all?" I asked. I wasn't really sure of how to handle kids at length. I mean I only dealt with them for two and a half hours per day, and there was rarely any feeding involved on my end. I just made sure they didn't kill each other, and sent them home after their parents got off of work. Plus Father Potter was only one hundred feet away at any point. This was a whole new ball of wax. I had never tried it before, but I figured I could handle it.

"Dawg, I'm starving'!" he exclaimed.

"Well, what do you want to eat? We can eat at the mall or we can get something on the way, it's your pick," I said.

"Well, which mall is we goin' to? 'Cause if we goin to LaBrea, it's dis bad fee up at da Chik-Fil-A dat I been tryn ta get at. But if we goin ova ta Rivahdale, din is dis female at deh lilluhl Greek spot dats feelin me," he explained. My eyes had crossed after the word "LaBrea."

"Well, first off, we aren't going to either place; we're going to Crescent Hills. Secondly, I know what we'll do for dinner. Thirdly, I didn't understand one word of what you just said. Where in the world did you learn to speak?" I said, clearly sounding exasperated. I had heard him talk on a regular basis, but that sentence was beyond my tolerance. He looked slightly embarrassed.

"Man, Mista Sullivant, dat's just how I talk. Dat's how e'rybody talks," he offered in his own defense. I decided not to beat a dead horse.

"We'll have to work on that. If you're going to be associated with me, you're going to have to get that together. You know what. I'll just go to the mall tomorrow. Have you ever had Casa D' Lorenzo?" I asked. His face soured.

"Dat boughie-ass Mexican joint?!" he asked. The indignation flashed across my face. He instantly reconsidered his words.

"The expensive Mexican place? Man, naw. Granny says if they don't take Ghetto Visa, we can't eat there either," he said solemnly. I was momentarily perplexed.

"Ghetto Visa…" I mumbled. I thought it was inaudible.

"Yeah, da food stamp card. We call it the Ghetto Visa. If you going grocery shopping, it's everywhere you want to be," he said in a mock commercial voice. I worked with everything I had to suppress a chuckle. I remembered those days. Mom struggled for a while. I didn't stop getting free lunch in school up until my sophomore year of high school. I knew all about food stamps. The ghetto visa concept was new to me though.

"Well no ghetto visa tonight. Casa D' Lorenzo it is then?" I asked. He was working to hide his excitement, but I could see it seeping out of his face. A smile was leaking out from behind the clay mask that comprised his hardened exterior. We drove to the restaurant.

The one thing I had forgotten about teenagers is that they consume massive quantities of everything. Food, money, time on telephones, toilet tissue. Everything. Bryan had to have eaten nearly thirty-five dollars worth of food by himself. I couldn't eat thirty dollars worth of food from there over the course of two days. He leaned back from the table, obviously completely satisfied.

"Was it good?" I asked him, expectant of the answer.

"Dawg, dat was da best Mexican food I eva had. Usually Brittany just throws one of those seasoning packets on a cut up hamburger or something. This joint had all kind of stuff. Dey ain't ever gone buhleave dis," he said, smiling. "Thank you, Mistah Sullivant," he said.

"You are most certainly welcome. Let's play a game. What do you think the total bill is going to be including the tip? I think it's going to be fifty seven dollars and thirty six cents. What do you think?" I asked him. He carefully surveyed the table.

"You ate maybe a third less than I did. I've got six dishes ova here an yoo only got foe', not countin da forks an stuff. I think I ate about thirty dollars worth so that means you wouda only ate about twenty dollars worth. I was keeping track by the menu, so everything should be aroun' fitty dollas. If I'm right den yousa lame tipper, 'cause seven dollas an thirty six cent is less den fiteen percent. My sister says that most cats tip about fiteen percent, which fa you right now is seven dollas an' fitty cent. If you want baby girl ta think you cool, you need to break her off a full ten dollas, dat uh be uh twenny pacent tip. Shoot, shawty bangin too, if I waz yoo I be tryn ta giv hah uh really big tip, n'yamean?" he said, crassly intimating at intercourse. I ignored the end of his statement in favor of the brilliance that he displayed right there. Did he just do all that in his head?! I was bright, but coming from him, I was shocked. I didn't want to show my surprise.

"So what's your guess?" I asked.

"It don't matter, either way it goes, yoo getting ready to drop 'bout sixty dollas, but if you beggin' me ta play, I'uhl say forty nine dollas and sixty-seven cent," he said as he leaned back confidently in his chair. The waitress brought the bill around. It was forty-nine dollars and sixty-six cents.

I had never in my life seen some one get within a penny. All the dates, all the times I had eaten out, not once. The girl I dated in college gotten within seven cents once. I had once gotten within a dime. Never had I seen that before. I handed him the check. His face lit up.

"I told chu main, dat boi got dem numbahs on lock. Clink-clink. Locked DOWN!" he said triumphantly. I laid sixty dollars in the payment booklet and motioned for Bryan to follow me out of the restaurant.

The meal took its toll on Bryan. I opened the sunroof, and the combination of the night air, the large meal, the soft jazz flowing from the speakers and the steady, gentle hum of the engine lulled him to sleep not five minutes into the half hour trip to my apartment.

# 5

"Jayson! Jayson, wake up! I need to talk to you!" Bianca said, nudging me out of my sleep. I bolted upright. Had she found what happened?

"Yes?" I asked nervously.

"What the hell is this?!" she asked furiously. She was holding the ripped condom. I felt my heart stop, and instantly, I died. My spirit literally began to float away from my body, just like in one of those Tom & Jerry cartoons. I started floating upwards toward heaven. She would have killed me anyway, so this at least got her off the hook. I floated up to the Pearly Gates. St. Peter looked at me, bewildered.

"Jayson Sullivant?! I don't have you scheduled for at least another fifty years," he said, checking the record book.

"If I'm early, can you tell me when I'm supposed to show up?" I asked, trying to get heads up. St. Peter shook his head.

"Sorry sir I can't. Company policy," he said, pointing towards the Throne. "What are you doing here?" he asked. I pointed to my lifeless physical form.

"My fiancée," I replied.

"Sheesh" He remarked. "Bianca's a real fire starter, huh?" he asked.

"Oh yes, all that and then some. Tell the Boss He did a phenomenal job creating her. I'm really going to miss her, but I'm safer here. So how do I go about getting in?" I asked.

"Considering you aren't supposed to be here yet, I'm going to have to make a few phone calls to see if we can get you in early. I can't send you back down there into that. It just wouldn't be right," he said protectively. He walked over to a desk and picked up a phone and started dialing a number. About midway through, a look of sheer terror seized his face Peter's face. He ran inside the Gates and locked them I began to panic.

"What does that mean?!" I asked, grabbing the gates.

"It means RUN!!" he yelled as he pointed behind me. A shadow began to envelope me. I turned around. To my horror, a giant hand eclipsed the sun as it reached for me. Bianca's giant hand. Her arm looked like a Stretch Armstrong doll. I tried in vain to run. She grabbed me by the foot.

"It's not going to be that easy! You are going to explain this!" she yelled. The hand had grabbed me by the leg and pulled me back to earth and into my body. When I came to, she was still sitting there and was still holding the condom condemningly in front of my face. "WHY JAYSON?! WHY?! SHE WAS GOOD ENOUGH BUT I WASN'T?!!" she yelled.

I awoke in a cold sweat. Bianca was sitting on the edge of my bed. "Poor baby! The medicine must be tearin' you up inside." She patted my forehead. "Don't tell the nurses, but I brought you some Sprite," she said, handing me a cold bottle of the beverage. I smiled weakly, thanking her as I unscrewed the lid.

"When I get out of here, do you want to go look at rings again?" I asked her. While it was understood that we were moving towards marriage, I hadn't actually proposed yet. Call it a flair for the dramatic; combined with the stress of the contract with Maclayne, I just didn't have the time to plan it the way she deserved. It was the most important thing I had to do. I just had to do it correctly.

"Don't worry about that. I just want you to feel better," she said, deferring the issue. I looked at the wall clock. It was just moments before three a.m. I was filling up with dread. At some point, I was going to have to tell her.

" Bianca, you know I love you right?" I started.

"And I love you left," she responded. I forgot she was notorious for bad jokes.

"That was so terrible! I guess I'm going to have to bring comedy to the marriage, because your jokes are always so LAME!" I said. Even from my weakened state I recognized her bad humor.

"The only thing comedic about you is your style. Who wears a shirt, tie and jeans? To work no less?!" She laughed.

"Your future husband," I replied I took a deep breath, and motioned for her to give me a hug. She leaned in compliantly.

"I love you. No matter what anyone says, no matter how bad things may seem, I love you Bianca Denise Windsor," I said as I squeezed her tightly.

"I love you too Jayson…Sullivant." Just then, the door popped open.

"Hey Bianca, Ms. Sullivant needs to talk to you for a second about something for the wedding. I'll stay with him for a second.", the voice said. Bianca lifted her head up. The figure filling the door was none other than Kymera. Bianca got up reluctantly and went to the door.

"I'll be right back sweetheart," she said. As soon as the door shut, Kymera was by my bed.

"How you holdin' up baby?" she asked me as she ran her finger down my cheek.

"Will you please just go back to hell and leave me and my life alone? I'm about to marry a phenomenal woman, and try to have a good life. I never did anything to you, why are you trying so hard to disrupt my life?" I asked, almost pleading for her to leave me alone. She abruptly got up, went over to the door, adjusted the blinds, and locked the door. She began to expose her breasts as she sauntered back to the bed and straddled me. I kicked as hard as I could, but the way my body was positioned, in addition to my medicated state, rendered my attempts at self defense futile at best. She grabbed my wrists and put my hands on her now exposed breasts. While ordinarily I could have easily removed her, the IV in my vein limited my range of motion significantly.

"Don't those feel good Jerry? Go ahead, squeeze them again, just like you did earlier," she said. I prayed for Bianca to come back. Anyone. I just wanted her gone. I started looking for the call button. I couldn't let this happen twice in one night.

"GET OFF OF ME!" I yelled. Moments later, I heard the door handle jiggle.

"Kymera! Come open the door!" It was Bianca. Kymera adjusted her shirt, and climbed off of me, and walked back over to the door.

"Oh, I'm sorry, it must have locked on its own," she said to the exasperated Bianca.

"I'm sure of it. Where was Ms. Sullivant at? I didn't see her," Bianca asked.

"Maybe the skank went home," Kymera said crudely. I was instantly incensed.

"That is my mother you are talking about!!" I yelled.

"I mean that in the playful way that all women refer to each other, you know, same way ya'll fellas call each other dog. Don't worry about it," she explained.

"Get out. GET OUT NOW!" I yelled. A nurse quickly arrived at the door. Assessing the situation, she identified Kymera as the agitator.

"Ma'am, visiting hours have long been over. I'm going to have to ask you to leave," she dictated, placing a hand on Kymera's shoulder to guide her out. I was instantly relieved.

"Thank you so very much," I said, feeling placated. Bianca walked back in to the room.

"That girl is a trip." Then she looked at my disarrayed blankets. "Is everything alright?" she asked suspiciously.

"Yes, ev.ev…everything is cool," I stammered. Then curiosity got the better of me. "Bianca, what was she doing here?" I asked. Bianca looked puzzled.

"I have no idea," she answered. We sat there quietly for a moment. The beauty of our love was that we could sit together silently and say more with our silence than most people could reading from an open dictionary. Then I saw an idea flash in her eyes.

"Scoot over!" she said, pushing me towards the IV. I complied as she crawled up the bed and rested her head on my chest. It was the best thing I had felt inside of the last twenty-four hours. The way I felt in that moment was how I wanted to feel forever, loved by someone that I loved. I slowly ran my fingers through her long, soft auburn hair as I proceeded to give her a kiss on the forehead. She looked up at me with her warm, adorable brown eyes. "What was that for?" she asked.

"It was because I love you Mrs. Sullivant," I said softly. She tilted her head to kiss me on the lips.

"I love you too, Mr. Windsor," she said, grinning at me.

"Here you go with that mess again!" I said. She was unfazed.

"You should think about it. Jayson Windsor has a much nicer ring to it than Jayson Sullivant. It sounds noble. You don't like it because it's my last name. It's okay for a man to take a woman's name, don't be so old fashioned. Or maybe we could try the hyphenated thing. Bianca Windsor-Sullivant. Doesn't sound so terrible does it?" she asked. Then she stuck out her left arm up in the air, and wiggled her ring finger, apparently admiring an imaginary engagement ring.

"Whatever it takes to get you to the altar is what I'm willing to do," I replied. I lay there, still running my fingers through her hair, lost in the beauty of the moment. Here I was at my absolute worst, and this woman was ecstatic about spending her life with me. It was going to be hard for me to say what I had to say to her, but I was confident that we would be okay. I looked down. Bianca had fallen asleep. Playing in her hair always relaxed her to the point of fatigue. I yawned, and smiled as I prepared to follow suit.

# 6

"Hello, this is Bryan Washington's uncle. He will be absent from classes today...Yes, ma'am. That's correct I am taking him to work with me today...Givend and Mosse Design...Yes really...Yes, I am single...I'm flattered but I really shouldn't. I can give you my extension at the office in case you need to verify anything else...304-6888 extension 513...Have a nice day...okay you as well...Goodbye," I said as I hung up the phone. I wasn't going to be able to get him to school and get to work on time, so I decided to be a little selfish. Plus I figured that he might gain something from seeing me in action. I went into the living room where he was sleeping and turned on the morning news. As soon as the television turned on, Bryan sat up.

"What was that?!" he asked nervously. He looked around the room in a panic.

"Relax man, it's just the t.v. It's time to get up anyway," I said.

"Man, I don't wanna go ta school!" he moaned.

"Okay, fine. You don't have to go. But if you don't go to school, you have to go to work," I informed him. He looked confused.

"But I ain't old enough to get a job," he answered.

"Okay, well then you can work for me. Go ahead and make yourself some breakfast, and I'll see if I have anything near your size to wear," I instructed. Bryan was relatively close to my size, so finding clothes for him shouldn't have been terribly difficult. I decided I'd give him some measure of control over the whole process. I took a quick shower, and proceeded to get myself dressed. Prior to tying my tie, I took a quick peek in on Bryan to see how he was doing with breakfast. He was sitting there watching BET while effectively killing my dream of having some Crunchberries for breakfast. I picked up the remote and turned back to the news. Bryan whipped around, spilling a couple drops of reddish colored milk on his white t-shirt.

"Maun watchu chang da channuhl fo'?" he asked with a mouthful of cereal. "Luda's new video was finna c'mon!" he shouted.

"Luda would rather you watch the news," I said. As far as I knew, I was lying, but he couldn't prove it. "Besides you need to get ready to go. Not only do you need a shower, you can't wear that into the office," I said. "Shirts and ties my friend, shirts and ties," he groaned.

"Man mistah Sullivant, ayaint on dat shirt and tie stuff. What's wrong with what I got on? I'm good in anybody hood!" he replied. Before I could answer, a special alert flashed on the screen. I turned up the volume. The newscaster started talking:

"A shooting occurred last night near the Riverdale Shopping Complex. Suspect is described as a black male, between sixteen and twenty years old, between five feet nine inches and six feet tall, and believed to weigh between one hundred and seventy five to two hundred pounds. He was last seen wearing a white t-shirt, baggy blue jeans and white sneakers. Police are asking for anyone with information to call the anonymous tipline." I turned the television down. That was exactly what Bryan was wearing.

"Now do you see why you need to put on a shirt and tie?" I asked.

"Naw man, 'cause dat description cuda been anybody. I don't undastand wat yo' point is. Dude cuda bin you," he reasoned. I masked my exasperation.

"Physically, yes he could have been, but you see I've lessened the chances of my being suspected by looking different. Bryan, if you already fit the profile, do you think it wise to also wear the uniform? How many people do you know dress like that description?" I asked.

"E'rybody. Matta uh fack, you da only pursun I know that don't, but that don't make dem guilty ov nothin', an it don't make you innnacent of e'erything. Most da time, da boys just be sweatin us fo no reason," he complained.

"Maybe not, but what are you doing when "da boys be sweatin' you?"" I asked.

"Man, nuttin, we just be chillin on the block, prolly spittin sum bars or tryna get at da fees dat be walkin around. Don't nobody be doin' nothin wrong, n'yamean? An din outta nowhere, here come da boys," he explained.

"I believe you, but you have to realize something. Not all police officers are bad—" I started.

"Man, you sound like a D.A.R.E. commercial or sum'in," he interrupted. I held up a hand.

"Let me finish. That doesn't mean that they are all good either. But they are all human, and like it or not humans judge, and they make mistakes. Bryan, a lot of times, they aren't looking for the right one, they are looking for anyone. I've been pulled over before because I "fit the description." I've never even had a parking ticket, much less a real infraction. So if it can happen to me, as straight laced as I am, what makes you think that it won't happen to someone who is wearing the exact same thing that the suspect was wearing? Bryan, to the system, we all look alike. You and I and any other black male you can think of, we all look the same. It may not be fair, but it is the system. You don't have to be guilty in order to look like someone who is. You have to put yourself in the best possible position. That means avoiding those situations where you put your life or liberty into jeopardy. I'm not saying you have to wear a shirt and tie all the time, I'm just saying you need to understand what you're up against. Sometimes the system just wants its pound of flesh, and it doesn't care where it comes from. I say if it doesn't have to come from you, why should you give it up?" I said. Bryan was taking it all in, though I wasn't sure of the depth of the effect that it had on him.

"A pounda flesh? What judges an nem is some cannonballs?" he asked.

"First off, the word is cannibal. Secondly what I mean by that is that sometimes people just want to see someone suffer for a crime, even if that person is innocent. That doesn't mean that everyone in prison is innocent, but it doesn't mean that they are all guilty either. You have to be extremely careful. Realize how precious a commodity you are and act accordingly," I replied.

"Ayaint neva thought of it like that," he said stoically. I looked at my watch.

"Get in the shower man! We are going to mess around and be late!" I ordered. He hopped up and went into the bathroom. I had laid out a couple of pairs of slacks and a few shirts for him to choose from. He left the bathroom and made his way to my bedroom while I sat in the front room watching the morning market report. He materialized in the room a few moments later. He picked out a matching set, but he had yet to fasten his tie.

"You gotta get your tie together man," I instructed as I began to gather my effects. Having pulled everything together, I went into the kitchen to get my keys. When I came back, I burst into full blown laughter. Bryan had tied his tie the same way that one would tie a pair of shoestrings. The pink and lavender striped tie hung from his neck like the world's worst bowtie. My laughter had caused him visible chagrin.

"Man, ain't nobody eva taught me how ta tie no tie," he explained.

"Sir, no one has ever taught me how to properly tie a tie," I corrected. I looked at my watch. We still had a few moments before we absolutely had to leave.

"Man you know what I mean," he responded.

"We're going to fix that today. I'm going to show you how to tie a tie," I declared. I undid his travesty, and retied it neatly for him. "This knot is called a four-in-hand. It's a very basic knot," I explained as I took it apart to show him slowly. After retying the tie on his own he looked dissatisfied.

"Man why is my knot all dinky and yours is all big? How I get mines to look like that?" he asked. I laughed.

"That's because we have two different knots. Mine is called a Half Windsor. This might sound silly, but I wore a tie with this knot on my very first date, and she kissed me, so from then on whenever I needed a little bit of luck, I tied my tie like this. Things go right when your Windsor's tied tight," I replied.

"Oh you got bars now? Yeah you right, dat do soun' funny. A lucky knot? An what was you doin' wearin' a tie on a date? Man yous a cornball. You prolly looked like Urkel ah' sumtin'!" he said derisively.

"I was going to Café Vive to perform for the first time that night and I wanted to look nice. Is that so wrong?" I asked in my own defense. Bryan mulled it for a second.

"Naw, I guess not. But anyway you said da knot is called a Half Windsor, you mean like my granny?" he asked.

"Yes, like your grandmother. Think about it though, how many times does you granny win at bingo, or on those little scratch offs?" I answered. She was the only person that I knew of that had to claim her bingo winnings on her taxes. He pondered my point for a moment before reconsidering his position.

"Man you think you can get mine lookin' like that?" he asked. The fact that he wasn't fighting me about it was more than enough impetus for me to help.

"Yes, I can. Pay close attention to me, okay?" I said as I undid the original knot and slowly retied the tie for him, and then we were off to work.

Arriving at the complex, I parked my car, and we got on the elevator, along with several of my co-workers. It was rare to see a child in the office, save bring a child to work days. Mark from accounting was the first to speak, as was the custom.

"I see Jayson brought one of those special kids with him" he remarked in a hushed snide voice, making a reference to Bryan. Fortunately Bryan didn't hear it. Everyone in the office knew that I volunteered at the Beacon. Most of them were content to write a check to some charity and feel at ease. I felt like my time was the more appreciated gift.

"Yes Mr. Faust, this is my assistant for today. My budget allows me to do that, bring in assistants. Bryan here is a wonderful young man, and highly capable of handling the tasks that being my aide requires. Besides that, he's a testament to the work we do down at the Beacon. You should stop by sometime, we'd love your help," I replied. He had a penchant for speaking recklessly. My remark, however served as the end of that conversation. Mark wouldn't go near a homeless shelter if there were a million dollars inside for the taking.

"Yeah well, I don't do "hood kids" so keep him away from my desk. Ya know what I'm saying homeboy?" he retorted in a mock hood voice. Bryan's eyes lit up.

"I will be certain to keep him as far away from your cubicle as he needs to be in order to complete whatever task I have assigned him to," I replied. Mark turned to Cheryl, my administrative assistant and started talking in an effort to ignore my remark.

"Yeah so Jennifer has a competition this weekend and—"

"She go ta Northridge don't she?" Bryan interjected. Mark looked confused.

"Yes, but I don't see how you would know her. That's one of the best private schools in Port Haven," he replied haughtily. I would have interjected, but I wanted to see where Bryan was going. Apparently everyone else wanted to see as well, because the other conversations on the elevator came to a halt.

"Oh fa sho, I go ta Westlake, but I know she be kickin it over at Crescent Hills Mall. She drive a Beemer don't she?" he asked. Mark was getting a little nervous.

"If by that you mean BMW, then yes, she does. How did you know that?" he asked as the elevator reached our floor.

"Remember last month when she was throwing up all the time and she asked you for some money but wouldn't say what it was for? Well first she was pregnant, but then we had decided to get an abortion," he said devilishly. Mark was ready to explode.

"YOU LITTLE NIG—"

"You little what?! I suggest very strongly that you mind your tongue Mr. Faust," I growled menacingly. It wasn't in my nature to be imposing, but some things could not be tolerated. There was no way I could let a grown man insult a child, even if the child was wrong. The doors on the elevator opened and the nervous crowd of people raced off to their desks. Mark glared at me angrily as he stalked towards his cubicle. As Bryan and I walked to my office, I took the time to rebuke him.

"Bryan that is an adult. You cannot speak to a man with an allegation as serious as the one you just levied against him. No man wants to hear that someone is sleeping with his daughter," I said. I tried not to be too harsh, because Mark had in fact started the entire episode, but my point was valid. Bryan smiled.

"Man Mista Sullivant, ayaint mess wit ol' dude daughter. I just sized him up. He work up here wit you, so he gotta be paid. Din when he said his "Jenny", he yaint say it like she was a little kid, so I figured she was my age. An' because she had a competition this weekend, I knew that it was a cheerleadin' competition goin on, 'cause they said it at school yestadey. A rich girl my age would only go to Northridge. An' e'rybody up dere drive nice whips. Most uh dem like drivin' beemers. And I figured that rich people like you an dem would only go to Cresent Hills Mall, cause that's where you said you go. Plus most uhv dem girls be tryin to be like models and stuff so they be starvin theyselves so they can be thin. Eitha that or dey be makin theyselves throwup. And they noramlly ask they daddies for money so they can buy expensive underwear, condoms, sum weed, sum meth, sum x or something fo dey boyfriends. That's why they don't tell they daddy what the money is for. I did used to sell to a girl named Jenny who stayed out that way, but it's prolly a million girls at that school named Jenny," he explained. I was thoroughly impressed. He had put all that together from only a cursory glance and a few pieces of conversation. That was beyond street smart, it was downright genius level.

"Bryan if you can put all that together, why can't you get your head right in school?" I asked.

"Man dat's dat Windsor in my blood. Granny be figgarin stuff out like dat too. I'ont know wat to tell you," he answered as we continued to walk down the hall.

Once we arrived in my office, I turned on my computer, and opened the blinds, revealing an expansive view of the city. Bryan walked in behind me a few moments later. His eyes were like saucers as he tried to take in the surroundings. In my receiving area, there was a micro suede sofa and two matching chairs all facing a forty-two-inch plasma television. It was primarily for viewing potential advertisements but during March Madness, my office was usually ground zero. Replicas of French Impressionist paintings adorned the rich oak paneled walls. The plush carpeting was also a nice touch. Givend and Mosse wanted to make sure that I never wanted to leave, so they had adhered to my specifications exactly. Thus, my office was nicer than the best room in some people's homes, a fact that Bryan quickly brought to my attention.

"Daaaaaannngg! Dis is nicer den da crib! You sure you ain't a D-boy? You one uh dem Tony Montana types ain't you? Mistah Sullivant, you Scarface, ain't you? When you flyin' out to see Sosa?" he asked me. I laughed.

"No sir, I just worked hard and I was rewarded for it. No yayo, no trips to see Sosa," I answered, referring to the movie. He was funny, even if a little misguided. He walked over to the window and looked at the city from a new point of view.

"I can't believe this is what the city looks like," he said in awe. "You look at dis e'ryday?" he asked.

"This is my office, so yes, I see this everyday," I replied.

"Man, I wish I could get ta som'in like dis," he said wistfully.

"You can if you work hard—Legally work hard. You still have enough time to make something of yourself, regardless of what anyone tells you," I replied. It looked like he was taking my words into consideration.

"It don't ev'n matter. Once I get out this program, I'm prolly gon hafta go back ta hustlin' anyway. If granny stay sick, da only way me an' Brittney can eat is if I move sum weight fa D'easy," he surmised reluctantly. I cringed. Bryan was only in the after school program at the Beacon as an alternative to juvenile detention. The other children were because their parents had enrolled them. Bryan was there because of a court ordered mandate that required he be supervised twenty-four hours a day. The court agreed to allow the Beacon to fill in the gap for the time when Mrs. Windsor was working Father Potter had agreed to fill in the gap from the end of the school day until Mrs. Windsor got off of work. So that, by proxy, made me responsible for him during that spell, and I was doing everything in my power to make sure that he didn't fall back into the lifestyle that had nearly claimed him.

"You know it doesn't have to go like that. I don't understand why you would take such a risk with your life. You're smarter than that. I bet you could do my job," I said.

"You foolin'! I can't do yo' job! You got all kind of degrees an' stuff, I'm barely in the ninth grade."

He said incredulously as he sat down on the couch with the remote. I saw an opportunity to kill two birds with one stone. I had a pile of expense reports that needed to be completed. I had done most of the technical work, but they still needed to totaled out before they went to accounting.

"Wrong. Today you are going to be my assistant. I need you to complete these and have them on my desk before lunch," I said as I turned off the television. He looked bewildered.

"But I don't know what I'm doin!" he exclaimed.

"It's just basic addition and subtraction. This paper will tell you how to do it. Remember, before lunch," I responded as I handed him a calculator, some scrap paper, and a pencil.

"I thought I didn't have to go to school today," he whined.

"Just because you didn't have to go to school, doesn't mean you can't learn anything," I rebutted. He started working as I turned the radio on and began with my tasks for the day. I had intentionally lightened my schedule because of my date with Bianca later the same day. The only major to do was a telephone conference with the heads of several departments. Bryan and I worked quietly for about an hour when a question broke the silence.

"You like Aint B, don't you?" he asked me.

"Who is Aint B?" I asked, visibly confused.

"You like my Aint Bianca, don't you?" he asked again. I felt myself blushing.

"I didn't know she was your aunt," I replied, avoiding the question.

"I guess you ain't answering questions taday. Aunt B is actually my cousin, but granny tol' me to call her aunt. Man, Mista Sullivant, you can tell me, it ain't like I'ma run back an teller or sum'in," he said. I still didn't want to say anything. I simply wasn't the kiss and tell type. Or the like and tell type. What went on between she and I needed to stay right there. Between she and I.

"Your Aunt Bianca is quite attractive, and yes I do enjoy our interaction," I said, attempting to placate him.

"I know that. You be makin' up reason's ta go up to da office. When Sistah Mildred was up dere, you use ta send dat dude Jonathan up dere fa stuff. Now you be gone fa like a half hour for some stupid stuff. How long do it really take ta get some staples?" he asked accusingly. He had me dead to rights. There really wasn't anything I could say.

"You got me man. I don't know how to respond to that," I answered. "Those still have to be done before lunch, whether your Aunt Bianca and I are dating or not," I instructed. Bryan smiled victoriously as he got back to work. We worked silently for about another forty-five minutes, before Bryan announced that he was done. I gave him instructions on how to get to Mark's desk, and told him to take the completed documents there. He walked out and completed the task and was back in five minutes.

"Mistah Sullivant, I saw dude's pit'sures, an' baby gurl is smacked. I wouldn't a messed wit her if somebody paid me to," he said. I was confused.

"Smacked?" I asked. He rolled his eyes heavenward.

"Mopped, hurt, busted, ugly?" he answered. I smiled.

"Be nice, everyone cannot not be blessed with aesthetic beauty. At any rate, are you ready to go get some lunch?" I asked. He nodded and we headed towards the elevator.

After a brief lunch, I remembered the video tele-conference that I had to have with the acquisitions team, and the finance department. I turned on my t.v. and set up for the event which was supposed to happen in about five minutes. I told Bryan to sit at my desk and be as silent as possible. I showed him how to get on the internet, and he was quietly occupied. I shut my office door and called Cheryl. There was no response.

"Cheryl? Ms. Knight?" I called into the intercom. "Is everything alright?" I asked.

"I'm sorry Mr. Sullivant. What did you need?" she asked in seemingly hurried voice.

"You to do your job for starters. There should be a call parked on extension 513. You can send the parties through to me," I said into the intercom. I was already nervous; I didn't need anything to go wrong.

"Okay Mr. Sullivant," she replied. The screen illuminated, and the images of three individuals came up on the television. We exchanged pleasantries and the conference began.

"Mr. Sullivant, Maclayne is looking for someone to be the face of their new urban marketing campaign. This person has to be highly marketable. No children out of wedlock, artistic, preferably young, under thirty, or at least looks under thirty, basically squeaky clean. I realize that sounds like a tall order, but that's what they need. If we can come up with a capable person, and organize a marketing blitz around that person, they are willing to pay handsomely," Mr. Largent, head of acquisitions started. Just as I was about to respond, my door burst open.

"YOU LITTLE THIEF! YOU STOLE MY PEN DIDN'T YOU!" Mark burst in.

"Excuse me gentlemen," I said hurriedly.

"Mr. Faust, what seems to be the problem?" I asked.

"My two hundred dollar Ecrive Droite pen is missing and this little miscreant took it!" he yelled. I could see the men on the screen growing disturbed. This needed to be resolved quickly.

"Bryan, I need you to be totally honest with me. Have you seen Mr. Faust's pen or know where it is?"

"No Mr. Sullivant, I have no idea what he is talking about. I promise I don't have it," Bryan said innocently.

"You have your answer. Please, I need you to leave now," I said, ushering him towards the door. Mark wasn't finished yet.

"Well, of course he said that. What, did you expect him to tell the truth? He's a criminal. But I guess you monkeys stick together huh?" he said invectively.

"You have overstepped your bounds at this point sir. You need to leave now before this escalates," I said as firmly as I could. Just as he was preparing to hurl another diatribe, Cheryl came running towards my door while fixing her skirt. Her make-up had been disturbed, a clear sign that she had been involved in some sort of recent physical activity. I noticed a smudge of lipstick on Mark's shirt.

"Mark, you left your pen in my office! I tried to catch you," she said, with the pen in hand. This whole drama had played out in front of my on screen guests.

"Mr. Faust that is not how we conduct business here at Givend and Mosse. I do not wish to be associated with anyone who behaves in such a reprehensible manner. I want your badge on my desk within the next seven minutes. Security will handle cleaning out your desk. Your services are no longer needed here at Givend and Mosse," Mr. Daniels said from the television. All of the associates in accounting answered to him as head of the finance department. Of all the people to display a lack of judgment in front of, he was the worst choice Mark could make. Mark turned pale.

"I can explain. It.it…it was a mistake, I was angry and I just thought that."

"Truly Mark, I am not interested in hearing anything you have to say at this point. Goodbye," Mr. Daniels said. Mark trudged slowly out of my office. I turned back to my guests.

"I apologize gentlemen. Perhaps next month I should requisition a better lock for my door?" I laughed, attempting to bring the situation back to normal. A slow laugh made its way through the room on the other side of the television. We talked about a few more points and then decided to meet in person to go over the particulars of the assignment. The activities of the afternoon had drained me, and I still had to get ready for my night out with Bianca, so I decided to call it a day.

"You ready to go man?" I asked.

"Yeah, les get outta here man," he replied. I shut down my computer, closed the blinds and turned out the lights. After shutting and laughing silently as I locked my door, I headed towards the elevator where Bryan was waiting. We went down to the car and headed towards his home. About a half an hour later, we pulled up in front of Bryan's house. He looked exhausted after the events of the past two days. Even though I wasn't in any hurry to have children, the experience showed me that maybe I could handle it after all. I looked over at him.

"You did some good work out there today man, I'm proud of you," he beamed.

"Really? Man Mista Sullivant, ayaint know you could get gutta like dat. When' ol' dude started talking all reckless, you let him know quick. Ain't nobody eva took up fa me like dat bahfo'," he explained. I smiled.

"It's innocent until proven guilty. If you say you're innocent, then we have to be able to prove you are guilty. I didn't think you were, and besides, he had no right to speak to you like that," I said. Bryan was still visibly appreciative of my gesture. I glanced at the clock. I was running late if I was going to meet Bianca on time.

"Alright man, that's enough of this. You know Mr. Sullivant has your back. Now get outta here so I can roll!" I said in my mock "hood" accent. He smiled as he opened the door to leave. Halfway out of the door, he stopped.

"What about yo' clothes man?" he asked.

"That's your uniform in case you ever have to go to work me again. Practice that tying that tie!" I instructed. His demeanor instantly brightened.

"Aw word? Aw fa sho, fa sho! Good look Mista Sullivant!" he chirped as he shut the door. I waited until he got into the door before I pulled off. I only had one hour to go to the dry cleaners, pick up flowers, shower, and write a new piece for tonight before I was supposed to go pick up Bianca. I wasn't sure how I was going to do it, but I knew it had to be completed. Just as I was racing towards the cleaners, I had an epiphany. I could get dressed at my mom's house. That would save me from having to return home, and would allow me the extra time I was going to need at the florist. I couldn't just get any flowers, they had to be the right flowers. Tonight was going to be special.

I arrived at my mother's house with a little more than a half hour of my original hour to spare. Our dinner reservations were for just over an hour from now, but the restaurant was easily thirty minutes away. I barged in the door with my clothes for the night which I had wisely put in the cleaners on Monday.

"Mom!? Brock?! Sammie?!" I called.

"Jaysee?!" a small voice called back to me. My little sister, Samantha, came from around the corner. She ran over to give me a hug. I picked her up.

"Whoa, you're gettin' heavy! How was your day?" I asked. Even though I was in a rush, I always had time for Sammie.

"It was good jaysee i practiced for my recital you're coming right?" she asked. I knew that she played the piano, but I didn't know that she had a recital coming up.

"Okay, just have mommy tell me when it is okay?" I instructed. "Where is Mom at, anyway?" I asked.

"Her and daddy are in the back with the merry man," she replied. I was perplexed. Merry man?

"Sammie, honey, what's a merry man?" I asked.

"Jaysee, you are so silly. when somebody wants to get merried they call the merry man and he helps them pick out what they want. I thought all grown ups knew that," she chided. It seemed odd for them to be sitting with a wedding planner, but I figured they must be preparing to try again. I walked to the back room to announce my presence. Brock and my mother were sitting there with the wedding planner, just as Samantha had indicated.

"Mom, I'm here, and I'm about to take a quick shower," I declared.

"Okay that's fine, honey. What are you doing on June $7^{th}$?" she asked excitedly.

"Nothing, why?" I responded.

"Because that's the big day! And we're going to go through with it this time, right honey?!" she asked, squeezing Brock's hand.

"That's right honey," he replied. I couldn't help but notice that he didn't seem overly excited with the idea. I don't know if it was because of the money or the "finality" of marriage. Either way, I decided to leave that alone. I still had two major tasks to complete. I showered quickly, and with about fifteen minutes before I absolutely had to pick up Bianca, I sat down in my old room to write a special piece for Café Vive . I didn't want to be working on it during dinner. I looked through my old notebooks. My mom hadn't changed my room since I left for college. The "you always have somewhere to come home to" sort of idea. I found a couple that I liked, copied them down quickly, and headed for the door. I gave Bianca a call to let her know I was on my way.

I pulled up behind her mammoth vehicle and walked to the door, flowers in hand. I rang the door bell. A woman in shorts and a t-shirt and physically as attractive as Bianca answered the door. I laughed internally. What were the odds?

"Quinn, I presume? Hello, my name is—"

"Jayson. I know who you are, she's been talking about you all week. I googled you yesterday, so I know exactly who you are, come on in, take a seat, she's upstairs getting ready," she directed. I complied as I entered the house and followed her to the living room. Her demeanor had put me on edge. She wasn't hostile, but she wasn't really warm and inviting either. "Can I get you a drink? I'm sure it will only be a few more minutes," she said.

"I'm fine, but thank you though." She smiled at me.

"So Bianca tells me that you work for Givend and Mosse," she started. I didn't really want to talk about my particulars, I was already nervous enough, but if she was to Bianca who I thought she was, I had to answer her questions."

"Yes ma'am, I do. I work on special projects. But I don't really like to talk about the specifics outside of work," I replied, trying to anticipate the next possible question.

"Oh. okay, that's nice. So what exactly do you do?" she asked. I was praying for Bianca to hurry.

"I help them design various facets of targeted marketing plans, but there is a non-disclosure clause in my contract, so I can't really say more than that. It's nothing personal, but I don't know you. I don't know who your employer is," I said, attempting to close that line of questioning. I effectively did the exact opposite.

"Non-disclosure clause? What are you doing that you can't tell anyone about? Sounds kind of fishy to me. Or is that just what you say to people because you don't really have a job and you don't want to have to tell anyone the truth?" she questioned intrusively. It was a delicate situation, because I couldn't get upset, but she was deliberately stepping on my toes, and as adult I felt like I needed to address the situation.

"It is exactly as I have said it is. Would you be so kind as to let Bianca know that I am here, please," I said, sounding as both cordial and assertive as possible. Quinn smiled.

"Okay, okay…" she moved towards the steps "…stands up for himself…" she mumbled walking past me. "Bianca!!" she yelled.

"Here I come!" she yelled back. I heard her moving down the stairs and I stood up, partially out of manners and partially out of anticipation. I wanted to see what I had been waiting on. Her white, open-toe sandals cradled her pedicured feet as she cautiously made her way down the stairs. I tried not to spend too much looking at her legs, but the rich copper hue overlaying the visibly toned muscles held my eyes as willing captives. The free-flowing pink cotton skirt that she had on liberated my eyes and gave them a new feast to consume. By the time I got to the white v-necked t-shirt that showed just enough cleavage, she was at the bottom of the stairs. Her auburn colored hair framed her face as it sat on her shoulder, and she didn't have on any detectable make-up, but from what I saw, she didn't need any. She was otherworldly beautiful, and I prayed that my mouth wasn't hanging open, but I don't think anyone would have held it against me if it was. I had practiced this moment in my head for the last day and a half, and in less than thirty seconds she had melted away thirty-six hours of preparation. She flashed her million-watt smile at me. I froze for a moment. Then I snapped back to reality.

"Wow. You look great. These are for you," I said, handing her the flowers. She grinned at me.

"How in the world did you manage to get flowers that matched my outfit?!" she exclaimed. Anything I could have said right there would have been a lie. It was just dumb luck.

"Maybe we've got a bond or something already," I sputtered. Quinn laughed.

"Are you serious? You are going to have to do better than that!" she said. Bianca shot her a look.

"Quinn, leave him alone!" she commanded, then she handed her the flowers. "Will you put these in some water please? I'd do it, but we're already running late," she explained. She took the flowers.

"I'll do it. You guys have a good night. Jayson it was nice meeting you, see you later," she said as we walked out the door.

"Likewise. I'll try to have her home at a decent hour," I said as I walked out the door. Bianca shut the door and scampered towards my car. We got in and made our way towards the restaurant.

The surprising lack of traffic and my expeditious velocity, allowed us to reach the Casa de Lorenzo roughly three minutes before our reservation. I checked in with the maitre'd and we waited for our table to be prepared. The conversation from the car continued to flow as we waited.

"Spiderman would absolutely *kill* Batman in a no holds barred street fight!" she argued.

"Are you kidding me?! Spiderman might get him in round one, but Batman would make some sort of formula and turn Spiderman back into Peter Parker in twenty minutes," I fought back. I was already in love. We were really talking about comic book heroes on our first date. She laughed as we sat down on a bench outside.

"Yeah, I guess he would. But he'd have to get out of round one. Spiderman is genetically enhanced; Batman wouldn't have any answers for that. Game over, I win!" she said. I let her have it. The Maitre'D looked up.

"Sullivant, party of two?" he called. I stood up and instinctively stretched my hand to help her up. She took it, but rather than drop it after she stood up, she interlocked her fingers with mine. I tried not to respond visibly beyond a smile. We were led to our table. The conversation took a different turn as we listened to the mariachi band playing.

"Okay, so Spiderman might give Batman all he can handle. I'll give you that one," I began. She smiled.

"Of course he would. Radioactive spider bite versus a rich dude who's afraid of bats? Uh. put my money on number one please," she said.

"You are too much! A woman that can discuss comic books? Where have you been all my life?" I joked.

"Somewhere looking for a man with a career and manners!" she shot back. I blushed. The waitress showed up to take our order.

"May I have the Muchachos Nachos and strawberry lemonade please? " I asked. Then she turned to Bianca.

"I'd like a steak, medium well, and a salad as well as a strawberry lemonade," she said, handing the waitress the menu. I had an incredulous look on my face. She really ordered a steak. No woman in my dating history had ever ordered a steak on the first night. Ever. She must have anticipated the reaction.

"You didn't invite me to soup and salad; you invited me to dinner, correct? Well I fully intend on eating. I feel like eating a steak. So let me eat my steak" she demanded. She had misread my expression.

"I wasn't surprised because you ordered a *steak*. I'm surprised because *you* ordered a steak. Where in the world are you going to put a whole steak?" I asked, referring to her lithe frame.

"It'll fit. I promise you that much, it will fit. You'd be surprised what I can fit in here," she said. I smiled at her.

"Most girls won't eat more than a tic-tac on the first date. You eat whatever you want sweetheart, I don't care," I said, trying to nudge the conversation away from a potentially volatile topic.

"I guess, but if you think about it, this isn't the first time I've eaten in front of you. Wednesday night counts. Maybe not as a date, but it counts as dinner," she said. Wednesday nights were when we fed the homeless in the Beacon's cafeteria. Usually a couple of children helped us, and we ate dinner with the people that we fed. She was right, she stayed to help this week, and we did eat together. Along with one hundred other people, but she was still correct.

"You're right yet again," I answered. The waitress brought our drinks and informed us that it would be another minute or so before our food would be ready. Bianca looked up from her drink.

"Did we really order the same drink?" she asked.

"Yes, ma'am," I replied.

"Awww, that is soo cute. They put little sombreros in our drinks instead of the little umbrellas," she noted. I smiled as I took a sip from my glass. It had been a while since I had been on a date and my rust was showing. It wasn't that we didn't have chemistry, it was more that it had been a while since I had been in the lab. I couldn't keep it moving the way I wanted it to go. Just as that weird first date silence was about to put out the fire that we had begun to kindle, Bianca looked at the mariachi band and the largely empty dance floor. Her eyes lit up.

"I realize this is going to sound crazy, but do you want to dance?" she asked. I was a horrible dancer, but I was more than happy to oblige. Just as we were preparing to move to the floor, our meal arrived. We both hastily sat back down.

"We'll dance one day," I said wistfully.

"I'm sure of it," she responded as she positioned her napkin. I was already into my plate of nachos. "If you like those, you should try my aunt Ky's Baja Nachos. She should patent that recipe, it's just that good," she said between bites.

"Aunt Ky?" I asked.

"Umhum. It's short for Kymera. She's my cousin a couple of times removed, that and she's like ten years older than me so I used to call her my aunt, but yeah, she makes these nachos that will absolutely change your life!" she remarked.

"Maybe I'll get to find out about that," I replied. We finished our collective meal and I asked the waitress for the check. Ordinarily I would I have played the "Guess the Tab" game with her, but that seemed like a crass move to make on a first date. I figured maybe we'd play on another date. I left the tab plus the tip in cash, and we headed to the car. Café Vive was next. I put on a cd of instrumentals I had created back in college. They always helped me get prepared for performances. Bianca looked at me quizzically.

"Who's album is this?" she asked.

"This is some stuff I did back in college. I like to listen to it before I go to Café Vive ." She still seemed a bit confused.

"So where are we going again?" she asked.

"Café Vive . It's a really nice little spot. Mostly spoken word, and they normally let local bands play. Tonight they have a featured poet performing, This guy named Jay Azariah. I think you'll like him. I hope you like him," I answered. That response appeared to placate her as she sat back in her seat and softly nodded her head as we rode. I silently practiced the pieces that I was going to do in my mind. This had to be perfect. I didn't know how much she would like it, but I couldn't live with myself if I did anything less than my best.

We got to the club and, after parking the car on the street, went to the door.

"Hey, Uncle Jeremiah!" I called to the man standing next to the bouncer. The owner turned in my direction.

"Hey, Jayaz…" I shot him a "not yet" look as I motioned towards Bianca. "…sssoon! How's it goin', man? The usual spot?" he asked. I nodded in agreement as he began to lead the way through the intimate audience. Small candles burned on every table giving the room its soft light as well as its vanilla aroma. Uncle Jeremiah led us to one of the many small sofa and table sets; this one was near the front of the nearly full room. He removed the reserved sign and we sat down on the small love seat. The stage lights went up as the act on stage concluded. The young woman got up, bowed and walked off stage. Bianca applauded softly.

"I'm sure she was good, even though we didn't get to see all of it. When's this dude Jazzarhea supposed to show up?" she asked. I tried to suppress a chuckle.

"Jay-Azz-uh-rye-uh, I corrected, and soon. They let all the in house participants speak first before they bring up the guest artist," I informed her. "Just be patient, dear," I said, boldly patting her knee. The remaining three in-house participants each performed their pieces. After the last performer, Uncle Jeremiah went up and got the microphone.

"Wasn't that lovely? All right ladies and gentlemen. Let's have some love for Mr. Homegrown himself, my favorite nephew and Port Haven's favorite son, Jay Azariah!" he said cheerfully as he smiled in my direction. Bianca looked at me, seemingly unsure of what was going on.

"You said you wanted to see if I was any good. I thought that maybe I'd let you be the judge." I quickly pecked her cheek. "Wish me luck," I said as I made my way to the stage. I climbed the stairs as a gentle round of applause filled the air.

"Awww, c'mon, ya'll can do better than that! This is one of our own!! This man has been puttin' it down for years now, the least ya'll could do is make him feel at home on his home stage!" Jeremiah said. I walked across the stage and shook his hand.

"Ya'll give it up for Uncle Jeremiah! This man has done everything in his power to keep this place open as a haven for us creatives. Give it up for Port Haven's favorite Uncle! Yeah, show him some love!" I ordered. The audience complied. On stage, with that mic in my hand, I was in complete control. It was funny, most people felt shy on stage, but that's when I felt most empowered. "I'm only Port Haven's favorite son because I'm its oldest son. I've been performing at these open mics since I was sixteen, right Uncle J?" I asked. He nodded in agreement. "Let's get down to it, shall we?" I asked the crowd. The applause served as positive reinforcement. "Oh, one more thing. How could I forget? How about a hand for the exquisite Ms. Bianca Windsor, who was so kind to lend me to you all tonight?" I asked, and again the crowd complied. Bianca smiled graciously. I started my set.

"How is everyone tonight?" I asked. The crowd signified their collective answer by way of applause. I sat on my stool and smiled.

"That's cool. I'm glad to hear it. For those of you that don't know, like Uncle Jeremiah said, I'm Jay Azariah. I knew I was doing a set tonight, but if I can be frank, there was only one thing on my mind today, and that was the lovely Ms. Bianca Windsor. So what I got for ya'll tonight is kind of a hodge-podge, if you will. I had promised that I would give ya'll one for Black History month, and even though I'm a couple weeks late, is there ever a bad time to talk about the struggle?" I asked.

"Do yo' thang, man!" a crowd member yelled supportively.

"I'm about to man, I'm about to, I promise. Well anyway this one is called: "Wearing the Flesh of our Dead Fathers." Check it out:

Eenie, meanie, miney moe, catch a tiger by the toe…

Where's that from? Do you know?

Let me help you, tell you something that you couldn't figure,

The orginal lyric in that song has you catchin' a nigga.

Yup, the childhood rhyme that's come out of everybody's mouth,

Originated down in the Civil War South.

I mean if you think about it, I'm sure it will amaze ya,

How many people had seen an animal native to Asia?

It's the information age and we refuse to open a book.

If you want to hide it from us, that's where we won't look.

We used to be the hopes and dreams of the slave,

Now it's like we rush to join them in the grave.

Sitting in our ignorance like a child in peed-in pants

We complain about what's fair, but won't give ourselves a chance.

You go to the school of hard knocks, spendin' tuittion on rims,

The house of prudence is destroyed by whims.

We don't feel we've made it unless we've got "King Kong in the trunk"

Just one more test that we as a people are going to flunk.

For the record, for those of you who let your "Chain hang low."

Gotta couple of facts that you probably need to know.

That chain was comprised of fingers, ears and toes.

Confederates cut them off of their Black Union foes.

For clarity, they were WEARING THE FLESH OF OUR DEAD FATHERS.

Please don't say I'm the only one that this fact bothers.

I'm not attacking music, it's just a cultural medium.

I am attacking the fact that we've got blind being lead by the dumb.

Dumb as in ignorant, and dumb as in speechless.

This level of idiocy is astounding, how did we reach this?This is our month and we insist on dropping the ball

We should be ashamed one and all.

Ordinarily, I'd end my poem with some modicum of hope and love,
Or some corny lines about Martin and Corretta watching from above.
But quite frankly that's what's wrong with us now.
Everyone knows what's up, but no one sees what's going down.
We've been castrated and catered too for so very long,
That we've lost the edge that once made us strong.
I'm won't write the end of this poem, I'll leave it a mystery.
It's up to the Blacks present to create more history.
I realize it's in mid-verse, so this is kind of abrupt,
However, this is a team effort, you it's your turn to pick up. Thank you," I said. There was a thoughtful round of applause. I could tell that that my words had found their mark.

"What ya'll think? Ya'll want sommore?" I asked.

"Yeah!" the crowd answered unanamously.

"Okay, let me see what I got here. I didn't really have a chance to write like I wanted today, so I'm might have to pull out of the oldies but goodies. Is that alright tonight?" I asked again. The audience cheered. "Boy I tell you, ain't no place like home. People say that because when you get out there, you know, away from home, people stop being nice, stop trying to build you up. They start going after you, trying to bring you down to their level. When I was doing my undergrad over at Halos State, I had this roommate that could never ever seem to just congratulate me on anything. It felt like every word out of his mouth was just pure hate. I couldn't get like that, or else I would have messed up my own karma, so ya'll know me, I put the feelings to words. Tell me what you think of this one:

You make a bad day worse, you can make the good days hell.
I've tried to get away from you to no avail,
More than make me sick, you make me deathly ill.
You inspire more anger than I care to feel.
Just the very sight of you makes me want to heave,
When you walk into the room, it's time for me to leave.
I'm serious, I've had enough of this I'm through.
Gotta find a way to break free from you.

My ability to thrive is limited by your proximity.
This must cease, I can't let you limit me.
I appreciate your outlook, no really it's great,
But why does it always soun like you tryin' to hate?
Ain't no "congrats," no pat on the back,
Just "man be careful" or "sounds like you gettin' jacked."
I understand that success isn't shared and nothing's communal,
Even so, it's time for this friendship's funeral.
Not just because of the differences, not just because of the rifts,
But because, in simplest terms, dude, I'm tired of yo' shit! Thank you," I said before I took the lid off my bottled water.

"I feel you dawg!" someone yelled from the back. I smiled.

"Thank you. Ya'll know me. I try to do stuff people can feel. I know ya'll getting tired of hearing me say this, but, can I get just one more round of applause for the phenomenally beautiful Ms. Bianca Windsor? We are on a date right now ya'll, so I'ma give ya'll one more, and then I'm going to get back to my date. Anybody that knows me, knows that I love my momma. If you know me, then you also know that Jessica was a baby with a baby. I love my mother for doing what she did for me, and this is one that I wrote just for her. Take a listen:

I make her sick everyday, I know it. She's not proud of our relationship; she's starting to show it. Even so, she's my everything, I can't let her go. I love her more than she'll ever know. I can sense her pain, because I embody her fear. I hope that she knows it will get better if I'm here. She says that she and I, we were a mistake. Even though I've done no wrong, the blame I take. She doesn't want me anymore, and now she has enough money to seperate us for sure. I kick and scream in protest. I don't want us to be done. She says that we are over tomorrow, right after she gets off the 21. What can I say? What promise can I give? I vow to love her for as long as I live. I confess my love and gratitude, praying that I can change her attitude. On the dawn of the day I believe to be our last, to my surprise, she watches the 21 pass. She swallows her pride and decides that for the rest of her life I'm along for the ride. So from that day to this, every chance I have I give her a hug and a kiss. I'm writing this now today, because 23 years ago, my mom let the 21 get away...

Thank you. I love you all. That's going to just about do it for me. I have to get back to my date. Thanks for listening. Uncle Jerry, it's all you!" I said as I waited for him to come and take the microphone from me. He hustled up to the stage, amid thunderous applause.

"That's my nephew, Mr. Jay Azariah. Ya'll give it up for him! Come on, ya'll can do better tha'nat! Show him some love!" he yelled. I smiled, waved and walked off stage. I walked to the couch were Bianca was still sitting, seemingly transfixed.

"Jayson, that was amazing! You should do that professionally! I'm serious!" she exclaimed. I laughed as I dismissed it.

"I work for Givend and Mosse professionally; this is what I do for fun. I'm glad you liked it. Are you ready to go?" I asked her. She nodded as she reached for my hand. We walked out to the car and headed back towards her house. We talked about the performance amongst other things on the ride home. I wished that there was some way the night could last forever. It was as perfect a date as I had had in the past year.

I pulled up in her driveway. I opened her door and walked her to the entrance of her home.

"Well sweetheart, I guess this is the end of the road for tonight," I said.

"Yeah, I know," she said fumbling with her keys.

"I had a wonderful time with you, and hopefully we can do it again soon," I said.

"Count on it. I'd invite you in, but Quinn would have a fit," she said. I wanted to invite her back to my place, or something. Not even for sex, but just because I wanted to find a way to keep the night going. I didn't know to do next. It seemed right to give her a kiss, but was it really? I didn't know what to say. I wanted to cap it off, but not be over the top.

"Okay, well, I'm going to go ahead and get lost, you have a nice night and I'll see you Monday?" I said.

"Call me tomorrow, maybe we can get into something else," she intimated. I smiled as I leaned in to give her a hug. She kissed me firmly on the lips.

"Make sure you call me," she said as she went into the house. "Goodnight" she said closing the door. I was so caught off guard that I didn't know how to react. As the door shut softly, I made my way back to car, trying my best to maintain my collectedness. The night was still young, but my fatigue and desire to preserve the perfection of the evening in my memory was enough to persuade me to call it a night. I drove to my mother's house to spend the night.

I walked into the house. Sportscenter was on as Brock lay sound asleep on the couch. I turned off the t.v. on the way to my old room. The beauty of the night replayed in my mind like a re-run of my favorite t.v. show. It couldn't have gone any better than it had. I lay awake in the bed for a moment, imagining the repetitions of the night, before finally the sweet rapture of the evening gave way to slumber.

# 7

"Awww, look at my babies! You guys are soo cute!" my mom cooed as she walked in on a sleeping Bianca and I, effectively waking us up.

"Mom...what time is it?" I asked, rubbing my eyes.

"Ten till five. Why? What time do you have to be there?" she asked.

"I don't have to be anywhere. I just want to know why you're here now," I asked. If she wanted to make sure I was okay, I didn't think she should have left.

"Bianca...Bianca...Wake up," I said, nudging her awake.

"What is it?" she asked drowsily.

"We need to make sure that you're on my insurance. Remind me to get that paperwork on Monday.

"Umb...okay," she replied from her slumber. She wasn't going to remember that. Just as I was preparing to go back to sleep, Father Potter entered the room with someone else in tow.

"Uncle Jeremiah?" I asked incredulously. "What are you doing here?" I asked.

"Well, when Father Potter told me about what happened, I thought I should swing by on my way home from Viveìììì. Gotta check up on my nephew. How you holding up?" Father Potter gave him a sharp nudge with his elbow.

"To the point Jeremiah," Father Potter instructed.

"City Council called me yesterday. They want to see if we can have a news crew cover your signing with Maclayne, and I wanted to know if you would be willing to do it down at the club. It would really help. It'll give downtown a boost, and it would be really good for Viveìiì. Good positive publicity never hurt anyone. The only catch is it has to be on Friday, since that's the only day that all of City Council can be present. I was going to wait until you came down to the club next, but then I thought maybe I should deliver the news in person "he explained. I looked at Father Potter for guidance. I had already planned on my signing it at the Beacon. He seemed to anticipate my question.

"It is okay with me if you decide for the change of venue," he said, assuaging my fears. I smiled. As long as I had his blessing, I felt okay with the change.

"Okay, Uncle Jeremiah, make it happen man, make it happen," I answered. I couldn't figure out why I was handling business at ten after five in the morning, especially from a hospital bed. The two of them proceeded towards the hall.

"Are you happy Jeremiah Potter? You came in here to disrupt this poor child, for a simple change of venue. "Father Potter scolded as they made their way down the hall. I thought about what I had agreed to in my mind. Friday was the day before my mom and Brock's wedding. My mom had only seen me perform a few times, but if there was ever a time I wanted her to see me at Vive, it was the night I signed my creative deal with Maclayne. It wasn't worth stressing over; Brock had never seen me perform. He said something about "the devil lives in dark places" or something silly like that. I brushed it off as nonsensical, kind of like ninety percent of the things I had ever heard him say. We were going to have to work on that, but it didn't really matter at present. I finally got to a point where I was able to clear out my mind and relax.

# 8

"I can't remember the cliché about funerals and rainy days, but either way, funerals are never fun. Death and dying is as much a part of life as being born. I know that's a bunch of stuff that you don't want to hear, but I'm telling you, it gets easier," I said. Bryan still looked like he was in a daze as we sat in the sanctuary.

"Still man, I hope it's sunny on Thursday. I'm already messed up, the lass thing I need is for it to be all rainy and depressing'. I jus can't believe she really gone. I loved my granny. She was like my moms. I don't know what Im 'on do now dat she ain't here," he said. I could tell that he was going to take this hard. I was never any good with grief counseling. According to my mother, my own father passed when I was two years old. So the only experience I had in dealing with death was well before my conscious memory. Even so, I had to help him as best I could. His grandmother was the single strongest influence keeping him from totally going over the edge. He had been showing steady improvement, but in her absence, someone had to step in and pick up the slack.

The funeral was four days away. Bianca had been busy getting everything arranged, largely in part to the dual role she played as the parish administrator, and as Mrs. Windsor's great niece. Her time had been crunched, and in light of the new role I played in her life, I was doing everything I could do to help her get through it. We may not have been together very long, but if there was one positive thing about me, it was that once I commit, I commit. Normally that's a good thing, right now though, it meant running countless errands and otherwise availing myself to her. I didn't mind though, because, if the roles were reversed, she would have done the same thing for me.

Bianca walked into the sanctuary where Bryan and I were standing. The urgent look on her face indicated that this was about to be another one of those errands.

"Jayson, I need you to do me a huge favor. Remember my cousin Kymera that I told you about? She's flying in today and I'm not going to be able to pick her up. Will you take my car and go pick her up for me please honey?" she asked. Bryan's ears perked up.

"Aint B did you say Kymera?" he asked.

"Yes honey, Kymera, your mom is coming into town," Bianca replied, smiling at him.

"She'll be gone as soon as granny is in the ground," he said dejectedly. I couldn't help but feel a little bad for him.

"I'll still be here," I said, trying to reassure him. He smiled weakly.

"Man, Mista Sullivant, yous a cornball.", he replied.

"Let's go to the airport," I said, placing my hand on his shoulder as we made our way to Bianca's car. The ride to the airport was silent, save for the background noise provided by the radio. Bryan stared blankly out of the window the entire forty-five-minute trip. He was normally a garrulous kid. His silence was almost moving. I tried to comprehend the stress that he was under. The only person you were certain loved you is about to be placed six feet under ground. Having to live with a barely eighteen year old sister and her twenty five year old drug pushing boyfriend and their child would have been enough to make anyone go crazy. This was his reality. I thought had it rough growing up but my own experience paled by comparison. This wasn't growing up, this was robbing him of his childhood altogether. He was still, in my estimation, a good kid, even if he was going though a rough spot.

We stood there in the terminal waiting on Kymera to arrive. Her plane from Dallas was supposed to arrive in a few moments. I realized that I had no idea what she looked like, and I assumed that it had been a while for Bryan, but I couldn't imagine him not recognizing his mother. We waited a half hour more before I decided to call Bianca.

"Baby, we've been here for almost an hour, and still no sign of her," I said.

"I was just getting ready to call you. She said she's taking a taxi to the hotel and she'll be over later. I'm sorry sweetheart," she explained.

"Okay. Bryan and I are going to get something to eat. I guess I'll see you later," I answered as we disconnected. I didn't want to tell Bryan that we had waited for nothing, but I had to give him an answer.

"She either ain't coming or she got one uhv her dudes to come get her. She cuda just stayed where she was at," he said, before I had uttered a word.

"Don't think like that, that's still your mother and like it or not, she did give birth to you. You may not like anything she ever does in your life, but respect her for the fact that she allowed you to have that life. I know it's hard, but you gotta try," I exhorted. He was unwilling to back down.

"If she was yo' mama, din you could say somehin'…I'ont even want to talk about it anymore," he said, effectively concluding the conversation. For the moment, I was willing to let his word trump my own.

As we drove back the parish, I decided to give it one more push.

"I can find out which hotel she's at if you want to go see her. Or we can go back to the apartment, it's up to you. I just want to feel like I gave you a real chance to spend some time with her before she—"

"Look Mistah Sullivant, no disrespeck, but can we drop it? This broad leff me an my sistah on granny's do'step and got ghost. This is the first time I've heard from her in fourteen years! What am I supposs'd ta say ta hur? Hi, how's it going? And then shake hur han'? It ain't goin down like that, an if you knew what was good for you, you wouldn't go nowhere near her. I don't want ta see hur, end ov discussion!" he exclaimed. His ire was so fervent that I simply had to respect it. I was trying to put someone into his life that I thought might possibly be a positive influence, or at least want to see him do well. I hadn't really thought about it from how he saw things. In his mind, in his view, this woman had abandoned both him and his sister years ago, and was only here now out of respect for her dead mother. I had just assumed that everyone's mother was as genuinely concerned as my mother had always been. But then again, my mother kept me with her every step of the way. Bryan was a completely different story.

The silence that Bryan had requested was interrupted by my ringing phone.

"Baby, I drove your car over to my house, can you meet me there? Kymera's here and she's cooking dinner for the family. Whatever you do, make sure you bring Bryan with you, Kymera wants to see him."

"Alright, we'll be there in a second."

"Okay, see you then."

"Okay, bye," I said as I shut my phone. I looked over at Bryan. I took a deep breath and prepared to tell him what was going on.

"Dude, you ain't even gotta speak on it. Aint B talk too loud," he said, pre-empting my statement. Even though he was upset, I had to maintain the structural discipline that I had used to govern our relationship.

"At the very least, I have not ceased to be anything less than Mr. Sullivant," I said. It was hollow, but I had to say it.

"Sorry, Mr. Sullivant," he retorted angrily. I decided not to push him any further. He was already dealing with enough, he didn't need another stressor.

We arrived at Bianca's house. I looked at Bryan. He normally didn't have a problem expressing how he felt about anything. This time seemed different. I put a hand on his shoulder.

"It'll be alright man. Just give it a chance. Don't think about it too hard. Just say hello. That's all anyone is asking," I said.

"I guess the sooner I start, the sooner it's over, right?"

"Come on. You can do it," I said. We exited the vehicle and went to the door. I rang the doorbell, and Bianca showed up almost instantaneously.

"Hey boys! The food is this way," she said in her cheery hostess voice as we entered the home. As we journeyed further back into the house, the overwhelming aroma of heavily spiced Mexican cuisine flooded the air. Each step took us further from Port Haven and closer to Mexico City. When we reached the kitchen, we saw the progenitor of the aroma. People were moving buzzing around hastily, but I somehow knew which one was the queen bee.

She stood over the island in the kitchen working on her masterpiece. If there was anything to be said about this family, it was that good looks were its hallmark. She was no exception to the rule. She looked like something out of a dream. A wet dream. Her face was a vision of angelic perfection. She could have easily passed for being half her age. She stood there in a v-necked t-shirt that looked more like a paint job than anything else. The stitching in that shirt deserved a plaque for the work that it was doing. She was asking a lot of it, but to be honest, I doubt it would have complained. Her raven black hair went to about the middle of her back. She was slightly taller than Bianca, who stood at an even five feet and three inches. And she had her beat by at most twenty-five pounds. But it was the *right* twenty-five pounds. It was like she had taken a pen and drawn the body she wanted. I wasn't sure how she got herself into the shorts that she had on, but I was sure that they weren't going to be the same after she took them off. If the shirt deserved a plaque, then those jeans deserved a congressional medal. A spot in the Smithsonian. Sainthood. Something. I wasn't sure what the perfect measurements were for a woman, but I was sure that they came from her body. She was a physical specimen, no questions asked. You couldn't tell that she had ever had a child, much less two. I understood why Bryan had told me I should stay away from her. I knew it wasn't for the reasons I was thinking, but the warning was still the same. My window of escape slammed shut as Bianca grabbed my hand.

"Aunt Ky, this is Jayson. Jayson, this is my Aunt Kymera," she said, introducing us. I extended my hand to shake hers. She grabbed my hand and pulled me into an embrace.

"Hello Jayson," she purred. At least I thought it sounded like a purr. Everything in me knew that I needed to release myself from this hold, but to be honest; I liked the way her body felt against me. The aroma of her pineapple body wash infiltrated my nostrils and threatened to hold me captive. The "acceptable embrace time" clock in my head was running low. I secretly wished I could have stayed there a little longer. Bianca felt nice but, if there was a difference between a nine and a ten, this was it. I stepped back.

"Hello, Aunt Kymera," I replied, looking into her eyes.

"He is sooo cute! You look just like that little mouse Jerry from 'Tom and Jerry.' I'm going to call you Jerry. That will be your new nickname from me. So Jerry, what do you do?" she said. I hated being called anything other than Jayson.

"I prefer to be called Jay or Jayson, and I work for Givend and Mosse" I answered almost stoically.

"Givend and Mosse? Ooooohh, Bianca sure can pick the good ones can't she? You got bread then, don't you? You think you're going to be happy with Bianca?" she asked, still holding, and now caressing my hand. The mention of Bianca's name was like a rope out of quicksand. I reached for my girlfriend.

"I'm comfortable, and Bianca and I, we are very happy. Aren't we sweetheart?" I asked as I gave her a kiss on the cheek.

"You are soo goofy! Look, Aunt Ky made those nachos I was telling you about," she said laughing.

"You mean she is making them," Kymera corrected. Then the oven timer went off. "That's the special sauce!" she said, turning to the oven. She removed the confection from the oven and the proceeded to pour it over a plate of tortilla chips that were already covered with every conceivable topping for nachos. Kymera stepped back, looking at her creation with a certain artistic pride.

"Baja Nachos, ladies and gentlemen," she said. Bianca looked at me expectantly.

"You're going to try them, right?" she asked. Considering the fact that I could smell how hot they were from three feet away, it just didn't strike me as a good idea. But I couldn't resist a challenge. I walked to the plate and took a chip that was had some modicum of every ingredient on it. I waited for it to cool down before I attempted to eat it. Once it was at a temperature I could handle, I bit down on it. Almost simultaneously, my eyes watered as my internal body temperature felt like it shot up at least one hundred degrees. My scalp started to sweat, and I hadn't even swallowed this piece yet. I hurriedly crunched the chip, attempting to swallow it before I chemically burned all of my taste buds.

"Ah ned sumtin ta drinhk!" I yelled with the remainder of the confection still in my mouth. It was still too hot to swallow. I was in pain. Bianca quickly went to the refrigerator and grabbed a beverage. She poured me a glass, which I hastily drank. It didn't taste like anything. I took a moment to regain my composure.

"How did you like it?" Bianca asked.

"Absolutely amazing!" I replied. Even though my tongue was probably chemically charred, it didn't take away from what I was able to taste.

"I told you you'd like them," she said. I looked to where Bryan had been standing. He wasn't there.

"Where's Bryan?" I asked Bianca. We looked around the kitchen. He had left. We started looking around the house. I found him up in Bianca's room on her Playstation.

"Weren't you at least going to say hello to your mother?" I asked.

"Not if I could avoid it," he replied.

"Come on, man, what happened to 'The sooner I do it, the sooner it's over with?'" I asked.

"Is that what it will take to get you to leave me alone?" he fired back.

"I'd like to think that I'm doing you a favor, but yes, that is what it will take," I replied. He put down the controller and trudged down the stairs. He progressed towards the kitchen, where his mother was still standing in front of the stove.

"Hello, Kymera," he said dryly. She turned to look at him.

"Hello, Bryan," she replied just as dryly.

"You wanted ta see me, I yaint wanna come. So what up, Kymera?" he asked. I could tell this wasn't going to be nice and neat.

"I supposed I deserved that. Do you think you could try Mrs. Randall, perhaps? I'll understand if you don't think I qualify for "Mom" yet," she relented.

"You lucky I'm even talkin ta you. You didn't think ta call once in fo'teen years. Da only reason you here now is cause Granny dead. I wish it was you insteada her!" he said as he turned to leave. Kymera's facial expression didn't change one bit, which I thought was odd considering her flesh and blood son had just wished death upon her. She just mumbled callously;

"For everything I had to go through for the two of you, neither one of you did me any good either." I heard her say it, but I didn't know quite how to interpret it. I was going to learn soon enough.

# 9

"I can't wait for my man to get home! Mrs. Brock Randall. That has a nice ring, doesn't it?" my mom asked me. Personally, I didn't care much for it.

"It sounds like two last names. Besides who names their child "Brock"? I mean seriously B-Rock? Whatever. I don't have to live with it, that's for you," I replied. I had taken the day off to help my mom at her rehabilitation center. I remember helping her study for all the exams she had to take to get her license. She and I had spent countless hours helping her learn terms, locations and names. I had picked up such a large amount of information, that I probably could have passed the state exam myself. She was a medical masseuse, and while I knew precious little about the subtle nuances of medical massage, I did know how to manage books. She asked me to take a look at her books to make sure that she could afford the wedding she wanted, so that's what I had spent the day doing.

"Oh shut up Mr. Jayson Windsor. At least my name follows the natural order of things."

"She's got you talking like that too, huh?" I asked. One night at dinner with my mom and Brock, Bianca suggested that if we got married, I should change my last name to Windsor, instead of her changing her last name to Sullivant. I thought she was just playing, but with Bianca, I could never really be sure. Her office phone rang.

"Sullivant Soothing Waters Spa…I'm sorry. I believe you may have dialed incorrectly, good bye." Then she turned back to me.

"Honestly Jayson, I think you two would fit really well together. You should think about it. It's already been six months. She is a phenomenal girl, and you know I don't say that about too many women, especially when it comes to my baby boy," she said as she gave me a kiss on the forehead.

"Jessica, we are in a place of business! You can't do that here!" I yelled playfully.

"Oh hush! We are in a place of my business! I can do what I want! I'm still momma regardless!" she shot back.

"I am not Brock; you need to wait for your man to get home for that nonsense. What is he doing in Dallas anyway? He should have taken you with him."

"He's meeting with someone about his severance package. They've been working on it for a while now; he should be getting paid pretty soon. But that shouldn't matter to you Mr. Givend and Mosse Design," she answered. The badinage could have gone on forever, but it was quickly interrupted by my ringing phone. I picked it up.

"Hello?"

"Hey Uncle Jay, do you think you cud come an pick me up from work?" the voice asked. It was Bryan.

"Yeah, but you're going to have to go to the Beacon with me," I answered.

"That's cool."

"I'll be there in a little bit," I replied as I hung up the phone. My mom looked a little disappointed.

"You're leaving? Will you do me a favor? Find out what you're doing on the weekend of January twelfth. I have to go to Orlando for a medical expo, and I need someone to keep Sammy for me," she said as I packed up my items. I hadn't but I was sure that I couldn't.

"I can look, but I'm pretty sure that weekend's locked up. Why can't her father keep her?" I asked.

"Brock's been in an out of Dallas so much lately, I don't know if he'll be here or not. I'd rather not depend on him for this one," she replied.

"But you're going to marry him? I don't know momma, sounds kind of silly to me," I responded.

"Jayson please don't. I love him, regardless of our problems, just like I love you. Okay? Let's just leave it there," she pleaded. I gathered my effects. This was the only place where we didn't see eye to eye, and I didn't want to start any sort of argument now.

"I love you too momma," I said as I made my way out to my car. Bryan had been released from the program last month on the condition that he maintained steady, verifiable employment, or was under the surveillance of an adult over the age of twenty one. Kymera still had matters to attend to in Dallas, so she left town immediately after the funeral, just like Bryan had predicted. However, she was due back before the first of the year in order to take possession of her mother's house. A unique clause in her mother's will stipulated that the only way Kymera could take legal ownership of the home was to reside there for five years, just enough time for Bryan to graduate high school. So in the mean time, for Bryan, the only other option was to get a job. Father Potter used some of his connections in the community to get him a job at a local grocery store, even though he was still a little too young to work at most jobs in the area. It didn't pay very much, but it kept him out of trouble. He was trying to improve. He had finally started to show signs of wanting a better life for himself. It was quite commendable. He was still pretty rough around the edges, but he was making an active investment in himself. Nothing could be more valuable.

Kymera was going to be gone until the beginning of the year, which was about a month from now. Bryan was going to be splitting time between my apartment and Bianca's house. It was a unique answer to a very difficult situation. Rather than allow him to wind up in juvenile detention, we decided to make an effort to work with him towards a solution. This however was coming at the expense of our relationship. Random check ups meant that Bryan had to always be with someone. Which meant that the moments Bianca and I had together alone were so few, that Haley's comet was more likely to appear again before we were alone next. It was a mixed blessing. It made me appreciate when I could see her that much more, but on the reverse, Bianca was extremely sexy to me. Not just attractive, but sexy. Even though I wasn't in a hurry to get to that next step, it didn't mean I wasn't trying to get there. Helping Bryan was putting a serious damper on those efforts, not that I minded, it was just that I noticed.

I drove to the store to pick him up. He was standing outside looking depressed. I pulled over so he could get into the car.

"Uncle Jay, main, dis ain't coo! I worked fa two weeks an' I only got two hunnad dollas. I mean, ya'll said ita get betta, but dis is sum bull. I cudda mad dis much workin' fa D'easy. By da time ah git sum minutes, an' sum new jeans, I ain't gon hav no cake left," he vented. I could understand the allure, but I had to keep trying to push him towards the right way.

"That's why you have to budget your money. I'm not going to lie to you, it's not easy. But you know that. You have to keep pushing. I promise it's worth it in the end. Think about it, that money is yours and you don't have to worry about anyone coming behind you, no looking over your shoulder—"

"I can't look over my shoulder cause I'm busy looking at the fingers that I'm working to da bone. Uncle Jay you an Aint B is doin' a lot and I appreciate it, but dis right here is not the business," he stated. There was something about how he said it that filled me with a certain dread.

"Bryan, you have a lot more than yourself to think about in all of this. Me, your Aunt Bianca, Father Potter, even your grandmother, we all believed that you were worth whatever sacrifices we had to make in order to try and get you to the right place. This goes beyond you. You have to understand that. Even if you don't want to do it for yourself, you represent more than yourself. You are the sum total of everyone that stands behind you. Think of it like that," I said, trying to pull him back. He still didn't look convinced.

"Imean, iss cool fa yall ta hav my back like that, but still, Ima live my life tha best way I know how, an I'ma live it fa me. You ain't broke, Aint B ain't broke. Father Potter don't need money and granny dead. I'm broke, an' this little bit a money aint gon get the job done," he declared. His dedication to making money reminded me of myself in a way, and while I had to respect his drive, I was afraid of where he was going.

"I had to work hard for years before I got this little bit of money. You know how much I got paid as an intern for Givend and Mosse? Nothing, not a dime. The restaurant I worked at only paid me one fifty every two weeks, hell I had to sell plasma in undergrad to get money to eat on the in between weeks. Not to party, to eat. I was eight years old the first time I helped at the Becaon. My mother had me around Father Potter as much as possible. Working at the Beacon still doesn't pay me anything. Your Aunt Bianca? Still has to pay back thousands of dollars in student loans. She had to work hard to get into school; again, that was just sweat equity. Father Potter had to give up…I don't know what he had to give up, but I'm sure it wasn't easy, and you saw how hard your grandmother worked. She was sixty five and still worked a fifty hour week to make sure you had a home. She could have sold that house and moved to Florida years ago. When you first got in trouble, the only reason she didn't sell the house was so that you wouldn't wind up in the system. No one gave any of us anything, and it wasn't easy at first, but with effort it gets better. If you stop trying everytime it gets hard, then you'll never finish anything. I care too much about you to let you go out like that," I said. Bryan sat contemplatively as we drove to the Beacon.

The holiday season was an interesting time at the Beacon. The proceeds from the Fall Fundraiser went directly to financing our holiday menu. We attempted to provide a meal for one hundred people every night from the day after Thanksgiving until Christmas, in addition to our normal Wednesday night meals. This of course meant added stress for Bianca, who had to find a way to coordinate everything, but as usual, she was handling everything well. We went inside the Bianca's office. She was on the phone smiling. She motioned for the two of us to come in.

"Hey boys! I've got some news for you. Apparently Kymera's managed to enroll at Port Haven Technical ahead of schedule. So instead of waiting until New Year's, she's going to come back this weekend. She'll be here on Saturday," she said. I could tell Bryan wasn't thrilled, but I was inwardly elated. I was glad to help Bryan, but I was seriously beginning to miss Bianca.

"Yippee," Bryan remarked sarcastically. I understood his disposition, but I was genuinely excited about my own good fortune. I tried not to appear too eager, but I had to strike while the iron was hot.

"It's been a while since we went to Vive; you want to check that out?" I asked impetuously. I instantly wished I could take it back as it was apparent I had hurt Bryan's feelings.

"Dang, you cudn't even wait fa her ta get here, youa just say dat in ma face doh?" he asked.

"It's nothing personal, really, I just miss my baby," I said playfully as I gave her a kiss on the cheek.

"Yall corny man," he said of our display.

"I have a little work to do, but I might be able to make that happen. As soon as I verify, I'll let you know," she replied. I smiled. Just one full day to wait. It was Bianca's night to watch Bryan. I said my goodbyes and headed for a decent night's rest. The next day at work was extremely important.

I had rescheduled the interrupted meeting from a few months prior to take place on today. The original parties where present, but there was someone else. It looked as though they had a representative of the client in the room with them. This was highly unusual. I normally knew about these things well in advance. I kept my professional cool and proceeded business as usual.

"Good morning gentlemen," I said coolly.

"Good morning Mr. Sullivant," they answered in unison. The third party in the room just quietly observed what was going on around him.

"Jayson, I'm going to get right to the point. Maclayne is looking to reach a more diverse, and particularly a younger, more urban crowd. They are looking for someone that can guide their marketing efforts in the right direction. Quite honestly Jayson, I believe that you are the right person to handle this project," the first speaker asserted.

"Thank you for that Trent. I have to ask though, what exactly is it that Maclayne Studios is looking for? How can I help them?" I asked.

"Well Jayson, they need someone that is as cool in a coffeehouse as he is in a corner office as collected in a back alley as he is in on the boardwalk. He's got to have both street appeal, and marketabilty. We need somebody universal. Young, no criminals, no daycare owners, no junkies, I mean this guy has got to be the total package. He needs to be good in any hood, and able to compete on Wall Street. Hey, maybe I could do it!" Trent said as everyone laughed politely.

"I mean that sounds a lot like me, I guess, but still, why not just go to a casting agency? " I asked. I realized that it seemed like the easy way out, but I wanted to get to the heart of the matter, find out their real intentions.

"This person has to have knowledge of everything that goes on behind the scenes. We can trot anybody out there, but this person has to have panache, he or she has to know how to react under any circumstance. We can't put our muscle behind just anyone. It's got to be the right one. Jayson, we basically need you to go out and find and exact copy of yourself," he said. I still wasn't convinced.

"What aren't you telling me Trent?" I asked. He took a deep breath.

"Jayson, Maclayne Studios has offered to buyout your contract, in exchange for a new one—with them," he said. I was confused.

"Well then why not just say that?" I asked.

"I realize it seemed round about, but I was trying to gauge your interest. Plus this was the list of questions as required by Mr. Tanaka. After seeing your track record, they approached us with a very handsome number, so you are going to be responsible for their project, which ultimately is your project," he admitted. The man in the back of the room stood up and walked to the front near the camera. I figured with a name like Tanaka, he was probably Asian, but it turned out, he was just as African-American as me.

"Mr. Sullivant, we are looking for a top notch personality to help run our newest venture. We are trying to tap a younger urban market, and we think you possess the perfect mixture of qualities to help us break into that market. The qualities that Trent was making reference to are all necessary, beacause you are going to have to deal with men in suits, and men in Timberland boots." I smiled.

"That was good," I said.

"Thanks I worked on it all night," he admitted. "We just need an effective go between," he concluded.

"What is the job description?" I asked.

"There isn't one. The only thing that we are concerned with is job status, and for you that needs to be or approaching "Done" at all times. We are prepared to compensate you one hundred and fifty percent above what you are earning currently, complete with a fifty-thousand dollar signing bonus. That's how serious we are." I nearly fell on the floor. I was already earning a shade under fifty thousand a year. One hundred and twenty five thousand per year was unbelieveable.

"I see why Trent didn't want to tell me. Can you send over the details?" I asked.

"We most certainly can. We are looking for one more person to add to our new marketing team. This person is actually going to be the face that the people see, and recognize when we start talking about connecting with the youth. You have a few months until our search is complete. The terms and conditions of the contract will be in your hands by Monday at noon, okay? It's all pretty much standard stuff, except for the 'purity clause.' This person, you, has to be squeaky clean. No kids, no drugs, nothing that could be viewed negatively. We need good publicity, and a good representative," Mr. Tanaka asked.

"Certainly, sir, and thank you very much for your consideration," I said.

"Congrats Jayson, you deserve it. We're gonna miss you around here," Trent said graciously.

"Thank you, Trent. You gentlemen have a nice weekend," I said as I turned off the monitor. I was beside myself with excitement. A new job?! A hundred and twenty five thousand a year?! I couldn't belive it. I hurriedly turned everything off and ran to my car. I was looking forward to picking up Bianca and going to Café Vive to celebrate. I didn't know what we were going to do with Bryan, but I knew I had to go out tonight and Bianca had to come with me. There wasn't any scenario that I could think of that I wanted other than that one. I decided I should call Bianca to inform her of my resolution.

"Hey baby, we gotta go out tonight. The meeting today was better than I could have ever imagined. One of the reps from Maclayne was there. They actually want me to spearhead this new campaign! Basically, they're going to buy out my contract with Givend and Mosse to give me creative control over this new venture! There are dreams that come true. This is way beyond one of those, so we gotta go out tonight! What do you think?" I asked excitedly.

"Aww babe, that is awesome! Meet me at my house at like nine thirty and we'll make it happen, okay?" she replied. I smiled.

"Great. See you then," I answered. I headed home to get some rest. I figured I was going to need it.

I showed up at Bianca's house at nine fifteen. I knocked on the door. Quinn answered it.

"Hey Jayson. Bianca!" she called. "You know the routine. Just hang out in here for a second. I'm sure that she's around here somewhere," she said reassuringly. A few moments later, Bianca materialized wearing a t-shirt and an a faded college t-shirt and a pair of gym shorts. It was cute, but I knew it wasn't club attire.

"Beeeeyyyyaaannnnccccaaa" I cooed softly. "You want to explain what's going on here?" I asked curiously. She had that "I-really-don't-want-to-tell-you-the-truth look in her eye.

"Babe, I got a joke for you. You ready?" I nodded. "What's five foot three and has to have the year end reports compiled by Monday?" she asked. I groaned.

"Are you kidding me? I thought we were going out! I was really looking forward to Vive tonight," I complained.

"I told you that I would see what we could do, but these reports have to get done. I'll keep Bryan tonight so you can still go to Vive," she said. I could tell that she was growing mildly exasperated.

"So I'm just supposed to go by myself? There isn't anyway I can change your mind? There's nothing I enjoy more than good poetry and the company of a beautiful woman," I asked as I wrapped my arms around her and kissed her softly on her cheek. I had grown used to her company at Vive.

"I'm sorry baby, but I gotta get this stuff done, otherwise it's going to be a long time before I see the light of day, let alone go out with you, or anyone else," she said as she wiggled out of my grasp. I understood what she was up against.

"I'll help you tonight and then maybe we can go out tomorrow night," I volunteered. I didn't really want to help her at all. I wanted to go to Vive and then maybe go another club after that, but I had to try and be supportive.

"Really? Baby I can't ask you to do that. I know how much you want to go to Vive. You should go," she deferred.

"It's cool, I really just want to be with you," I answered. I wasn't really trying to score any points with her, but having the right words to say didn't hurt.

"That's what makes you such an unbelievable boyfriend. How in the world did I ever get so lucky?" she asked as she gave me a kiss on the cheek. I blushed. I was giving up a night out, but gaining a world of approval in her eyes. The trade off seemed favorable. I was just about to take off my shoes and settle in for a long night of tax forms and other associated headaches, when I heard the door slam.

"Bianca?" the voice called.

"Kymera?" Bianca replied as she went into the front room. I stayed seated. Moments later, the two of them appeared in front of me. "Look honey, it's Kymera," Bianca stated redundantly.

"I.I see. Hello Kymera, I thought we couldn't expect you until tomorrow?" I asked politely.

"I missed you, so I thought I'd come back today," she said. Moments before the wave of disbelief completely washed over my face, she smiled. "I'm kidding sweetheart, it was cheaper to come back today, and the sooner I start living in this house, the sooner I can sell it and get out of here," she answered. At least she was honest.

"Well Kymera, we've got to get on this paper work. Are you taking Bryan with you?" Bianca asked. Kymera smiled as she opened her full length mink coat, revealing a scant red minidress. I prayed to God that my mouth wasn't hanging open. It was like a work of art. Even better than the t-shirt and shorts when I first met her.

"Does this look like I'm trying to take Bryan anywhere?" she asked.

"Were you going to ask me to keep him?" Bianca asked.

"If I were still in Dallas, he would have been here, right? So just pretend I'm still in Dallas" she responded, crassly imposing on her younger cousin. "I'm sorry, that's rude of me. It's just that I haven't been out in so long, and I thought that I was going to get to go out tonight, but my husband can't seem to get rid of his girlfriend for the night. So of course I'm stuck in the house on a beautiful Friday night. I just want to go out, I don't want to get into any trouble, just out of the house," she opined. Then she looked at me. "Jerry, you sure are dressed nice to sit at home and do paper work." I froze. There are times when a man just shouldn't say anything, because every answer he provides is going to be the wrong answer. After taking a few moments to consider my response, I spoke.

"I was trying to impress my girlfriend," I answered weakly.

"You should come out with me. Bianca won't mind, and besides, she tells me your poetry is beautiful." I looked at Bianca incredulously. I didn't believe in sharing intimate details, regardless of how trivial they may seem. Some things are just better between the parties involved.

"We talk. And your poetry is good. You should be happy to share that with the world," Bianca answered as she worked.

"C'mon Jayson, we should go to Vi-vay, is that what it's called?" Kymera whined. I couldn't lie, I did want to go, but I knew that there was no way this would work out in my favor.

"I'm just going to stay here and help Bianca. I appreciate the offer though," I replied. Bianca was clearly growing agitated.

"Jayson, I have to get this stuff done. Not almost, not partially, but all the way done, no questions asked. You are probably going to be a distraction. Please take her to wherever it is she wants to go," Bianca said, in what for her was a cross tone. Kymera turned and went to the kitchen. Once she was out of earshot I turned to Bianca.

"Are you sure you want me to take her out? That doesn't seem like a bad idea to you?" I asked. It sure seemed like a bad idea to me.

"Jayson, first off, I trust you. Secondly, Kymera is like a sister to me now, and thirdly, anything she's got, I promise mine is better. I'm not worried about any of it. Go have a good time and I'll see you tomorrow," she said as she gave me a kiss on the cheek. Kymera came back into the room.

"Do you really want to go to Vive?" I asked.

"Yes, I'd love to go, it sounds a lot better than sitting in the house," Kymera responded. I put my coat on and we headed out to my car. I opened the door for Kymera, who was seeming shocked by the procedure.

"Bianca said you had manners, but wow!" she remarked. I smiled. Sometimes I wished I could get past the force of habit. The last thing I needed to do was significantly endear myself to this woman.

"My mother taught me well," I replied.

"That's so adorable, a man who loves his family and especially his mother. Who is responsible for raising such a well mannered individual?" Kymera asked.

"Jessica. Jessica Sullivant," I replied. She looked like she wanted to say something, but had decided to hold back.

"Oh, okay…So I know you, but I don't know anything about you, Jerry, tell me a little more about you," she requested. I never enjoyed speaking about myself at length, I almost always sounded arrogant.

"I work for Givend and Mosse—"

"Ooooh, how much does a job like that pay?" she asked eagerly.

"Enough. I eat and I have a place to stay, so it pays enough," I answered. That was why I normally didn't tell people that I worked there, because that was ordinarily the next question.

"Okay…Do you have any other family?" she asked, seemingly gathering that fiscal questions were out of bounds.

"My dad died when I was little and my mom never remarried, although she did have another child with her boyfriend Brock," I answered.

"Brock? That is an interesting name. I nearly named Bryan Brock," she replied.

"I don't like it, it sounds like a last name. Or a really terrible nickname. And then on top of that, I don't think he's good enough for my mother."

"Oh really? Why is that?" Kymera asked, appearing strangely intrigued.

"I just don't feel like he loves her the way she should be loved. I mean from what I see, it looks like his heart is somewhere else. I mean from what I've seen, he and my mom are like wearing a pair of shoes that are two sizes to small. You can try as hard as you want to, but they just won't fit. Even if you can somehow get your foot all the way in, it will never be comfortable," I surmised. Kymera was drinking it all in.

"So why do you think they're together?" she asked.

"I don't know, probably because of Samantha," I answered.

"Does Brock have any other children?" she asked.

"Not that I know about. My mom wouldn't date someone with kids, just because she wouldn't. Apparently I was enough," I replied. Kymera laughed politely.

"Well look how well you turned out, I can't imagine why your mother wouldn't want to insert herself into more families."

I was confused.

"I'm sorry, I don't follow. What do you mean by that?" I asked. Kymera laughed again.

"Just that your mother shouldn't have ruled out joining someone with children so she could influence more young lives," she answered. I wasn't all the way convinced, but for the moment I was sufficiently placated. I honestly wasn't that interested in finding out about Kymera, and any thing that I might have asked about would have seemed like I wanted to know more, and the last thing that I wanted to do was to give her any type of sign that I might be in the least bit interested. We sat silently for a few moments before Kymera decided to re-break the ice.

"Do you prefer producing material, like the writing part, or do you prefer performing material?" she asked. Asking questions about writing was the one way in that was never closed.

"I like both parts, but performing it is the best. People hear what I have to say and they apply it to their own lives. It's a beautiful thing to know that I might be helping someone, or sparking a light in someone's head," I replied.

"Have you ever tried putting you work to music?" she continued.

"I'd like to think that I can do that. I've never tried it," I answered. "Maybe I'll give it a real effort sometime."

"That would take a lot of talent. I bet if you could pull that off, you could get a deal, like be a rapper or something," she said, placing a hand on my shoulder.

"I already have a career. This is just what I do for fun," I said. I shifted gears sharply so that her hand would fall off of my shoulder. I didn't need any further temptation.

At Vive, Uncle Jeremiah seemed a bit confused when he saw Kymera. I couldn't blame him, I had been showing up with Bianca for the past six months, so to see me with someone else should have been a shock. He led us in to my usual spot and we sat down to watch the open mic performances. About an hour in, Kymera's eyes lit up.

"Can I go up there and do something?" she asked me.

"If you want to I can get you on the list," I replied.

"Can you do that?" She seemed excited. I motioned to Uncle Jeremiah. He came over from his perch just offstage over to where we were sitting.

"Will you put Mrs. Randall on the performance list for me please?" I asked him.

"Yeah, but she's got to be quick, I've got something special lined up for tonight," Uncle Jeremiah said as he scrawled Kymera's name on the list. "She's the third one on after the intermission," he informed me. The onstage act was finishing and he went up to the mic to call the next performer.

"Monica Longmire? She must have stepped out. Okay how about Ms. Mahogony Jones? Wow, she's not here either? Oh my God, where is everybody? How about this: He didn't know I was going to ask him this, but how about we get Port Haven's favorite son up here to bless us? What ya'll think?" Uncle Jeremiah asked. The crowd applauded in agreement. I smiled weakly as I climbed up on stage. I hadn't prepared anything at all.

"Uncle Jeremiah, you REALLY shouldn't have...How ya'll doin' tonight?" I asked.

"Good" the audience replied in unison. Without a prepared piece, I found myself needing to improvise. I looked over at the small house band. I had an idea. I pulled the mic out of the stand and moved the stand out of the way.

"Can you play "I'm a Little Teapot for me?" I asked. The band looked at me for a moment but then complied with my request. "I call this song right here, "Writer's Block" Tell me what ya'll think:

More garbage lyrics, bars that don't fit,

I can't think of anything, but I won't quit.

My thoughts keep on crashing, rhythm won't hold.

I went from being white hot to ice cold. Thank you. I'll try and do better next time, I promise.

I got down off the stage. Kymera was ecstatic. "Oh my GOD!! That was soo good! Bianca wasn't lying!" she exclaimed. I blushed.

"It wasn't that good. I messed up a little bit towards the end," I said, trying to defer the attention. I noticed Uncle Jeremiah in the corner talking to someone that looked vaguely familiar. They shook hands and Uncle Jeremiah rushed hurriedly to the stage. Past the glare of the lights, I recognized the man as Mr. Tanaka from my meeting. "Ladies and gentlemen! Your attention please! Café Vive is going to be the new home of Maclayne Pictures new reality show series! Every week local and national acts are going to be featured! Café Vive is on the map!" he said cheerfully. A thunderous roar of applause went up from the crowd. "That's not all! Guess who they want the host to be ya'll? My friend and yours, Port Haven's favorite son, Jay Azariah!" he yelled as a spotlight swung to where I was sitting. I couldn't believe it. I thought they just wanted me to direct their marketing efforts, I didn't realize they had planned to design the efforts around me. I was speechless. I smiled and walked dreamily to the stage. "Say somethin' Jay!" Uncle Jerry ordered.

"Uhh. Wow, I don't really know what to say. The details are still getting worked out, but like Uncle Jerry said, we are definitely on the map now ya'll!" I said excitedly. I hadn't even seen this coming. I climbed down from the stage, still euphoric from the new revelation. Kymera and I sat there for a few more acts. She decided that she didn't want to perfom after all, and asked me to take her home.

Kymera was convinced that she had been the sole cause of my new found good fortune.

"Now see, if I hadda let you stay home with Bianca, you wouldn't have been seen by that talent scout, and you'd still be working for Givend and Mosse," she repeated for no fewer than the tenth time. I had stopped correcting her after repetition number four. I knew the truth and I was convinced at this point that she knew it as well, even if she was wanted to believe otherwise. I drove a little faster than normal to get back to Bianca's house so that Kymera could get her car, and the evening would be completed. It wasn't that I didn't enjoy myself, it was just that she wasn't Bianca, and in a way, that cheapened the experience for me. I got Kymera back to her car at Bianca's house. I had never been more excited to drop someone off in my life. I sat there with the car idling while Kymera gathered her effects. I wasn't paying her any attention as my focus was on going into the house to talk to my girlfriend. Kymera seemed to be taking a little longer than I might have liked for her to be taking. Just as I was about to voice my concern, she leaned in quickly to try and kiss me. I turned just quick enough so that her embrace landed on my cheek as opposed to my lips.

"Thank you for a lovely evening, Jerry," she said. I was beside myself, but I tried to contain my anger.

"I had an enjoyable evening with you as well. However in the future, I'll have to ask you to respect my relationship with your niece," I asserted.

"Bianca is my cousin, and I'll respect whatever it is you have, just so long as you promise that when you're ready for a grown woman, you'll come here first," she said seductively.

"I appreciate the invitation, but there is a grown woman inside of this house that suits me just fine," I answered. My phone rang. It was Bianca.

"Yes, dear?" I answered.

"Are you going to stay here tonight?" she asked. I hadn't really thought about it, but I wasn't going to refuse an invitation to come in.

"If that's an invitation, then sure I'll be in a second," I answered loudly. I was hoping Kymera would see what was going on. Her facial expression seemed to indicate that she got the hint.

"I'm leaving, but my offer still stands," she said as she winked at me. She got out of my car and sauntered over to her own, and in moment, she was gone. I was so busy watching Kymera that I forgot Bianca was still on the phone.

"Baby! Are you coming in or not?!" she yelled, snapping me back to reality.

"I'm staying, I'm staying!" I answered.

"Well, stop shining you lights in my window and get in here!" she ordered. I hastily complied with her directive. When I knocked on the door to announce my arrival, the I found the door was already cracked. I cautiously stepped inside.

"Bianca?" I called.

"I'm upstairs," she replied. I shut and locked the door behind myself, and slowly tread up the stairs. The faint scent of Bianca's perfume hung in the air. I reached the top of the staircase, and turned towards her room. I knocked on her closed door.

"It's open Jayson," Bianca replied seductively. I pushed open the door. The light of no fewer than twenty candles emanated from various points in the dimly lit room. I walked in, and took off my coat. Bianca, who was lying on the bed stood up. I nearly fainted when my eyes finally adjusted. She sauntered towards me slowly in an untied black satin gown. There in the candlelight, with the soft music playing, I realized just how fortunate I was. At this point, she had become the living embodiment of my fantasy. Her normally flawless face was accented by light touches of make-up. I could just make out the eyeliner. Her hair sat softly on her shoulder, exactly the way I loved for it to be. She stopped walking just out of my reach and placed her hand on her hip, forcing the gown completely open and revealing the treasure underneath. Her black satin bra held her breasts like a glove. I let myself get lost in the lines of her flat stomach until I arrived at the border of her matching black thong. Her toned, long legs, ended in a pair of new black pumps. She looked better than great and she knew it. I stood there transfixed as I slowly drank in her essence. She had me in a trance, under her influence, and my eyes were reveling in their inebriation. She took another step towards me and gently took my hands in her own as she looked into my eyes. Neither of us spoke. There wasn't anything left to say that hadn't already been said with our eyes. She let my hands go as she wrapped hers around my neck and craned her neck to kiss me. I put my hands in my back pockets in order to warm them a little bit before I touched her. Feeling as though they were warm enough, I began to gently caress her back as we embraced each other slowly. I held her as close as I could; the heat from her body was beginning to light my fire. She slipped her hands under my shirt and ran her fingers over my defined abs. She pulled up on my shirt, and without losing momentum, I pulled the shirt over my head. The kisses intensified as I began to explore her body with my hands. I reached around her back and unclasped her bra. The garment fell to the floor, and she stood there in front of me uncovered. I lifted her into the air and she wrapped her legs around my waist as the kisses began to get even deeper. I began to kiss her soft supple breasts and we moved towards the bed. I held her for a few moments more and I laid her down gently. She looked at me as though she had completely relinquished control of the situation. I began to kiss the nape of her neck, and slowly I made made my way down her body. Bianca was my drug of choice, and like any fiend, I needed my fix. She was like crack; I was ready to inject her. I kept working my way down her body, taking my time to make sure that I paid every square inch of her body the time it deserved. I reached the top of the black panties that she had on, and I gently bit down on the top of them, and started to pull them down. She arched her back to help me. Before I had gotten them past her thighs, there was a loud thud from the back bedroom. Instantly she froze.

"Jayson, what was that?!" she asked.

"How would I know, I'm in here with you?!" I responded.

"Go find out please," she asked, redressing. "My bat is by the door," she directed. I walked angrily towards the door and picked up the aluminum bat. Whomever or whatever was in this room was not going to have a good night. I was going to see to that.

"I don't believe this!" I said incredulously walking towards the source of the noise. I opened the door slowly, with the bat cocked to do as much damage as possible.

"Wait don't swing!!" the person yelled. I turned on the light. It was Bryan.

"What are you doing? I thought you left with your mom?" I asked. I could see his face twisting as though he was about to say something false. Before he could speak, the doorbell rang.

"Save whatever lie you were about to tell. Just stay here and be quiet," I instructed. I walked back past the Bianca's room.

"What was that babe?" she asked.

"Bryan," I replied.

"Who's at the door?" she asked. I threw my hands up.

"Babe, I'm upstairs, I haven't answered the door yet, I don't know. " I replied. I stalked down the stairs and opened the door. Two police officers stood at the door.

"Hello Sir, I'm Officer Morian, and this is my partner Officer Giraud," the first speaker said as they flashed badges at me. "We were following a suspect in a narcotics investigation, and we believe that he may have come here. We would like to look around very briefly if you don't mind," he said as they moved towards the door. I impeded their progress.

"I do mind. Without a warrant, you won't enter this house tonight. I answered curtly. "What makes you think that anyone is here? You gentlemen are ruining what had started out as a beautiful night for my girlfriend and me," I answered. They didn't look happy with my decision, but they had little in the way of options.

"If you don't have anything to hide, why can't we come in?" Officer Giraud asked.

“Because I know my rights and unless you come back with a warrant, you won’t get in here at all,” I said. The officers walked away seemingly defeated. I noticed that they weren’t walking to a cruiser, but to a busted older model car. I was surprised that it was even functioning. “And for all the money I pay in taxes, you guys need to do something about that car. It’s an eyesore!” I yelled out after them antagonistically. It was a bit uncalled for, but considering that my night was ruined, I felt mildly justified in it. After watching them get in the car and drive away, I locked the door. I walked up the stairs and to the room where Bryan was. He was sitting there apprehensively. I didn’t know what to say to him.

“Call your mom. Tell her to come and get you,” I instructed. I couldn’t think clearly enough to discipline him correctly. I would have taken my anger out on him, and that wouldn’t have been fair. I walked back down the hall to see how Bianca was doing. Much like I expected, she was asleep. She had been working long days as of late, and I couldn’t blame her. I walked back down the hall.

“Uncle Jay, my mom wants to know if I can just stay here tonight, and she’ll come and get me in the morning,” he suggested.

“That’s fine. Are you okay?” I asked. Angry or not, I don’t know how I would have responded if the boy got hurt.

“Yes sir, thank you,” he answered gratefully.

“It’s fine. Get some rest, and I’ll drop you off in the morning,” I instructed.

With Kymera assuming responsibility for Bryan, things between Bianca and I sped along. We were emotionally where most couples are in a year in only about nine months time. It wasn’t so much that either of us was rushing, it was more that we just clicked. Our thought processes were similar. We had similar goals, likes, dislikes. She was what I wanted in a woman, and I felt like I was what she wanted in a man. It was funny, I felt like a complete person before I met her, so it wasn’t that she completed me, but it was more like she made me better somehow. I didn’t like who I was without her around. I wasn’t as good as I could be when she wasn’t there.

One night, about a week and a half after New Year's Day, Bianca and I were sitting at in my apartment watching "One Night with the King." I wasn't much for love stories, but I had promised her a quiet night at home, and this is how she elected to spend it. About half way through the movie, Bianca, who was lying in my arms turned over to look me in the eye.

"I always wanted curtains around my bed. I brought that canopy bed and just haven't had a chance to put up the posts or the curtains. It's all just sitting in my closet, gathering dust. I just think that is so romantic. Maybe I'll have someone come and do it one day," she said refering to the movie. Then as the main characters moved towards the same bed on their wedding night, she looked as though she had more to say. "Baby, it's been almost ten months, and we've never had sex. I'm not complaining, but at the same time, I just wonder. I mean, aren't you even the least bit curious?" she asked. I didn't really want to have this conversation. If there was ever a time that I would have rather watched a love story, this was it. I looked into her big brown eyes.

"Bianca, I…I…I don't really know how to explain this—"

"Ohmigod, you're gay! I knew it! That's the only way any sane man could pass on all this!" she exclaimed. It was a rare moment that one saw her seem proud.

"No! That's not it! Just let me talk. Remember when we first met, I told you why I was single right?" I asked.

"Yeah, you said because you got your feelings hurt in college, but Jayson, there is no way that a mild injury in college could still be hurting you now," Bianca reasoned coarsely.

"Let me explain. My junior year in college, right when I started my internship at Givend and Mosse, I met Amina. She was beautiful, inwardly and outwardly, and before her, I had never had any strong romantic inclinations towards anyone. I had always been focused on trying to get my degree. I was a nerd. I'm still a nerd, but anyway, I'm saying it started out as a friendship. We would hang out from time to time. It grew to be more than that and pretty soon she and I were virtually inseparable. I mean we did everything together—"

"None of this explains why you haven't made a move yet," Bianca interrupted. I had never seen her quite this antsy. I laughed.

"Baby, give me a second, I'm getting to it. Everything was great. We used to have so much fun with everything, whether it was playing cards, studying, going out, whatever. The friendship started to change. There was this undercurrent of sexual tension. I wanted her, and I could tell she wanted me, but neither of us was willing to take the risk of messing up the friendship. Then one night, while we were studying for an Economics test, I went for it. I kissed her. She kissed me back. It was exactly what I thought it was going to be, and then some. From there it escalated, and before long, we had done everything sexually there is for two people to do. I mean everything. But the friendship was still there and still strong. And I felt myself falling. As far as I was concerned, she was perfect. I tried not to let it affect me, tried to play strong, but she had me head over heels. I thought I loved her. I really did. I decided to tell her how I felt, and so one day, I went to her apartment. I found the door was open." I felt tears welling in my eyes. Bianca sat there, transfixed.

"Let me guess she was having sex with the captain of the football team or something," Bianca interjected.

"No," I replied softly. "She was having sex with a man that I later discovered was her fiancé. Apparently he lived a couple of hours away. She had never mentioned him, never even pretended like he existed. The part that bothered me wasn't the sex, I could have forgiven that in time. It was the fact that she was already engaged. She already had love, and here I was thinking that maybe she was the one for me. I was nothing more than a toy. My heart was on a string, and she was content to play with it as though it were a yo-yo. I was never going to be anything more than a fling. We stopped hanging out after that. I never spoke to her again. Most guys with a story like mine, just turn into womanizers. Hurting women, bed hopping, basically becoming a dog wasn't something that I could do. My mother taught me better than that. I couldn't inflict the pain that I felt onto someone else. So rather than lash out, I just shut down. Love was for other people maybe, but it wasn't for me. I couldn't handle the way that made me feel, so I poured myself into my work, trying to block it out. I worked so hard at Givend and Mosse that my mentor recommended me for the job I have now before I graduated. Evenings at the Beacon, weekends at Vive, days at work, nights alone. It keeps me safe. Or rather it kept me safe. That was all true until the day she walked in. She floated in like a dream. And all of a sudden, I believed in love again. I thought that maybe there was someone for me after all. She was it. I saw our lives merging into one. My life flashed before my eyes, but not because I was dying. It was because I was being reborn, into someone that had a chance at love. I saw everything, the fights, the love, the laughter, the growth. I saw us growing old and eating applesauce on the porch watching the sunset together. In one instant, my world had changed. I knew she was it. My heart's resurrection, the effective rebirth of my soul. In that instant, I knew that it was possible for me to love again. It had to be because she was finally here. She stood there in front of me, like a vision of perfection. There was only one thing left for me to know. Her name. What was her name? I was still standing there transfixed when she walked over to me and said simply; hi, my name is Bianca," I said. Bianca's eyes were filled with tears as she reached up to hug me. "So you see I haven't "made a move" not out of disinterest, but rather out of extreme caution." I was unsure of how to say what I felt was coming next. I turned off my mind and let my heart speak. "Bianca, you are the first thing I think about when I wake up, and the last thing I think about when I go to sleep. When I get dressed, I think about how much you are going to like what I have on. The other day I almost put on a blue tie that didn't match just because I know how much you like the color. I think about the smile on your face when I send you flowers. I talk to your picture when you don't answer your phone. I've called Cheryl "Bianca" so many times, she's thought about having her name changed. You consume every free thought that I have and it's driving me crazy. When I close my eyes, I see your face on the back of my eyelids. Bianca, my mother used to say I wouldn't have to write a poem for a woman if I truly loved her. At first I thought she was being silly, but now I understand why she said that. I don't need to write you a poem.

Sweetheart, you are my poem. You are every song, every sonnet that I could ever hope to write. I'm not in a hurry to make a move because, in my mind, in my heart, I know that I have a lifetime for that. It's funny, for all the words I know to say, there is really only one way to say what I feel right now. I love you Bianca," I finished. Bianca was crying at this point. I was nervous. I was pretty sure she felt the same way, but sometimes you just never know.

"That was beautiful…I love you too Jayson," she replied as she kissed me softly on the lips. "No one has ever expressed that emotion like that to me before. I'm sorry about what the last girl did, but I'm not her. I won't hurt you Jayson. I promise, and whenever you're ready, I'll be here," she said as she turned around and settled back into my arms. It wasn't that I didn't want to, it was just that she was so special that I didn't want to ruin it. For her, I felt like everything had to be perfect. She deserved the absolute best, and that was what I was determined to give her. We lay there quietly watching the movie, until sleep claimed us both.

The next morning, I felt inspired to make Bianca breakfast. I managed to slide from underneath her without jostling her, and proceeded towards the kitchen. Keeping Bryan had forced me to procure a variety or breakfast foods, and since I normally grabbed something on the way to the office, most of the non-perishable items were still in the cabinet. I surveyed my supplies, and deciding upon what to make, I went to work. My scrambled eggs, pancakes, ham and freshly squeezed orange juice wasn't gourmet by any standards, but I felt like I had done a good job. Bianca had been aroused by both my clangor in the kitchen and the aroma of the meal, and sat up in eager anticipation. I placed the meal on a tray and brought it over to her.

"Jayson, you shouldn't have!" she exclaimed. I smiled.

"I hope you like it," I replied. The sheer joy on her face was reward in and of itself. I sat and watched her for a moment, before I got up to go and fix myself a plate. She turned on Saturday morning cartoons. I laughed quietly. She was as big a kid as I was. After preparing my meal, I joined her on the couch. We ate and watched old reruns of The Justice League. I couldn't be happier. With all the stressors that we both faced on a daily basis, it was nice to retrogress into the safety of the confines of childhood. I took the plates into the kitchen and she sat there in my arms as we settled in to watch television.

"Do you hate Amina?" she asked. I had to think about it for a second.

"No, I don't hate her; I just wish I could have met her without having to go through the pain that she caused me. But then again, without her I wouldn't have met you. So for that reason, I don't hate her, but before you I thought that her plus two dimes and four pennies wasn't worth twenty-five cents," I recounted. Bianca took my words to heart, but then apparently sought to lighten the mood.

"Okay so in a foot race is your money on Superman or the Flash?" she asked me.

"If it's a footrace, it's got to be the Flash. Superman would have to fly, and that wouldn't be a foot race. Plus Superman is just faster than a bullet, but The Flash is on something altogether faster, like the electricity or something" I reasoned. She nodded thoughtfully. Conversations like this were pretty normal.

"Do you think Wonder Woman wears a wonder bra?" she asked.

"Was that a joke? Oh my God, that was terrible!" I answered. She hit me with a pillow.

"No, I'm serious, do you think she does?" she reiterated, laughing.

"I would guess she has too, I mean she fights dragons and stuff, but still looks great in her uniform. You would know more about that than I would. I mean either way she's phenomenal. What do you think?" I asked. She gasped.

"Speaking of phenomenal women, Kymera asked me if I knew anyone that could help her in an anatomy class that she's taking. She's got to pass that class in order to get her degree and she feels like she is going to have a difficult time unless she gets some help. She asked me if I could look into either you or your mother could help her or suggest someone that. I remembered you telling me about having helped her study for her masseuse license. So I figured maybe you could help." I was had a bad feeling about it. I just didn't trust Kymera. It amazed me that Bianca trusted her so blindly, and how in the world would Kymera know that?

"Babe, I told you I get bad vibes from her. I just feel like she's just up to no good," I pled. Bianca laughed.

"Why? Sure she's an attractive woman, but I promise you she's not a bad person, and she doesn't have any ulterior motives. She does like attention from men, but that doesn't mean she's going to rape you or anything. Jayson, we're talking about my nearly forty-year-old aunt. You're a baby to her, why in the world are you so nervous? Besides that she's married," Bianca said.

"Married?! To who? Where is this mystery husband? Who is this mystery husband?" I asked.

"I've never met him, and she doesn't talk about him, so I don't know much. Apparently he's due some money of some sort, and she's trying to make sure she gets her cut or something. That's all I know about it, because she doesn't talk about him much," Bianca explained. I nodded understandingly.

"I'll ask my mom if she can help, and if she can't then I will." I prayed my mother could help her.

"I promise she won't bite you. I'm sure she'll appreciate it," Bianca said thankfully. I smiled weakly as she turned back around. I just couldn't help but feel weird about the whole situation. We watched television for about another hour or so before Bianca got up to leave. I walked her to the door.

"Honey, I should have told you earlier, Kymera was looking to start studying tonight, so you'll have to work quickly," she said. I frowned.

"Babe, my mom is out of town at that medical massage expo. She won't be back until Tuesday," I said.

"Well then I trust you to do a good job," she retorted.

"Only because I love you" I said as she walked out the door. She smiled as she turned to give me a kiss.

"I love you too honey," she replied. I put on a pair of sneakers and walked her to her car. We were silent the entire trip. Sometimes you can say more with silence than you can with a pre-written speech. She climbed in her SUV after one last salutatory embrace and was gone. I walked back into my apartment to prepare for the day. As I was closing the blinds, I noticed that the sky had suddenly become ominously dark. It looked like a storm was coming. I smiled weakly in an effort to reassure myself. I was sure it was nothing to worry about, but I couldn't quite shake the way I felt. I thought about it for another moment more before I got dressed to leave. I had promised Father Potter that I would drop him off at the airport so he could make it to his guest speaking engagement in Orlando. Hopefully, whatever foreboding was hanging over me would dissipate before then.

After running my errands for the day, I went to Kymera's house. The feeling that was hanging over my head from earlier had only multiplied by the time that I reached her door. If I wasn't doing this as a favor to the woman I loved, I would have turned around and gone home. The condition of the house helped to inspire that feeling of dread that I was feeling. The gaping cracks in the sidewalk looked less like minor imperfections and more like passageways into the abyss. Every facet of the exterior of the house needed some modicum of attention. The blue shutters had faded to some odd shade of gray. The originally white paint covering the rest of the house had begun to yellow. The shutters were just barely hanging on to the structure. Considering the way Kymera presented herself in public and the fifty thousand dollar BMW in the driveway, the house was the complete antithesis of what I expected from her. I didn't remember it looking like that when Ms. Windsor lived there. It was as though her physical presence was enough to maintain the appearance of the home, as though the very spirit of her home died with her. I took a deep breath and reached over to the passenger side to gather my mother's old text books, and made my way to the door. I rang the doorbell. Moments later, Kymera appeared.

"Hey, Jerry!" Kymera said, opening the door.

"Jayson," I corrected dryly. I had to nip that in the bud, otherwise I'd be Jerry forever.

"Are you going to stand there and sulk or are you going to come in? She asked. I entered the house.

"Lead the way," I replied, stepping into the door. She shut the door and walked past me. The visual image was similar to the first night I met her. An extremely loose t-shirt that barely covered anything for a top and an equally inadequate pair silk boxers for bottoms. She started walking towards the back of the house. I was trying not to look at anything other than the back of her head, but it felt like her butt had its own gravitational pull and my eyes were its lone victim. I couldn't look at it. Not because I couldn't look at it, but rather because of the temptation to want more. I figured out of sight, out of mind. I tried to act the way I would act if Bianca were standing right there. Besides, if she found out that something had happened, that would certainly be the end. I was actively losing the battle when we walked past a mirror.

"You can look, I won't tell Bianca" Kymera said as though she knew what was going on in my head.

"Look at what?" I said innocently. I saw the mirror, but I didn't think she saw me looking.

"Jerry please don't take me for a fool. You're a man and I have a nice ass. Who can blame you for looking?" she replied. I couldn't argue with anything she said.

"I'm sorry, it won't happen again," I said ruefully. She laughed.

"It's no big deal, it'll be our little secret. Besides, Bianca ain't the only person in this family worth looking at," she replied. "I'm studying in here, so if you want to set up shop in there, feel free," she instructed. I walked into the room and sat on the plastic covered couch. The coffee table was littered with pens, pencils, notebooks and text books. Diagrams and pages of notes sprawled about, each with about a gallon of highlighter ink on them. It looked like she was really trying, even if she was really confused. I said a silent prayer for myself. If this woman's sexuality didn't overwhelm me, her apparently cluelessness might. I sat alone for a few more moments before Kymera appeared with a few cans of soda.

"I didn't know if you were thirsty or not, so I thought I'd bring you one as well. The kids are at their Mrs. Randall's house, so we can study with no interruption," she announced. I nearly choked.

"Mi…Mi…Misses Randall?" I asked. I thought back to my conversation from a day prior. Why would my mother be keeping her children?

"What? They're at their father's mother's house, as in they are spending the weekend with their father's mother. She wanted to see all of her grandchildren this weekend. Why are you trippin?" she inquired. I had to regain both my composure and control of the situation.

"Never mind, I was thinking about something else. What are you studying for tonight?" I asked.

"Muscular identification. I have to know where each muscle in the body is located and what its name is. To be honest, they all look the same to me, and I don't know where to start," she confessed. It wasn't going to be easy, but then again, it wasn't going to be extremely difficult either. This was the crux of what I had to help my mother learn for her exam, so most of in was fairly well ingrained in my memory. About twenty minutes into it, Kymera had a defeated look on her face.

"Jaaaayyyyssssooonnn! I can't do this! It's too hard!" she whined. I hated to hear a woman crying under any circumstances. "Is there an easier way to learn this stuff?!" she continued.

"Sweetheart, it's anatomy. The study of how the human body is put together. You are nothing more than a walking answer sheet," I responded. "Here's something that helped my mom. When you name a muscle, touch where it's located on your body, that way you remember it a little better," I suggested. If it worked for my mother, I couldn't imagine why it wouldn't work for her.

"Maybe it will work better if *you* touch where it's located on my body, then I'll really remember it," she countered. I couldn't believe it. That was the last thing in the world that I wanted.

"To be honest—"

"What? You wouldn't feel comfortable with that because Bianca wouldn't approve? Look Jerry, I'm not trying to make a move on you, I just need help to learn this material. I 'm not going to tell Bianca anything, and I'm sure you aren't going to say anything. Quit acting like you aren't attracted to me at all, and help me learn this stuff. I'm not saying cop a feel, but I'm not saying act like a virgin either. You aren't a virgin are you?" she fired.

"That's really none of your concern," I responded. I wasn't but I couldn't see why that was of any importance.

"So then you must be waiting on an upgrade from what you have now, because that's the only reason I can think of for why you still haven't tried to get at Bianca, or rather in Bianca," she said. I was incensed, but there wasn't anything I could effectively do at this point, Kymera wasn't at fault in my mind, Bianca was. Even so I would address that issue with her. My objective at this point was to keep my cool and get through the next hour.

"None of this has anything to do with where your muscles are located. Can we please get back on topic?" I asked firmly. Kymera looked like she wanted to say more, but decided against it.

"Just think of it like this; if I fail this class, I'll be begging Bianca to help me find a tutor again, which means she'll come and ask you again and you'll be in the same spot. Besides that, you don't want me to fail, because that means you'd have let Bianca down, and you don't want that, now do you? I could have had any of those pimple faced nerds help me with this stuff, but I wanted it to be you for a reason, okay? I really think you'll like me if you give me a chance and get to know me. Even if you don't like me, you owe me. It was cool for me to make you get down to Vive and scoop up that nice contract, but now you want to pitch a fit about returning the favor? That's not how this is going to work. Now, I'll call out the muscle and you come and touch where it is on my body," she said as she picked up one of the many worksheets that was lying on the table. I didn't know how to respond. I don't know how she was able to orchestrate things the way she had, but I had to respect the way she had pulled everything together. Even so, I still wasn't comfortable with touching her in any way, shape, or form, but if that's what it took to get through the next hour, then I was willing to do it. She read names off of the page and I showed her where they where. There were two muscles I noticed she hadn't called, and of course they were the two I could have left without hearing about.

"Pectoral," she said. I quickly pointed to the area just above her breast.

"It's right there," I answered. She frowned.

"Jerry, you're supposed to touch it!" she yelled as she grabbed my hand and forced it onto her breast.

"That's not you pectoral, that's your breast. The pectoral is here," I said as I moved my hand up to the correct location.

"Oh…my fault," she said, feigning remorse. "Okay last one, Sartorius," she announced. I crouched down to trace out the muscle's path just above the surface of her inner thigh. In between her toned bronze legs was the worst place in the world for me to be at that point. Especially when I could tell that she wasn't wearing any underwear.

"The Sartorius is here. Feeling like you can ace that exam Monday?" I asked relieved. I started hastily packing up my things.

"I'm pretty sure I can, thanks to you. Why are you in such a hurry to leave? You should stay so we can talk. I'd like to get to know you Jayson," she said invitingly. It seemed rude to pass up such and offer, considering how nicely she had asked, but I knew I had to or else it would have only ended badly.

"It's getting late, and I think I'm going to head out," I deferred.

"That's too bad. I was looking forward to making you some of my Baja Nachos," she said.

"Maybe next time. I'll let myself out," I said. I made my way to the door, which I found, was locked. Kymera sauntered up behind me.

"Well, Jerry, it's been fun. We have a test once about every two weeks or so. If you could stop by once every two weeks to help me study that will help me get a passing grade. Bianca thinks that's a wonderful idea." Then she moved in closer and whispered in my ear, "When you get done playing in the kiddy leagues, you should get into the adult division. I'll be here. See you later baby." she leaned in to kiss me on the cheek. The fact that my hands were full eliminated my ability to effectively avoid the coming insult, not to mention the celerity with which she carried it out. She then unlocked the door for me. I scurried out to the car and quickly sealed myself inside. I reached into the glove compartment and grabbed one of the wet-naps that I typically keep in there. I didn't know if Kymera had left any lipstick on my face, but I didn't want to take any chances. After scrubbing my face as best I could with a moist napkin, I put my car in gear and raced back to the safety of my own home.

# 10

It was dawn. The bright sunlight crept through the cracked blinds, infiltrating my eyelids, and softly urging me to awake. I looked down at Bianca, who was still resting on my chest. I softly ran my fingers through her hair. The slight touch roused her from her slumber.

"What time is it?" she asked groggily.

"Just before seven," I answered. She smiled. In my eyes she was even beautiful in the morning. She reached up and gave me a kiss on the cheek before she wiggled out of the bed.

"You feeling any better?" she asked me. Physically, I was fine. My mental status was completely different. I was still besieged by the fact that I had to tell her what had happened.

"Ye…yes. I do feel better Mrs. Sullivant," I responded. She winked at me.

"Were you serious last night when you asked me what I wanted to do today?" she asked with a half smile on her face.

"Yes, I do want to go looking at rings today as soon as I get home and get cleaned up. It wasn't the medicine talking. That was all me," I answered. Her face lit up.

"Really?! You're serious? I can't wait?!" she exclaimed as she hugged me. We were in mid-embrace when Doctor Ross walked in.

"How are you feeling this morning Mr. Sullivant?" he asked.

"Better," I answered.

"I need to discuss some things with you," he stated as she looked over at Bianca. Apparently they were private matters. Bianca looked puzzled, but nonetheless compliant.

"It's fine, I'm going to go downstairs and get something to eat," she said as she made her way towards the door, visibly confused. She pulled the door on her way out. Dr. Ross turned to me.

"Mr. Sullivant, I wanted to caution you about the usage of recreational drugs. There was an extremely large amount of ecstasy in your system. Your blood work isn't complete, but that's what the preliminary results seem to indicate. I'm not here to pass judgment or tell you how to live, but I will say that this is a nasty habit to pick up, and at your pace, you won't be able to sustain it very long," he started. I didn't know whether to be appreciative or incensed. I had never used any sort of drug in my life; it was a fact that I prided myself on.

"Dr. Ross, let me assure you that I have not now or ever in my life knowingly consumed any drug in any form. If what you allege is in fact accurate, in this case it wasn't deliberate. I didn't intend on doing anything. I didn't know I ingested anything, let alone ecstasy, and I most assuredly didn't do so knowingly," I said, half explaining and half defending myself.

"That may be so Mr. Sullivant, but the sheer amount that was in your system indicates otherwise. I have to believe that you would have noticed such a large quantity of something that, quite frankly, tastes terribly acrid. Whatever the answer is, I simply wish to advise you against taking such needless risks. You are young, and you have a wonderful life ahead of you. This simply isn't the way to go. This isn't a path that you want to go down," he said. I felt like my honor was being assailed.

"Dr. Ross, I understand your intentions here, but at this point you have offended my sensibilities beyond what I can rationally tolerate. I am going to have to ask you to leave now," I said as politely as I could.

"I understand. A nurse will be by shortly with your discharge papers," he responded as he made his way to the door. Bianca walked in just moments after the doctor left.

"What was that about babe?" she asked. I kept my cool.

"Nothing. The doctor was just advising me on getting in better shape and reminding me about getting check-ups more regularly. That's it," I answered. How was I supposed to tell her that I was in the hospital because I had a ridiculous amount of ecstasy in my system and I had just slept with her cousin?

"Uh-huh...Well, did they say when you could leave?" she asked. I couldn't help but feel like she didn't entirely believe me, although I wasn't sure why besides the fact that I was lying, but she didn't know that, did she?

"Doctor Ross said that a nurse should be by with my discharge papers pretty soon. Do you still want to go look at rings later on today?" I asked. Her demeanor brightened.

"Yes! Of course, I still want to!" she responded. Then I saw her face twisting the way it always did when she was about to ask a question. "When's the last time you had an HIV test?" she asked. Under normal circumstances, that question would have been clear out of left field. But I decided to humor her.

"After I walked in on Amina, I went straight to the student health center. I haven't had sex since then," I answered. She looked placated if not altogether convinced.

"Are you seriously telling me that you haven't had sex in nearly three years? Do I look stupid to you? Be for real!" she demanded. I was mildly incensed.

"I was trying to wait until I got married. Is that so wrong? So no you don't look stupid to me, and yes I am being for real," I retorted.

"That may be so, but before anything happens over here, we need to get tested," she said.

"Definitely, I don't have a problem with that," I sputtered. I didn't like this line of questions, but I had to deal with them. "Why don't I just have them test for it now?" I asked.

"Not today, you've had enough happen to you. We'll do it a little later," she replied. We sat there silently for a few more moments, and then a nurse walked in with a wheelchair and my discharge papers. She unhooked me from the machines and both she and Bianca helped me as I climbed into the wheelchair. Bianca rolled me to the front desk, where I signed all the required insurance billing forms and then Bianca went to get her vehicle while an older orderly waited with me and the wheelchair.

“Quite a woman you have there. Has she been here all night?” he asked.

“Yes, sir, she has been. That’s crazy, right? Most guys at best will only ever get a woman that’s half as good as she is. I don’t know what I would do without her,” I gushed.

“That’s serious. Don’t let her get away. She seems like a once in a lifetime type of girl. You better make sure you treat her right, even if you have to do something that you don’t want to do. You make sure you treat her right. An always tell the truth, you hear me. Always. It may not seem good at the time, but it’ll work out, you can truss ol’ Malachi on that,” he said. I had just resolved to sweep this whole mess under the rug. The last thing I wanted or needed was a pang of consciousness.

“Yes sir, I hear you, but what if the truth is going to cause her undue pain?” I asked. I didn’t make a habit of sharing stories with strangers, but he seemed different somehow.

“It may not seem like it at first, but she’ll respeck you more for telling her the truth now, than she will for finding out you lied to her later. I know it may seem hard to believe, but it’s the truth,” he replied. “Have some courage about yourself. Respeck yourself as a man and have some integrity as well.” His words were all directly on the mark. “Is she a good Christian woman? Ya’ll aint shackin’ up is ya?” he asked rather intrusively. I decided to keep the conversation rolling.

“No sir, we aren’t shacking up—” I liked my personal space way too much for that. “—and she is a good Christian woman. I’m trying to figure out the best way to propose to her now.”

“Let me help you out. The best way to propose to her is right now. The Bible says, “He that findeth a wife findeth a good thing, an now, women like that, they don’t wait for long and with good reason—they don’t have to, ’cause they know that somebody gon find ’em. Son, take it from me, I watched the best women I ever had walk away because I was out here messin’ around. I realize you’re young, but you won’t be young forever.” Bianca pulled up. “Well son, that’s my piece, you think about what ol’ Malachi had to say,” he said to me as Bianca came around to open the door for me.

"Thank you for the advice sir, I will make sure to take it to heart," I assured him. He winked at me as he turned with the wheelchair and walked back inside the hospital. After we were both secure in our seatbelts, Bianca smiled at me.

"You survived!" she exclaimed. I laughed.

"We'll see about that," I replied nervously. I had to tell her as much as I could remember. We didn't keep secrets, and I didn't want to start.

"What do you mean?" she asked solemnly.

"Babe, Kymera lied to you, and up to this point, I've lied to you by omission. I didn't have an asthma attack last night. In fact I haven't had one in nearly ten years. I got rushed to the hospital because I passed out in Kymera's bathroom, and she called 911. Dr. Ross said that I had a large amount of ecstasy in my system, that's what we were talking about," I said nervously. Bianca's face turned a shade of red that I had never seen before, which considering her African-American heritage was saying quite a bit. I could see the veins in her hand as she squeezed the steering wheel. I thought she was going to lose control of the vehicle, but she amazingly managed to keep driving.

"What were you doing with X? I thought you went over there to help her study! You guys just go and get high?! I thought you said that you got rid of that stuff!" she yelled as she smacked the steering wheel.

"Let me explain. Because it was our last session, Kymera made some of those infernal nachos of hers. The next thing I know I'm in the hospital. Doctor Ross said that I had a large amount of the drug in my system. I don't know how it got there. It had to be in something that I ate. The rest of the night from there was a blur. Please don't be angry with me. That's the first time something like that has ever happened, I promise. I got rid of the stuff I had ages ago. Father Potter was with me when I did" I explained. She was quiet. We had never really fought over anything. In fact, we rarely fought period, save our superhero discussions. Normally we talked things out and they were okay in a day or so. Bianca being completely silent was new. I was scared. The tears that looked they were going to fall stopped just before they left her eye.

"If I cannot corroborate your story with Kymera, you don't have to worry about ring shopping or anything else like that. If you're getting high with her, there's no telling what else you're doing with her," she asserted definitively. If nothing else, Bianca was a strong black woman. She wasn't going to let me see her sweat at all. Even so, I felt like I had told her enough of the truth to grant me permission to speak.

"I understand that you are upset, and I totally respect your right to say whatever you want to say right here, but remember I told you that she gave me bad vibes. I never wanted to go there in the first place. You insisted that I go help her. So before you get all irate with me, and threatening me or whatever, consider the circumstances," I said in my own defense. Retrospectively, I should have just left the matter alone.

"So this is my fault?! I tell you what, since I'm supposed to 'consider the circumstances', how about you do the same?!" We had just passed the Beacon, and the bus stop where she first picked me up was about one hundred feet ahead. "These are your circumstances! If I had never picked you up, then I wouldn't feel the way I feel right now! Get out!" she yelled. I wasn't sure if she was serious or not. But I decided to call her bluff, seeing as how I was admittedly a mixed bag of emotions. But even in my medicated state, my masculine ego stirred itself and forced me to find the strength to climb out of her truck.

"If this is what you want, then fine, go ahead and leave. I told you that I didn't want to go there, that I didn't trust her and that something bad might happen. You didn't listen. No girl ever listens. I'm supposed to hear everything you say, remember every little detail, but what do you know about me? Anything at all? The only thing you think you know is that we haven't had sex and I may have had sex with your cousin, or rather she may have drugged and raped me. That's all you know. You don't know anything about me, you just want someone to marry you. That's all any of you really wants. If you knew anything about me, you would know that something was wrong and something beyond my control happened. If you knew anything about me at all, you'd believe me right now. You'd trust me over your cradle-robbin' gold diggin' aunt! But of course you can't. Bianca, you poured A1 sauce on me and fed me to the wolves and now you have the audacity to get upset because I got eaten. I did the best I could. If you really cared about me and not so much about how Kymera views you then we wouldn't be having this conversation now. You would have been blind not to see how she kept throwing herself at me, and because you wanted her to like you, you just kept throwing me out there, like a sacrifical lamb. Bianca, I'm not some object in your perfect world. I'm as much a person as you. I thought that you could see that. But I guess not. Girls are all the same. As soon as something better comes along, or my usefulness is outlived, boom! Out with the trash! Do I get the chance to make a mistake? Of course not, even though every girl swears she's different, but at the end of the day, she doesn't care. None of ya'll really care! As far as I'm concerned, right now, you aren't any different than Amina!" I yelled as I climbed down to the curb. I wished I could take it back. I only said it because I knew it would hurt her. She looked at me unflinchingly and said dryly.

"If that's true, then call Amina and see if she wants to be Mrs. Jayson Sullivant, because right now, she's your best option," she sped off before I could even slam the door like I wanted to. The celerity of her exit caused the door to shut under its own weight. I stood there, still woozy from the medication and with my head spinning, I had to figure out how I was going to get back to my car. I sat on the bench and called Father Potter. In a crisis, he was usually the best option. I let the phone ring. No response. I decided to try and call my mother. Again the phone rang and there was no response. Momentarily distraught, I decided to rely on the one person I knew I could always count on, myself. Kymera's house was about a seven minute walk from my mother's house. I could take the bus to Rock Canyon and then walk to my car. I loved Bianca with everything I had in me, but I couldn't stop living just because she was upset. I had to keep going.

# 11

I was never really big on Valentine's Day. I liked expressing how I felt; I just didn't like doing it on the same day as the rest of the country. As far as I was concerned, it was just another Hallmark holiday. Besides that, in my eyes, Bianca was way more special than other girls, so why should she celebrate our love along with the rest of the women on the planet? It seemed like a simple equation for me. I decided that since the holiday fell on Saturday, I would celebrate it for the whole week leading up to the holiday. She was worth at least that much to me.

It had been a while since I had anyone to dote on, so my romantic creative inklings had been suppressed, but with this newfound chance to show them off, I was prepared to let them run free. Unlike most men, I looked forward to this sort of thing. Flowers, cards and candy were all "just because I thought of you" gifts. So for Valentine's Day I had to go above and beyond. From the outside, it may have seemed like a lot of effort, but I looked at it like this: If I could make Bianca happy in the short run, then in the long run, she will make me twice as happy as I make her. So in the end it was really an investment in me. It was really very simple logic in my mind. I didn't understand why more men didn't pick up on that. I decided to keep the knowledge to myself and just utilize it for my own gain. On the Saturday prior to Valentine's Day, I called Quinn. I couldn't pull this off without an accomplice.

"Hello?"

"Quinn? This is Jayson. How are you today?" We didn't talk much, so I conceded the fact that I was going to have to suck up a little bit.

"What do you need Jayson?" she responded dryly. I forgot how matter-of-fact she could be.

"I need to get into Bianca's room tomorrow for about an hour or so."

"For what?! Why don't you just ask her for a key and—"

"Because then it wouldn't be a surprise. You gotta help me out here," I interrupted.

"Okay, but you have to figure out how you're going to get her out of the house, and I'll let you in, but if you do anything stupid, I didn't have anything to do with it, agreed?" she relented.

"That's fine dear, whatever it takes. Thank you!" I replied.

"Whatever. Anything else sir?" she asked.

"No, ma'am, that's all I needed. Thanks again and I'll see you tomorrow. I answered as we disconnected. That was the hard part. Now I had to contrive a way to get Bianca out of her house for an hour. After a few moments of heavy thinking, the answer came to me. I picked my phone back up.

"Mom, what are you doing tomorrow?" I asked.

"Going to church like I do every Sunday," she replied.

"Okay after that?" I asked. Had I been thinking a little more clearly, I would have made that connection.

"Nothing, do you need me to be doing something?" she asked.

"I need you to take Bianca to brunch for me," I responded.

"Why can't you take her? She's your girlfriend," my mother reasoned.

"I can't really explain right now, I just need you to take her out to brunch tomorrow. You have to keep her out for at least an hour. I'll pay for it, but I'm begging you to do this for me mom, puhleeezee," I pled. It was more important than she knew. This was our first Valentine's Day and I wanted it to be perfect.

"Okay, but only because you asked so nicely," she replied.

"Thank you so much!" I answered. That was all I needed, a window of opportunity. Having completed the most arduous portion of my plan, I got up to go out and gather everything I needed. I only had a couple of hours to get everything that I needed for what I had in mind.

I always laughed at how most men seemed to turn into honey bees during this time of year. There's always a gaggle of them anywhere that you could find flowers. All just buzzing around, trying to find some salvageable bouquet that was nice looking and yet as cheap as possible. Because it was still a week prior, many of the stores still had plenty of roses, carnations, and other highly regarded blooms left. As the fourteenth drew closer, the selection was going to begin to dwindle and eventually, some poor girl was going to get stuck with a bouquet of half dead dandelions, with a crab-grass accent. Fortunately for me, the crux of my plan had nothing to do with flowers, even if they were an ingredient.

I stopped by the florist, a toy store, a pet shop and a craft store before making my final stop at the grocery store. I had been running all day, but I felt like it was worth it, even if I wasn't one hundred percent sure of how much she would like it. I looked at my chronograph. It was just after nine o'clock. Bianca and I were supposed to go out at ten. There was a movie that she wanted to see and while I was generally opposed to movie dates at the beginning of a relationship, at this juncture, they were permissible. I lugged my haul into my apartment as I didn't want her to see what was going on before I had a chance to pull it make it a reality. I sat down and inscribed on the card that I had purchased, then I cleaned myself up and picked up my phone to call Bianca. Before I could push her speed dial button, my doorbell rang. I walked over to the intercom.

"Yes?" I asked.

"Baby, let me in, it's me." It was Bianca.

"Uh…okay," I stammered, trying not to sound caught as unaware as I had been. I was supposed to pick her up. The theater was closer to her house, so it only made sense. I buzzed her in, and then began frantically trying to hide everything. With all the work I had put in to this point to execute this grand scheme I had, I couldn't just let it go to waste now. I managed to get everything hidden away in my bedroom closet under a pile of blankets, and not a moment too soon as I heard Bianca's all too familiar knock on my door. I opened the portal.

"Hey, sweetheart. I thought it was my turn to drive," I said as I opened the door while obstructing her progress.

"Let me in means move so I can come in silly!" she said as she playfully pushed past me.

"What brings you by? I thought we were going to the movies. I was on my way, I promise," I said, trying to be as cool as possible.

"Well, I was already downtown, and I remembered that I left a pair of earrings over here, and I figured since I was already dressed, I'd just swing by here and pick up both my earrings and my boyfriend," she said as she walked around my home. It was apparent that she was looking for something else. She was looking in every conceivable hiding spot that existed in my apartment. I didn't know who had tipped her off to anything, but I figured I had to try and beat her to the punch.

"Which earrings were you looking for honey? Maybe I can help you find them," I volunteered.

"Uh. that one pair. The ones you brought me for the Fall Fundraiser. The jade ones with the silver trim," she answered. If those were missing, I definitely wanted her to find them. They weren't cheap.

"Well if they were anywhere, they'd be with the rest of my accessories, although I don't remember picking them up at all," I said. "I'll go look in my room, just in case."

"Thank you baby," she said. I looked at her outfit. Those jade earrings would have gone nicely with what she was wearing. My desire to help her find them intensified. I had only taken about seven steps when I realized she hadn't lost her earrings. Bianca wouldn't lose a pair of earrings if I paid her to do so. I turned around and crept slowly back into the front room. She had effectively moved the couch three feet away from its normal position.

"Now how in the world could your earrings be both behind my couch and in your ears at the same time?" I asked. She stood up, smiling through her chagrin.

"Okay, I'm caught! I just wanted to see what you got me," she said.

"I didn't get you anything. Valentine's Day isn't for another week, so I've still got time. What made you think I had gotten you something?" I asked. My initial thought was that Quinn had said something. Still I couldn't react, because Bianca was looking for some sign to contradict what I had said.

"Kymera just said that I should expect something from you before Valentine's Day. She said she got her information from a credible source." I was puzzled. The only people that knew anything was going on were my mother and Quinn. I just couldn't picture either of them talking to Kymera at length; it just seemed out of the ordinary.

"Well Kymera was wrong. Even if I had gotten you something, do you think I would be so crazy as to hide it somewhere that you might find it? Let's get out of here," I said.

"Was she? So then why does your mother want to take me to brunch tomorrow?" she inquired.

"Because she wants to have a relationship with her future daughter-in-law independent of me," I answered. Bianca's face lit up.

"Future daughter-in-law? Are you serious?" she asked excitedly.

"Doesn't that feel like where things are eventually headed? I'd be crazy to let you get away!" I said. Bianca was positively euphoric. You would have thought I actually proposed at that moment. I turned out the lights and grabbed my keys.

"You know what, I don't want to drive back out near Rock Canyon and then have to come back out here. Why don't we just do something near here?" she suggested as we walked to the parking garage. It made sense to me.

"Get something to eat and play a little pool? Sounds like a plan. Let's go," I asserted. "Your car or mine?" I asked.

"I'll drive," she answered. We walked to her SUV, got in, and headed off towards downtown and the entertainment district. Normally I would have taken the main roads, but Bianca decided it would be faster if we took the back roads into the entertainment district. Just as we came up to the point where the financial district meets the entertainment district, I saw a suspicious, albeit familiar-looking teenager standing on the corner. I wanted to get a closer look, but I didn't want to alarm him.

"Bianca, pull over," I whispered.

"What for? Why are we whispering?" she asked.

"I think that's Bryan," I answered. She pulled over. We sat with the lights off watching the shadowy figure. Cars slowly pulled up. The passenger would exchange a few words, and then the teenager would reach inside the vehicle very briefly, and the car would drive away. In between vehicles, the teen would look around cautiously. The Financial District was normally crawling with law enforcement during the day, but after the close of business, it was a veritable ghost town, save for the homeless people that normally squatted outside the buildings.

Bianca squinted hard. "Oh my God! That is Bryan!" she exclaimed.

"Shh!!" I whispered. We were about half a block away from him. The fact that he hadn't seen us yet was odd considering the moderately low amount of traffic that was coming through this particular area. If we were able to watch him like this, I could only imagine how easy it would have been for the police to do the same.

"Jayson, we can't leave him out here, he's doing something he doesn't have any business doing. Call his phone, to make sure it's him," she directed. I called his cell phone. I watched the figure across the street answer the phone.

"Bryan?" I asked.

"Uncle Jay? What up, man?" he asked.

"I was calling to see if you wanted to go watch that new Jet Li movie. I was going to take your Aunt Bianca, but she's got paperwork to do," I lied.

"Uh…naw, I'm cool. I already saw it," he stammered.

"When? It just came out, and I thought you had to work last night and tonight?" I pushed. An oddly familiar, banged up, late seventies model Pontiac Bonneville drove slowly along side Bianca and I. I recognized the two men sitting inside as the plain clothes officers who had knocked on Bianca's door a couple months back. I didn't recognize them so much as the car. It was so God-awful that they might as well have had lights and a siren put on it. There's no way there was more than one of that car. They slowed at the intersection, and then drove past the corner where Bryan was standing.

"I saw a sneak preview. Man, Uncle Jay, I gotta go," he said, snapping the phone shut. I watched him put the phone back in his pocket.

"Bianca, we have to go get him now! I want you to be ready to drive," I asserted firmly. They were going to circle the block, much like the other cars had. I didn't know how much time I had, but I knew it wasn't more than five minutes. I got out of the car and started walking towards Bryan. I wasn't really sure how this was going to work out, but I knew that I had to get him into the car before Officers Giraud and Morian circled the block. Bryan was only fifty yards from me, but he was so intent on watching for this next sell, that he wasn't checking around himself. I pulled my scarf up around my mouth and pulled out my cell phone. My soft soled shoes muffled my approach. I wasn't sure what I was going to do, but I knew that I had to somehow prevent him from selling anything to the undercover officers that were on their way around the block. I formed a plan in my head as I closed the remaining seven yards. Seconds later, I was in arms length. I grabbed him forcefully by locking my forearm around his neck.

"I know you holin' lil' man," I said gruffly. I wasn't really sure of what to say. That didn't matter. Bryan was scared out of his mind.

"I-I-I don't know what you talkin' about man! I'm jus waitin on ma people ta show up! I ain't holin nothin'!" he said, panicking. I jammed my cell phone into his back as though it were a gun.

"Quit tryna game me! I seen you out hurre fa like a week! You dat lil' cat wit all da work, ainchu?! I'ahl hav you lookin like swiss cheese right now if you don't come up off what you holin! I want da pieces an da doe!" I yelled.

"A'ight man, a'ight!" he said as he started emptying his pockets. He put a sandwich bag full of little pills and a wad of cash in my hand. I knew he had more. Bryan was smarter than to hold everything in one place. I had to clean him out.

"Gimme wat's in yo' shoes too lil' nigga!" I yelled. The words tasted disgusting on my tongue, but his life was worth it to me. I had to make him believe he was in peril. He reached into his socks and pulled out a secondary roll of bills.

"Dat's it man, dat's e'rything!" he said ruefully. "D'easy is gon kill me," he moaned. I hadn't thought about how I was going to get away. I imagined I only had about a minute left before the car came back around the corner. At this point I was guilty of theft and possession, with the apparent intent to distribute, amongst other charges.

"Lay down on the ground and close yo' eyes! Don't try nothin neitha, just get down!" I yelled. He complied.

"Count to a hunned! You bet not get up until you get to a hunned neither!" I commanded. Despite his best efforts, I could hear him sniffling as he began to count. I felt my heart breaking as I ran as hard as I could. I hated to scare him like that, but it was the only thing I could come up with. I sprinted hard back to the Pathfinder. Bianca already had it running. I climbed in and she drove down the street.

"Jayson, what did you do?!" she asked.

"I made sure that when those police officers tried to buy something off of him, he didn't have anything to sell them," I answered.

"How did you know they were police officers?" she asked me.

"Long story," I answered. I kept the bag in my coat pocket. I had every intention of destroying the pills in my fireplace when I got home that evening.

"Do you still want to go eat?" Bianca asked me. In all my exertion, I had worked up an appetite.

"Sure. No point in wasting a good night." Oddly enough I felt good. I had just saved Bryan from throwing his life away, and maybe I had scared him straight, even if I was going to have to deal with it later. For the time being, I was still with the woman that I loved, and I couldn't see any real reason to scrap the evening. It was a couple of minutes before ten o'clock. We continued on our trip as though nothing had happened.

After the dinner and a couple of games of pool, Bianca dropped me off back at home. I pulled the bag that I had taken from Bryan out of my pocket along with the cash. There were about twenty little pills that all had the letter X engraved on them. I counted the cash out. It was just over three hundred dollars. I understood the allure this must have had for him; after all he had made double his salary in one night, and had the potential to maybe quadruple it, depending on what the value of the bag was. But I couldn't help to hope that his experience tonight was tantamount to a rock bottom event for him.

I went back and forth for about an hour on whether or not I should destroy the drugs. I decided to call Father Potter. He'd know how I should deal with the situation.

"Father Potter?" I asked. By now it was close to midnight, I hated to wake him up, but I had to get some answers, and he hadn't failed yet. I scrolled through my phonebook until I got to Jacob. Jacob Potter. I looked back at the bag as I hit dial. The phone rang a few times and then a woman's voice answered the phone.

"Hello?" she asked groggily. The voice was so familiar that I almost threw my phone down.

"MOM?!" I exclaimed. Instantly the other line died. I looked at my phone in utter disbelief. I called back. Father Potter answered on the first ring.

"Jayson? What's wrong, son?" he asked. As I screened the sentence in my head, I realized how terrible it sounded, but I decide to go with it.

"I saw Bryan out on a corner selling again, and I robbed him," I answered.

"You did what?!" he asked incredulously.

"There were police rolling by, it was the only way that I could get the stuff out of his possession. That's not why I called. I need to know what to do with it. I feel like I should destroy it, but I don't know how much it's worth. That and I don't know how to tell him that I was the one that took it from him," I said.

"One at a time, son. Okay first off, what did you take from him?"

"I don't know pills of some sort they've all got the letter X stamped on them," I answered.

"Ecstasy. Okay, how many are in the bag?" he asked.

"I don't know maybe a dozen or so," I replied.

"That's anywhere between one and two hundred and fifty dollars. Did you take any cash off of him?"

"Just north of three hundred dollars," I answered.

"That's right around five hundred dollars of money and product. Someone is going go be looking for him with that much missing. Don't destroy it unless you are ready to pay for it. Cash," he informed me. I wanted to ask how he knew so much, but then I considered how many people he must have counseled, how many confessions he must have heard over the years, and it made sense to me.

"Okay, so how do I tell him that I took it from him?" I asked.

"You don't have to worry about that. He's going to come to you for help," Father Potter answered. "Where is he now?" he asked.

"I don't know. Hold on a second Father, my other line is beeping," I said as I placed him on hold. "Hello?"

"Uncle Jayson, it's Bryan. Ah need sum help." He sounded scared out of his mind.

"Okay, hold on one second," I instructed as I clicked over. "Father, this is him now. I am going to find out what's going on," I said.

"Okay. Find out where he is and get to him quickly. He may be in more trouble than you know. Make sure that you don't tell him you were responsible for what happened. You'll inspire a sense of false confidence in him. That is the exact thing we are trying to guard against," he advised. It made sense.

"Very well Father. Thank you for your time," I said. I thought that I could make out a woman's voice in the background, but I wasn't certain.

"Goodnight, son," he responded. I clicked back to the other line.

"Hello?"

"Uncle Jay! Thank God! Man, imen trouble. You think ah cud stay wit chu tanight?" he asked. I had never heard him sound so afraid in my life.

"Calm down, calm down, now where are you?"

"I'm near da Beakin. I can't go home, 'cause Kymera gone an Brittany got D'easy an nem ova da crib," he blurted.

"Okay, so why is that a problem?" I asked coolly.

"Uncle Jay, can you jus come scoop me?" he asked me. He still sounded like he was moments away from a nervous breakdown.

"I'll be there in a moment. Where are you exactly?"

"Im by da Beakin," he answered.

"What are you doing there? And how did you get there?" I asked. It was nearly twenty miles from the Entertainment district to the Beacon.

"The Beacon wuz da safess place Ah cud think ov, so I caught a bus and rode out herre," he responded. Alright, just stay right there. I'll be there in a little bit," I instructed.

"Please hurry. If I ain't back tuh da hous by one, D'easy gon come lookn fa me," he pleaded. I looked at my watch. It was about twelve thirty and the Beacon was easily a half hour away from me, while only being five minutes away from where I presumed D'easy to be. I placed both the money and the contraband in my top drawer, grabbed my keys, and ran down the stairs to the parking garage. Even though I was trying to teach him a lesson, the idea of him in danger because of my interference was rather harrowing. I don't know if it was the guilt, or the fear that he might really be in trouble, but when I got in my car, I was overcome by a sense of urgency. I had to get to him and I had to get to him now.

I had only pushed my car to its mechanical limits once before, and that was the day I brought it, just to see what it could do. Tonight, it appeared, would be the second time. I hurriedly threw the car in gear, and stomped down on the gas as I sped out of the parking garage. I decided to take the freeway, simply because there weren't any red lights there. I raced to the on-ramp and shifted flawlessly through my gears. It was as though my Z could sense my need to move faster than our normal pace and was feeding of my desire to do, almost as if our collective wills had fused into one. I had just merged onto the moderately empty expressway and I was already moving at seventy-five miles per hour. I kept my foot welded to the accelerator as I tightened my grip on the steering wheel. I simply had to get to him first. I couldn't let anything prevent me from reaching him. The car seemed to almost take over, as though it understood the situation. I looked at the speedometer. Eighty-five miles per hour. Not fast enough. I easily had twenty miles to cover. I silently cursed myself for having put him into this situation. Then I recanted. I hadn't done this to him; he had done it to himself. Ninety. Still no letting up. No music, just the throaty hum of the engine and the sound of the rubber on the road. The few cars on the road were little more than decorations; I had caught up to and wove past most of them before they had a chance to put on a turn signal. Ordinarily I'd be worried about the police, but to be honest. They would have had to follow me to the Beacon. I simply couldn't let anything that may have happened to him rest on my conscious. One hundred. My phone rang.

"Baby, where are you?" It was Bianca.

"I'm on the highway going towards the Beacon," I answered.

"Brittany just called me. Bryan hasn't been home yet, and she's afraid that something may have happened to him. She hasn't been able to get in touch with Da'Rell either. Do you know where Bryan is?" she asked.

"I'm on my way to get him now," I answered, still concentrating on the fact that I was moving in excess of one hundred and ten miles per hour. "Where is his mother at?" I asked. I didn't want to start assigning blame, but I had to ask.

"She's out of town, but baby, that doesn't matter right now. Right now I need for you to locate my nephew and get him somewhere safe please, and you be careful as well, okay? I love you and you better come back in one piece, understand?" she asked assertively.

"I love you, too, babe. I gotta go," I answered as I flipped my phone shut. My exit was in about a mile. Even though my car normally stuck to curves like a matchbox car in a loop-de-loop, I knew I had to slow down a bit before I exited the freeway. I might be able to bend the laws of the land, but the laws of physics were immutable. I reached the Rock Canyon exit and pulled off of the express way. I still had a few city blocks to go before I got to the Beacon, but having knocked out the bulk of the distance via the freeway, I felt marginally better about my chances of getting to Bryan before anyone else. After about five minutes of going sixty miles an hour on the surface streets, I reached the Beacon. I expected Bryan to be by the pay phone in the front, but he wasn't there. I slowly drove around the building, searching desperately for any sign of him. After my second lap around, I parked my car and called Father Potter.

"Hello?" It was that same groggy female voice that I thought I heard earlier.

"Father Potter?" I asked.

"I believe you may have dialed incorrectly," the woman said as the call was disconnected. That felt strange. She sounded like my mom, but I knew I had called Father Potter. I relegated it to things that I had to think about later. Right now the objective was to find Bryan. I got out of my car to look around. As I did I noticed the same beat up late seventies car from earlier creeping by slowly, this time with its lights off. My phone rang.

"Uncle Jay is you here yet?" Bryan asked.

"Yes, I'm around the back. Where are you at?" I asked.

"I'm back here too, hol' on," he instructed. Almost simultaneously, the lid on the dumpster popped open, and Bryan materialized. He dusted off the refuse that had covered him as he sprinted towards me. "Man, we gotta go!" he asserted as he ran to the car. I unlocked the doors, climbed in, and put the car in motion. Pulling out of the parking lot, the Bonneville that I had seen earlier was coming back. Bryan looked like he had seen a ghost.

"Uncle Jay, we need ta get missin right now!" he yelled. "That's D'easy an 'nems goons! You gotta go now!" he ordered. His intensity inspired fervor of my own as I threw the car forward. Bryan was slinking down in the seat. I looked in the rear view mirror. The car was coming down the street with its brights on, effectively blinding me. I looked at Bryan.

'Put your seat belt on!" I yelled. I had decided to play to my strength. I couldn't out fight them, but I knew I could outrun them. My tires squealed as I mashed down on the clutch, and shifted into gear. I couldn't get back on the expressway right away, that would lead them back to my house, and my objective right now was to get as far away from here as possible, until I could figure out what was going on. I drove towards the manufacturing district, a twisted maze of old buildings, railroad tracks and no traffic lights. I looked back. They were still giving chase. I spurred my car on even harder. I looked over a Bryan. If I was ever going to get some straight answers, it was now.

"What is going on?! Why am I being followed? And DO NOT LIE to me!" I boomed. A new wave of fear washed over his face. Dejectedly, he put his head down and took a deep breath.

"Man Uncle Jay, I know you gon be mad at me or whateva, but I quit ma job ova at Quiggly's. I wasn't seein no kinda money, an' I can't be broke. So I went back ta D'easy. He said he was workin ona new hustle, an' dat I cud get down."

"You quit your legitimate job to go back to violating the terms of your release, okay, continue," I instructed.

"So tanite I was down by da innatanment district tryna move some pieces an' I got jacked. An nees fools caught me from behind. Dem cats took errything I had on me. I had my whole supply for like the next two weeks on me. It was like ten uhv 'em, an' they all pulled dey heat on me, so I just let it go, but now I'ma be short half a stack. D'easy is gonna kill me," he moaned, at this point, on the brink of tears. I wanted to tell him that I knew he was lying about getting jumped. That and the fact that I had everything and that he was going to be alright, but how would he learn? What if he had been robbed and it wasn't me? I had to follow through. By this point we were about ten minutes away from the Beacon. The Bonneville was still behind us. Apparently I had underestimated the vehicle, as it followed me very easily at seventy miles an hour. I was going to let them follow me for about another five miles until I could get back on the expressway and open my car up. I had paid for all three hundred horses under my hood, and they were all going to earn their keep tonight. I still had more questions.

"So how long have you been selling?" I asked.

"About two months now. Erry since Kymera been at da hous. It ain't like she care any way. She prolly be in my stash anyway," he replied.

"You do know that if you get caught, you are going to prison? Not juvy Bryan, prison! Bryan when are you going to see that you aren't the only person that is affected by your actions?! I'm out here running from God knows what. My mother is up worried about me, your aunt is worried, your sister, Father Potter, the list goes on. Do you know how many people called me to find out what's going on?" I asked. At this point I had exaggerated a few points and taken some liberties, but I had to try and get through to him. "Bryan, you are getting to be an adult and this stuff isn't cute. In fact it's getting old." The highway was coming up in about three minutes. I was going to get on, going towards my house and floor it, defying them to keep up. It wasn't much of a plan, but considering my limited experience with high speed chases, I thought it was pretty good.

"Uncle Jay man what can ah say? I'm sorry. Iyaint know all dees people was concerned wit my life. I mean im jus out here tryna make some cake. Dats it. I ayaint usin or nothin', jus pushin' it." I still couldn't follow his logic.

"Bryan, I still don't understand. You are going to throw your life away and for what? An extra two hundred dollars a week? This makes sense to you though? How? You don't have to do this. You aren't paying rent. Your mother works. You are just searching for ways to throw your life away, and I'll be honest, I'll only be able to catch you so many times before I come up short. These bail outs aren't indefinite. You've got to decide that you want to do better for yourself!" The Bonneville had given a valiant effort, but now it was time to stop playing. The car behind me was giving everything it had to maintain its current pace. There was no way that they could keep up if I pushed it for real. I took the on ramp to the expressway going back towards my house. I was going to lose them by sheer force of will. I started accelerating. I felt the car feeding from my desire as I drew from its performance. It was a symbiotic bond. The faster I wanted to go, the faster it went, and the faster it went, the faster I wanted it to go.

"Iyain't gonna go ta colledge, so I gotta get my cake while I can—"

"Who said you can't go to college? Why not?" I asked.

The stress from the evening was beginning to take its toll on me. Twenty minutes of driving at just over a hundred was outside of my normal pattern, but it looked like it had worked. Convinced that I had lost them, I pulled off of the expressway and into a gas station. I needed to call Father Potter. I pulled out my phone, and dialed the number from memory. It rang three times.

"Hello?" a woman's voice answered his phone for the third time tonight, and again she sounded like my mother.

"Mom?" I asked. The voiced laughed.

"No, son, this is Sister Mary Margaret. How can I help you?" she asked.

"I'm looking for Father Potter. Can you get him for me?" I requested.

"Certainly, just one moment," she said. Moments later, Father Potter answered the phone.

"Yes, Jayson," he answered. I was perplexed.

"How did you know it was me?" I asked.

"Who else has my cell phone number and would call me at two a.m.?" he reasoned. That didn't strike me as a definitive description. That could have been anyone. I decided to get to the heart of the matter.

"I found Bryan. We got followed by some guys for a while, but I think I lost them. I'm going to take him back to my apartment and we'll go from there."

"I'm proud of you son. That is a great length for you to go to for anyone. In time he will come to see it," Father Potter surmised.

"I can only hope that you are correct," I replied.

"Trust me on this one son, you are," he assured me.

"Goodnight, Father," I said.

"Likewise," he answered as we disconnected. I started the car back up and Bryan and I headed for my apartment. He was sitting there silent. I noticed the tracks of tears on his face. He was in a hell of his own creation. I didn't want him to suffer, but he had to want to do better for himself.

"So how are you going to get the money back?" I asked.

"I ont know. It ain't like it's jus twenny, or even a hun. Im missing half a stack worth uhv product an' cash. Aint no comin' back from nat." he answered. In that moment, I figured out how I was going to correct his behavior and push him to be greater.

"I got a proposition for you. You need five hundred dollars right now, correct?" I asked. He instantly bolted upright.

"Yup, an I ont know where ta start," he answered.

"Here's the deal. I'll front you the money. Five hundred dollars cash. But only on the following conditions: First you have to go back to Quiggly's. I'll talk to Joe, and you'll get your job back. That means no selling, just working at Quiggly's, and you are going to bring me one hundred dollars a month until the debt is paid. Secondly, you are going to get in school and you are going to maintain a three point grade point average—"

"Uncle Jay, I can't do that! I ain't that smart!" he whined.

"Bryan, that's bull! Anyone that can put numbers together the way I've seen you put numbers together absolutely is smart. Right now it doesn't matter if you think you can or not, it's the only way you are going to get the money. Thirdly, you are going to promise me that you will do better. Start thinking like a man, and not like such a little boy. You have so much potential, and yet you refuse to use any of it beyond trying to make a quick buck. Lastly, you are going to be my shadow. If I need it, I expect you to be there with it," I stipulated.

"An' yull gimme da cash?" he asked.

"Yes. But the second you don't line up with any part of this, you won't have to worry about Da'Rell. I'll kill you myself. Understand," I asked. He looked at me somberly.

"Thank you so much Uncle Jay. I promise I won't let you down this time," he vowed.

"I know. You don't have an option to let me down. Even if you did, this isn't about me, this is about you. You have to start thinking about your life, and about your future. I see a lot of the same drive in you that I see in myself, that's why I work so hard to help you," I explained. About five minutes later, we reached my apartment.

"Uncle Jay, I gotta take dat cash ta D'easy in morning," he said.

"Okay. You can take it to him after you help me do some work at your Aunt Bianca's house. Okay?" I asked. It wasn't like I was affording him an option; I just didn't want to seem like a tyrant.

"Yessir. Mannass cool wit me," he asserted. We went inside. I remembered that I hadn't called Bianca back. I decided to do that shortly after I had gathered some blankets for him.

"Babe?" I said softly into the phone.

"Did you find him?" she asked. I had awakened her.

"Yeah, I found him. Poor kid was hiding in a dumpster," I recounted.

"That's terrible. Are you guys alright?" she asked. I decided not to tell her all the gory details. The last thing I wanted to do was get her worked up.

"We're fine. I picked him up, brought him back here. He's in the shower now. The situation has been taken care of. You get some sleep, okay? I love you," I cooed.

"Okay baby, I love you too," she replied before she hung up the phone. I smiled. I grabbed some pajamas for Bryan, and set my alarm. After he got out of the shower, Bryan materialized in my doorway.

"Ay Uncle Jay. Ah jus wanna say thank you man. I mean you be tryn so hard to keep me outta trouble, an' I always be findin' ways to pull myself back inta it. Thanks fa not givin' up on me. Imean, Iyaint even yo' kid, you jus talkin' ta ma aintee," he said gratefully. It made me feel a little bad about the fact that I had robbed him six hours earlier.

"It's okay. I see a lot of the same hustle in you that I once saw in myself. It's just that I had someone pointing me in the right direction. I think if someone would take the time to show you, or a lot of other people the right way to go, they would get to somewhere great. So I can't take credit. If I were languishing in the pits of my own ignorance, I would want someone to help me out as well," I replied.

"Langushing? Uncle Jay, you be usin' some wild words man. Wat dat mean? You doin' laundry in your ignorance?" he asked. I wasn't sure if he was being funny or not, but it gave me another idea.

"One more thing you are going to have to do. You are going to have to start reading books. I'll pick them out. Maybe if I show you the world beyond Port Haven, you'll desire more than Port Haven," I reasoned. He let out a faint groan, but then smiled.

"I guess dat's cool" He agreed.

"I guess THAT IS cool," I corrected. I wasn't going to change him, just smooth out the rough edges.

"That's what I meant. Good night Uncle Jay," he said as he walked away. I took a bottle of cologne from my dresser, and then I went to the closet and pulled out all the bags from my shopping earlier. I took everything into the front room and placed it all by the door. We weren't going to have much time to sleep, because I was still going to surprise Bianca. I went over my design in my head once more before finally allowing myself to go to sleep.

# 12

I felt like I had only blinked my eyes as opposed to having gotten a full night's sleep when my phone rang.

"Jayson, I'm standing here talking with Father Potter. I'm going to pick Bianca up in about ten minutes, so I suggest if you aren't up, you wake up and get it in gear," she barked into the phone.

"Yes Sister Mary Margaret," I quipped drowsily.

"Who? You know what, never mind. I'm leavin in nine minutes. Get to it!" she directed. I dragged myself out of bed. I went to get Bryan. His blankets were folded and rested neatly in the corner of the couch. I was moderately impressed. He was sitting there watching what looked like the news. I was amazed.

"Wow. The news? I was just expecting you to start making an effort. I didn't expect overnight reform," I said. He laughed.

"I wasn't gonna watch dis, but they started talkin' bout how much mo' money a college graduate makes than a high school graduate and then someone who hasn't finished high school. An' they started talking about different ways to make money legally. I ain't know it was so many different hustles out dere," he remarked. I was pleased. I guess the problem wasn't his desire to change, it was that no one had been speaking his language all along.

"Well sir, I hate to interrupt, but we've got things to do today. Let's get everything handled, shall we?" I asked as I turned off the television. Bryan stood compliantly and we walked to the door, picked up the bags and went down to the car. Once we hit the open road, I decided to let Bryan in on the day's agenda.

"Here's the deal. I'm going to stop at an ATM to get the cash for you. Then we are going to go to Aunt Bianca's house for about an hour or so, and then I'm going to drop you off at home. Okay?"

"Iss whateva man. Uncle Jay I meant to ask you where you learn how ta drive? I mean you got ghost last night. I know this thing is supposed ta move, but I yaint know it got out like dat," he recounted. I smiled. We got to an ATM. I took out two hundred dollars. Apparently he was watching.

"Uncle Jay, I need five hunned," he said neverously.

"I know. I got it covered," I assured him. I reached in my pocket and took out the money I had taken off of him last night. "Here you go. Five hundred dollars cash." I handed him the money. He looked at the bills strangely, and then just put them in his pocket. We drove to Bianca's in silence. We were around the corner when I called Quinn.

"Is Bianca gone?" I asked.

"Yeah, she left with your mom about ten minutes ago or so. The door is open," she said matter of factly.

"Okay, thanks," I replied, hanging up the phone. We pulled up into the driveway, got the bags out of the trunk, and ran inside the house.

Decorating a room isn't at the top of the "Most romantic things you can do for someone" list, but the degree of thought that goes into it has to count for something. I didn't really require Brian's help beyond taking everything up stairs because I had planned to do everything on my own, so he got relegated to being the lookout. I took a look around the room and after assessing the situation, I decided that I might need Bryan's help after all.

"Bryan!" I called. He came bounding up the stairs.

"Yeah Uncle Jay?" he answered.

"Change of plans. I do need your help. You see the bag from the craft store, with the curtains in it? Bring that over here please, and look in the closet, there should be a box with wooden beams in it. Grab that also," I instructed. He gathered the items I requested and brought them over to where I was standing. We were going to assemble the canopy on Bianca's bed, as well as hang drapes in her favorite color around it. Fortunately for us, Bianca had purchased a do-it-yourself style frame. The process was moderately onerous, but we completed it in about twenty minutes. After hanging the blue drapes around the bed, I remade it as best I could. Then I pulled the contents out of the toy store bag and the pet store bag. I put a stuffed Batman and a stuffed Spiderman on the bed and put little somberos on their heads. Then I placed a chew toy steak in the middle of them on a plate that I had Bryan get from the kitchen. Bryan looked perplexed.

"Uncle Jay, I don' get it. I know Valentine's Day finna happen but I don' undastand, what is this? I thought that it was 'posed ta be hearts an' flowers an' candy. You got Spidaman and Batman and some curtains. What is that about?" I understood his confusion.

"That's a good question. Let me answer that with another question. What's your favorite food?"

"Uh…I'ont know, pizza," he responded, even though he still seemed confused.

"Okay. Now imagine that someone will give you pizza whenever you want it, at anywhere or at anytime, and so you always eat pizza. Now that same person tells you that they are going to make you a special meal. Do you want that person to give you another pizza, or are you going to want something else, like some chicken or steak?"

"So what is you sayin'? You ain't cheat on ma Aint B didchu?" he asked. I laughed.

"No. What I'm saying is, I send Bianca flowers and candy all the time. I get her cards just because I'm thinking of her. Flowers and candy are ideas for men who don't know where to start. It's a bail out. How hard is it for you to do what everybody else is doing? It's like, "I'm not really putting any thought into this, what's the easiest thing that I can get away with? Uh…here we go flowers and a box of chocolate. My girlfriend is special. She deserves something extraordinary. So I'm going to put in the time to make sure she gets what she deserves," I explained. Bryan still looked bewildered.

"Dat don' explain Batman an' Spidaman, or da stake," he said.

"Persistent. Everything you see here is something that we either talked about, or something that happened. Batman and Spiderman have to do with our first date. She's going to appreciate the fact that I remembered it. I'm going to be doing nice things for her all week. This is just item number one. The better I make her feel, the better she is going to make me feel," I explained. Bryan twisted his face up.

"I'ont wanna hear about you an' Aint B gettin' it on!" he whined.

"That's not how I meant it. Love is about more than sex. It's the bond that two people share. It's how they support each other and build each other up. The more that I build her up and support her, the more support she can offer me. This then means there is more than I can offer her. You have to put something in in order to get something out. Just like anything else," I explained.

"I guess. Does all that stuff work? Like did you usta have mass fees, cause dat sounds like game." he asked.

"I wouldn't call it game, just a loose understanding of how to treat a woman. If you stick with me, you'll have more dates than you want," I answered. "But we'll talk about that later. We've got to get out of here; otherwise this is going to be pointless. Grab those bags and go ahead downstairs, I'll be there in a second," I directed. Bryan followed my directions. I reached in the last bag and pulled out a card and two packages of pulled rose petals. I put the card in Spiderman's hands and opened the rose petals and sprinkled them sparingly on the bed and the floor. Then I took my cologne and sprayed a little on the sheets and in the air before I closed the doors. I went downstairs and out of the front door. Bryan was waiting inside the car for me. I put the car in gear, and we headed off towards his house. I needed to let my mother know that I was clear and that she could go ahead and bring Bianca back.

"Mom, we're done. You can go ahead and bring her back now," I said.

"We're at the mall. I wanted to get some stuff for when Brock comes home and Macy's was having a sale so we're here, take your time," she explained.

"That's cool. What do I owe you for brunch?" I asked.

"Don't worry about it," she answered.

"Thanks. I'll talk to you later, Mom," I said. A couple moments later, I pulled up at Kymera's house.

"She still ain't back yet? She should just stay gon," he opined. I started to ask what was going on, but I decided to dismiss it.

"Make sure you handle your business, and make sure that's the end of it. I trust I don't have to say anything else to you about this. You don't owe D'easy any more, you owe me now. I won't be as easy to shake as those dudes from last night," I asserted. "I tell you what else. I'm going to go ahead and call Joe right now. You are still going to have to talk to him yourself, but I will make it a little easier for you. You need to be ready to go back to work on Monday, okay?" I said.

"Aight Uncle Jay, thanks again," he said as he exited the vehicle. I waited for him to get into the house before I pulled off. As he walked into the house I called Joe Quiggley. The phone rang.

"Hello?"

"Joe? Hey this is Jayson Sullivant. Do you have a minute?" I asked.

"Sure, anything for Jay Azariah, what's up?" he retorted.

"My nephew Bryan was working for you not too long ago, and I wanted to know if there was any way he could get his job back. He got mixed up with the wrong crowd, and I'm trying to get him back on the straight and narrow. Do you think you can help me out here?" I asked. There was a brief pause.

"I tell you between you, ol' Papa Potter and this kid... Yeah, but he needs to come talk to me himself. I'll let him have his job back. He was a good kid and a hard worker, just seemed a little bored... Yeah, bring him by the store next week, and if he sounds like he wants to be here, I'll give him his job back. You ain't gonna forget about ol' Joe Quiggley when you start working for Maclayne are you?"

"No Joe, I promise you I won't. Thank you for helping my nephew. It means a lot to me. I'll bring him down sometime next week. Is that cool?" I asked.

"Definitely man! I'm glad to help. See you at Vive ," he responded.

"Sure thing. Thanks again," I answered as we hung up the phone.

I made it home safely and after walking into the house, I collapsed on my bed. With my last bit of strength, I turned my phone off. I needed to go to sleep.

I was awakened a few hours later by a heavy knock at my door. I got out of bed and went to investigate. Father Potter was standing at my door.

"I called you several times and I was unable to get through. I thought something may have happened, so I thought I would stop by. How are you son?" he asked.

"I'm fine, nothing to report here. I was just trying to catch up on some sleep is all. You may come inside if you would like, I need to get up anyway, and otherwise I'm not going to be able to sleep tonight," I offered. He took me up on my offer. He came inside and sat on the couch.

"Jayson, I have watched you grow from a boy to a man. I remember the first time I saw you, I thought you were so beautiful. I know that's weird to hear an older man say about a boy, but it's the only word that applies. When your mother explained the situation to me, I decided that I would do everything in my power to help her and make sure that you had a positive role model in your life. I can't say that I saw all of your potential, but I knew you were going to be special. That's why I've always been nearby. You really went above and beyond last night. I'm proud of you. You made a plan and you executed it. You did execute it, right?" he asked.

"Yes, Father, I did," I answered.

"So how did you get rid of the pills?" he asked. I couldn't remember. In fact, I had completely forgotten that they were still in my possession.

"I...I...I don't quite recall," I answered. I started racking my brain trying to remember what I had done with the drugs. Then it came to me. "They're still in my drawer," I informed him.

"We have to get rid of those now. I'll start a fire," he asserted. I went to get the pills and Father Potter kept up his end of the bargain. I unceremoniously threw the pills into the flame.

"I can't believe he'd throw his life away over this stuff," I said as the fire consumed the pills.

"That's one of the dangers of having children. You have to be there every step of the way or they will fall in to mischief," he said stoically.

"If that's the case, then I don't know about having children Father. I'm only responsible for Bryan by proxy. I look out for him because I choose to, not because I have to, and quite frankly, I don't know if I could do so for any one else if it wasn't for my own volition. If I were responsible for my own kids, I don't know how I would handle it," I answered. Father Potter looked at me quizzically.

"Jayson, I contend that you would in fact know how to handle it. There is a natural parental instinct that develops when one takes on that role. My own started to develop when your mother first introduced me to you. You exercised it last night when you did everything that you did to help Bryan. If you had sat down with a pencil and paper and tried to script the best way to help him, do you think you would have come up with the plan you unveiled last night? Probably not. It was irrational, unusual and highly unorthodox, yet it was wildly effective. He probably came in here last night and read the Bible." He laughed.

"Not the Bible, but he was watching the news this morning," I replied.

"And my son is my point. You may not have known exactly what to do or even how to go about it, but by simply following your instinct, you were able to affect the best possible solution. Sometimes Jayson, you have to simply trust yourself, even if you don't have the best plan in the world. Just do things the best way that you know how and don't worry so much about what it looks like. You will make a wonderful father, because you will love your children and that love will cause you to do things in their best interest. Much like my love for my children makes me do things in their best interest," he explained.

"Do you mean real children, or metaphorical ones?" I asked.

"You and I both know that I was not privledged to have raised my own child. Having adopted the neighborhood's children as my own, I do things in their best interest. That's why the Beacon provides after-school care. What father doesn't want to see his children everyday?" he answered. I sat back, feeling reasonably satiated.

"That may be so, but I first need a mother for those children," I blurted. I had wanted to talk to him about this for a little while now, and this seemed like the perfect segue into it.

"So you are thinking about marriage? Bianca is a very special girl, and I don't know if it gets much better than her. I can see why you'd be thinking about it. We are talking about Bianca, correct?" he asked.

"Of course! She's the only woman I've been able to think about. The only person at length anyway, except for Bryan. I just feel like I'm rushing into it. I mean I'm just barely twenty-four years old, and I love her, but it seems a little impetuous to me," I answered. He twisted his face.

"That is the wrong way to look at it Jayson. I don't normally advocate rash decisions, but in this case I will encourage you to view the situation like this: you don't know how many chances at love you will get in a lifetime. Only you know how good or bad this one is. Let me ask you, compared to Amina, how do you feel about her?" he asked.

"If Amina were a lighter, then Bianca would be the sun. There simply is no comparison," I answered. Father Potter smiled.

"If that's the case, then why would you take a chance on someone else taking your sun?" he inquired. "The more time you spend with her as your girlfriend, the less time you can spend with her as your wife. You can handle it Jayson. I'm not saying bring her down to the Beacon tomorrow. I'm saying maybe it's time. Do you really think you are going to find anyone better? If it were me, I'd do it. I'd be on one knee faster than Nancy Kerrigan," he joked.

"Was that a joke? Father, that was terrible! But I see what you're saying," I answered.

"How does she feel about it?" he asked. I realized that I had never talked to her about it.

"I don't know. We've never really talked about it, as in our own marriage. Other people's maybe, but not our own," I answered sheepishly. Father Potter looked at me disapprovingly.

"Don't you think you should maybe have that talk? I mean if it's a partnership, one half of the unit is in the dark," he advised. Then, almost on cue, there was a knock at my door.

"Who is it?" I asked.

"It's me Jayson," she replied. Father Potter looked up at me.

"You two are behaving yourselves, right?" he asked.

"Yes we are," I responded.

"You'd tell me that either way, but I believe you. I'm going to go ahead and get out of your way here. Think about what I said. She is a wonderful person, and you two would have beautiful children, assuming they take after her." I laughed as I walked over to open the door.

"I guess it's better that they take after me than after some ol' ugly preacher," I said. He made his way towards the door. Then I remembered one other thing that I wanted to ask. "Who is Sister Mary Margaret?" I asked. His face flushed.

"There is no Sister Mary Margaret," he answered.

"So then who answered the phone last night when I called your cell phone? She gave the name of Sister Mary Margaret," I reiterated.

"I'm sorry, but there simply is no Sister Mary Margaret. She died about twenty years ago," he answered. Something was distinctly wrong, I could feel it, but I didn't know how to get my questions answered, so I let them go. Plus Bianca was still waiting outside the door.

"If you say so Father. I suppose we will speak about this at length later," I suggested.

"The matter dies here my son. The matter has died here," he answered. I opened the door. Bianca's million watt smile was the first thing I saw on the other side of the portal. She jumped on me and started peppering me with kisses.

"Jayson baby, I love what you did to my room! I can't wait for you to come over and put me on the bed and—"I coughed loudly while motioning towards Father Potter. Bianca looked over and instantly jumped down and smoothed her skirt.

"Good evening, Father," she said, seeming mildly embarrassed. Father Potter simply grinned.

"It's alright, my child, I was just leaving," he replied. "I'll see you both tomorrow," he answered as he walked out of the open door.

"Goodnight, Father," I said as I shut the door. After I turned the deadbolt, Bianca tackled me onto the couch.

"I love you soo much, Jayson Azariah. That was so thoughtful of you. I can't believe you remembered all of that! And you fixed my bed, and hung the curtains! It was all so beautiful! And the Mexican Batman and Spiderman with a steak! How in the world did I get so lucky?!" she exclaimed. I was blushing as much as my skin tone would allow.

"I just pay attention when you talk. A woman will always tell you what she wants; you just have to be smart enough to know it when you hear it," I replied. My mother had given me that little pearl of wisdom, and now I found myself quoting it verbatim. Bianca just gazed at me lovingly.

"I have the best boyfriend in the world," she said. I frowned.

"I don't like it when you call me that. Maybe we can come up with new titles?" I asked, thinking back to my conversation with Father Potter.

"Comme mon petit copain, et ma petite copine?" she said, showing off her bilingual knowledge. She had apparently forgotten about my own.

"No because all you did was say boyfriend and girlfriend in French. I'm talking about something a little more…progressive," I answered. She paused for a second while considering what I could be talking about. Then her face lit up.

"Jayson are you serious? You really want to take it there?" she asked.

"Take it where?" I asked. I wasn't convinced that she knew what I was talking about.

"I don't know, I was trying to bluff you into telling me," she admitted.

"Well baby, Father Potter was here because I wanted to talk to him about marriage. Not just saying that to keep you around, but seriously. I just want to know how you feel about it, like what are your thoughts on it?" I asked. She smiled at me.

"Jayson to be your wife would be like winning the lottery. How could I say no? I want to get married and it would be nice to have children with you, even though I hope they take after me. Cause you're cute but in a gremlins sort of way," she joked.

"Is everybody blastin today, or do I just have a target on my back? First Father Potter, now you? I don't care what either one of you says, if I were really that ugly, you wouldn't say it to my face. No one ever tells a really ugly person that they are ugly to their face. So hush. I'm fine and my kids will be fine," I argued. Bianca laughed as she kissed me on the cheek.

"I know baby, our kids will be fine. Seriously though, I thought we were moving in that direction the whole time. I love you, and I can't think of a single reason why we shouldn't be together. Plus I'm almost twenty-seven; I ain't got time to waste. That and the fact that you just signed that fat contract, I ain't goin' nowhere!"She said playfully. As we lay, I thought about how bright and comfortable my future was shaping up to be. A beautiful wife, a career that I loved, a contract that ensured my family would be taken care of for a long time to come. I just pictured myself in the interview on Oprah's couch. Talking about all the things I had to overcome, how I helped at the Beacon, gushing about Bianca, talking about my new position at Maclayne. I let myself get lost in the moment. I felt like my stock was rising, and I wasn't sure that there was a force under Heaven that could bring it down. In fact, I was certain that there wasn't a force under Heaven that could bring it down.

The rest of the week was relatively run of the mill. Everyday I sent her flowers that started with a letter of her name. Except for Friday, because she hated carnations for some reason, so I sent her chocolate instead. On Saturday we went to Casa de Lorenzo. The next six weeks were like the Golden Ages of our relationship. We grew closer and closer, almost to the point of becoming a singular unit. Even though I was spending more time at the office preparing for the move to Maclayne, we were still moving right along. We decided to wait until we got married before we had sex. It may have seemed old fashioned, but considering we had already gone eleven months without it, it wasn't that much of a strech. Plus it was just one more tie that binded us together, because with that kind of stipulation, marriage was no longer an if, but rather a when. I was going to propose, but only when the time was right. The only real hangup that I could identify was the fact that I still had to go help Kymera every two weeks.

Kymera was becoming steadily more aggressive. Every time I went over there, it was becoming more and more difficult to get away. One night she ripped my shirt trying to get me to give her a kiss. I tried to explain it to Bianca, but Kymera continously beat me to the punch. My ripped shirt simply got caught on a doorknob. Her meeting me at the door naked was watered down to I came in the house before she was ready for me. I was getting discredited at every turn. I felt like I was marching myself to the slaughter. That's the only way that I know how to describe it. Besides that, the next six weeks went by without a hitch. I had circled our last study session on my calendar, in my phone and on every device I had that recorded the date. I wanted this whole mess to be over, and if I could make it without any significant injury, I would count that a blessing. The sun came up that morning; I had a really good feeling about the day. However by about six o'clock, a storm rolled into town and somehow, I just knew that this was going to be a nightmare. I just prayed that somehow, someway, I'd wake up from it.

# 13

Cats and dogs are never outside when it's raining cats and dogs. I always found it funny that people said that. I parked my car and ran to the door. After a significant soaking, Kymera showed up at the door.

"Aww, my wittle Jerry's all wet. Why don't you come inside so whe can get you some dry clothes?" she said. After the ripped shirt incident, I knew better than to go there without a change of clothing.

"I have my own. Give me a moment to gather my composure and we can begin," I answered. *You aren't going to get me that easily*, I thought to myself. It had almost become a game. I stepped inside the house.

"Well, while you're doing that, I'm going to get the nachos, and make sure the camera is set up," she called. The nachos I didn't mind so much, but the camera seemed odd, she had never used a camera before. I finished getting dressed and went towards the den. Kymera came and sat down.

"What do you need a camera for? You've never used one before," I questioned.

"The final isn't until Thursday, but it's a comprehensive final, so tonight we have to review everything starting with the very beginning. I know you're a pretty busy guy, with the contract signing coming up this week, so I figured I'd just tape the session and review it every night until the exam," she explained. For the first time in life, I agreed with her logic. I didn't bother to tell her that I had taken the whole week off in order to get prepared for the signing on Saturday. She didn't need to know that and besides, her misinformation was going to get me out of every having to come back. Feeling relatively comfortable in her presence for the first time, I sat back on the couch.

"Well, let's crack open a book and get started," I said. I didn't want to be there very long, but if I had to be there, I was going to at least be effective. She had a look of dismay on her face.

"I knew I forgot something!" she yelled and she raced upstairs. After what I thought was a considerable amount of time, she reappeared.

"Sorry, I couldn't remember where I had left it," she said explaining her absence. I wrote it off as another quirk of her personality.

"That's fine. Let's get started," I said dryly. She got up and went over to the camera turned it on and focused it where I was sitting.

"Okay Jerry. Aaaaannnnddd, action!" she said as she came back to join me on the couch. We started reviewing old tests and notes. Rather than use her body to point out where things were, we just used the diagrams in the books and on the notes. I felt like I had finally convinced her that I wasn't interested. Either that or her will had subsided. About thirty minutes in, a bell rang. "Break!! It's time for a break, the nachos are done," she yelled as she moved towards the kitchen.

"Great, I'll go with you; I'm actually pretty hungry," I said greedily.

"NO!" she yelled. "You stay here; I'll bring them to you," she said, leaving the room. I didn't understand her objection, but I didn't fight it either. Moments later, she brought the searing plate into the room. I cleared a space on the table. If nothing else, she could cook. She looked sincerely in my eyes and said: "Jayson, I know I've given you a lot of headaches, but you've stuck with me the whole way. I'm going to pass this class and get my degree because you hung in there with me, and I just wanted to say thank you. So enjoy your nachos, I know how much you love them. Hopefully they help you keep your strength up for tonight," she said, and she bent down to give me a hug, which I accepted. Then, as soon as she stepped away, I went for the plate.

I survived longer than I had on our first encounter, but only by two and a half minutes. My eyes started to water. My mouth was engulfed by veritable flames.

"Ky mer uh! Ah need sumtin ta drink!" I yelled. She got up slowly and went into the kitchen. After what seemed like an eternity, she came back with two glasses. I assumed they were Sprite, but they may as well have been water, because I couldn't taste a thing. I drank all twelve ounces like a shot. Even if I could taste, I doubt it was on my tongue long enough for me to decipher any iota of flavor.

I consumed the entire plate. It was a little bitterer tasting than what I remember, but I just barely noticed, considering the damage I had already done to my tongue. "These taste a little different did you try something new?" I asked.

"I just tried some new spices in the cheese is all. I think it's called exta…mexi…lente…Extamexilente, yeah that's what I used," she explained. That sounded like total nonsense to me, but for some reason, I didn't think to correct her.

"Let's just get back to the review," I instructed. We dug back into the notes. We had gone through the skeletal and cardiovascular systems when I started to feel a little weird. I couldn't get my eyes to focus. No matter how hard I tried, I just couldn't get my eyes to focus. And I was getting hot. Like summer day in the middle of the Sahara with a sweatsuit and thermal underwear on in layers. I started to sweat. I felt like the heat may have been on too high or something. "Kymera, can you turn the heat down? It's baking in here," I asked. She smiled at me.

"Baby, the heat isn't on. Maybe you're still hot from dinner. Maybe you should take your shirt off, that might help," she suggested.

"No, I don't want to take my shirt off, that won't help. I'm just going to go and get some water," I said. I tried to get up, but Kymera forced me back down on the couch.

"I'll get it for you, you stay put right there," she said. I obeyed. She came back with a glass of water. I took one sip and spat it out.

"Kymera, do you have anything in a bottle? This is by far the vilest tasting water I have ever attempted to swallow," I said, realizing how rude it must have sounded, but not really caring enough to do anything about it.

"You don't have to be so rude about it! I'll see what I have," she said. I was embarrased.

"I'm sorry. Gimme a hug," I said. She smiled and then leaned down to give me a hug. I could see her unfettered breasts inside of her loose fitting t-shirt, and I simply could not make myself look away. They were nearly perfect, from what I could tell. She hovered for a second. Then she said.

"Let's study some more." She walked in front of me slowly, and I couldn't take my eyes off of her butt. It was so perfectly round and perfectly sized. It looked like two Christmas hams or something. Delicious. She stopped about half way across the room to tie her shoes. She bent with her back, leaving her butt in the air. I was beside myself. Normally I could look away, but now it was like a siren's song and it was calling to me. I simply couldn't turn away no matter how hard I tried. She finished tying her shoe and walked back over to the couch.

"Jayson, lets skip the rest of this stuff and go to the part that I have the most difficulty with, can we please do the reproductive system? Everything's got so many names, and I don'r remember what does what and it's just a mess, can you help me please?" she asked. There was a war going on inside my head. The last sane part of me was screaming at me to get out of the house. Unfortunately, the insane portion was screaming to stay, and it had a microphone and speakers.

"Ohkay," I responded. She smiled.

"Can we do it the way I learned the muscles?" she asked. It felt like a bad idea.

"If that will help you learn, yeah, we can do it like that. Wait, no! We shouldn't. I can't help you like that. That's not a good idea," I said. She moved closer to me and took my hand and placed it high on her inner thigh. I couldn't fight; or rather I didn't want to fight it. She looked me in my eye. "Jayson ask me what muscle this is," she said seductively. I couldn't think.

"Uh...Uh...the pectorial, I mean the sartorious," I answered. She moved my hand to her breast.

"This is the pectorial Jerry. These are my mammary glands," she said. I left my hand there. I felt like I should move it, but I wasn't sure why I should move it.

"Yes, Kymera, this is where your mammary glands are located," I responded. My lingering hand seemed to be more of an invitation to mischief than anything else.

"Do you want to see my mammary glands?" she asked. I needed to say no. I knew I had to say no. But I couldn't control my mouth for some reason.

"Yeah, I want to see them. I mean no!! No!! That's bad" I said, but it was too late, Kymrera's shirt was up and over her head before I had finished my sentence. She took my hands and placed them on her exposed breasts.

"Feel how soft they are Jayson. Bianca's aren't like this are they?" she asked me. The mention of Bianca's name caused a momentary insurrection.

"You're married! I have a girlfriend! I shouldn't be doing this! Our session is over Kymera!" I shouted. She looked at me repentantly.

"You say married like I've seen my husband in the past seven years. Ever since he ran off with that therapist of his...I know. I'm sorry. But you can't leave yet, because we have to go over the man parts" she said. Before I could move, she reached for my groin. "That's the penis," she said innocent ly. Instantly, the blood flow that was sustaining my last functioning brain cells was rerouted away from them. She massaged it gently, and I began to feel myself engorge. The last remaining brain cells gathered their strength and made one last desperate plea which I vocalized.

"Kymera I don't want to have sex with you, I have a girlfriend that I love. I—" She covered my mouth.

"Shhhh. We aren't going to have sex. I know you have a girlfriend. Are you still hot?" she asked me. By this point, I could feel the beads of sweat starting to form.

"Yeah, I am," I answered. She moved her hands from where they were to the top of my jeans. She quickly undid my belt and fastener and then pulled my pants down, revealing my boxers and erect penis. I was losing it. Kymera was beautiful. Sexy even. Why was I fighting her so hard?

"That's just how it looks in the diagram! Jerry, you should be sharing this with the world." She swung my feet up onto the couch and covered my body length with her own.

"Jerry, I know we've had some differences, but I really like you, and I hope that you aren't angry with me over anything, because I think a lot of life's problems are easily solved," she said as she kissed me softly. I was positioned oddly, so I couldn't get my arms from under my back. "Don't you want me Jerry? Aren't I sexy?" she asked. I was silent. I felt like I shook my head no, but I wasn't sure She sat up with her hand on my chest, and because of how I was positioned, she had effectively pinned me. She sat there just inches from my erect penis. She grabbed her book off of the coffee table and after a few moments of looking, produced a condom.

"Jerry, you are going to love me for this," she said, slipping the contraceptive out of the wrapper. As she positioned it for use, I felt my mind shutting down. The one time I desperately needed my mind and I couldn't focus. It was like I was there, but I wasn't there. My mind was gone, and everything started to blur. It was like being in surgery, but being completely awake and unable to speak. I thought I heard myself say no, but it could have been "slow" or "go." I don't remember what I did or didn't do, or what she did or didn't do exactly, but I do know that I came to once I felt the condom break.

# 14

The bus finally came. I climbed aboard, and just as I was about to pay my fare, the driver covered the recepticle.

"I couldn't charge you if I wanted to, you can just go ahead and take a seat man," he said to me.

"Do I look that bad?" I asked. Medicated, broken-hearted, whatever, I still had my pride.

"Worse," he answered softly. I sat down humbly and rode to the Rock Canyon stop. The thoughts ran rampant through my mind. I didn't know how to fix it. I didn't even know that I could fix it. More accurately than that, I didn't know quite which problem was fixable. The only thing that I could think of was that my world was on the rocks and there wasn't effectively anything I could do about it. I got to my stop, and just as I was exiting the bus, the driver called out: "Good luck man!" I nodded my thanks to him. The bus passed in front of me and I crossed the street and began to trudge down the street. Even though it was a relatively short hike, not more than a half a country mile, the myriad of emotions running rampant in my conscious combined with my sheer physical exhaustion made the trip nearly unbearable.

About halfway through my journey, I tried to call both my mother and Father Potter again. Again, no response. Of all the times to be alone, this wasn't it. Another half an hour later, I reached my mother's door. Oddly enough Father Potter's car was sitting in the driveway. I didn't want to get worked up about it, but I knew that something wasn't right. I used my keys to get in the house.

"Mom?!" Brock?! Hello?" I called. No one answered. I looked in the garage. My mother's car was missing. I figured they must have ridden together in her car to see me at the hospital. I decided not to worry about it too much and went to make myself something to eat. After scrounging up the semblence of a meal, I went and sat on the couch. There was an indentation in the cushions. *Brock must be on the couch again*, I thought to myself. I sat down and watched t.v., or more accurately stared at the television set while the events of the past tweny-four hours ran roughshod through my head. I couldn't believe that this was really happening to me, and like this. What could I say? What could I do? I had never felt so out of options before in my life. I had told Bianca the truth as I knew it, and it had netted me nothing. I felt myself spiraling downward. Before I could sink any lower into my self pity, the phone rang.

"Hello?" I answered.

"Hello, this is Nadine, the caterer. Is Mr. Randall present?" she asked. This was ordinarily out of character for me, but I decided to try and help.

"Speaking," I lied.

"I got your message about the potential cancellation on your order. In order for us to meet your requests we are going to need to know what you and Ms. Sullivant decide to do by this time tomorrow. Also, assuming that you do decide to go through with it, we also need to know if you are interested in having your special day filmed. Have you and Ms. Sullivant come to some sort of conclusion?" she asked.

"We have not, but I will have an answer for you by this time tomorrow, okay? Thank you very much Nadine, goodbye," I said, hanging up the phone. Why would he have cancelled the caterer? Something was wrong, but I didn't know how to address it. Should I call Brock out on it, or should I just let it go and pretend like I didn't know. I know it's generally bad policy to cover one lie with another, but in this case, they balanced out. I called Brock.

"Hello?" he answered.

"Hey, this is Jayson. I'm at the house and the caterer just called," I said.

"What did she say?" he asked.

"Something to the effect of you have twenty-four hours to confirm your order or it's going to be cancelled," I answered.

"That's odd, because I didn't cancel that, Jessica must have changed her mind about using Nadine. Okay, well, can you call you mother and let her know for me? The last thing I want to do is deal with that. I'm tired of all this wedding stuff. That's why I didn't want to do it the first time," he said gruffly. I understood. Weddings were the one thing I couldn't stand. If I didn't have to be there, I wouldn't go to my own. Assuming I would ever have one.

"I'll call her for you, it's not a problem. When are you going to Dallas?" I asked. It was slightly odd considering that historically Brock and I never spoke much. There really wasn't anything to talk about. He was sports, I was business. He was fishing, I was poetry. The only thing we had in common was my mother, and Samantha, who was a function of my mother.

"I actually just touched down about twenty minutes ago," he answered. Maybe we never talked because we never gave it an honest effort.

"That's cool. I'll give my mom a call for you. You be safe," I said. I didn't really have a good salutation for him yet.

"Thank you and you do the same," he replied. Apparently he didn't have a good one for me either. I hung up the phone and went back to my ham and cheese sandwich and the Monday morning television, which was surprisingly good, considering what I was expecting. I heard myself screaming at the television during the Price Is Right.

"You moron, there's no way that car is only eleven thousand dollars!" I said, laughing at myself. Then the phone rang again. A man with a very official sounding voice was on the other end.

"Hello is either Ms. Sullivant, or Mr. Randall available?" he asked. Somehow lying to this guy didn't seem like the best idea.

"I am Ms. Sullivant's son, but neither of them is available at present. May I take a message?" I asked.

"Certainly. My name is Craig Washington and I work down at the courthouse. Ms. Sullivant tried to apply for a marriage license, with a

Mr. Brock Randal but there was a problem with it. Just have either party give me a call at the number that showed up on your caller ID, extension 808. Thank you," he said quickly.

"Am I allowed to know the nature of the problem, just so I know what to tell them?" I asked.

"No, I can't give you that information, unfortunately. I can only discuss it with the parties that are involved. Just have them call me please, alright? Goodbye." Dial tone. I didn't even know what to say, but I knew that things weren't quite what they seemed. I decided to try and call my mother one more time.

"Hello?"

"Father Potter?!" I asked incredulously. Why was he answering my mother's phone?

"Yes Jayson?" he answered cavalierly.

"Why are you answering my mother's phone?" I asked.

"This is my phone, Jayson. Check the number you dialed. You probably fat-fingered it and dialed Jacob instead of Jessica," he said. I pulled my cell away from my face. He was right, I had called him.

"I'm sorry, Father; it's just that it's been a long couple of hours," I bleated.

"Where are you now?" he asked.

"I'm at my mother's house. Why?" I inquired.

"Why aren't you with Bianca? What happened?" he asked. "You must have told her what happened. Sheesh. Did she put you out on the spot or did she drop you off?" he asked.

"On the spot. It was horrible. I caught the bus and then I walked all the way down Rock Canyon until I got here. You haven't seen my mother perchance have you?" I asked.

"Yeah, she's right here. You want to talk to her?" he asked.

"Please, that way I don't have to pay for this call twice," I replied.

"Jessica Sullivant," my mother replied.

"Mom, I'm at the house and there's a problem. Apparently, there was a cancellation placed on the order with the caterer, and she needs to know what's going on within the next twenty-four hours. Also there was a problem with the marriage license and you have to call the

Bureau back. They wouldn't tell me what was wrong, but they said either one of the parties involved had to call them back to get it straightened out," I said.

"Okay, I'll take care of it. Brock must not have filled out the papers correctly. Thank you Jayson," she said nonchalantly. I was confused. The wedding was scheduled to take place on Friday, as in four days from today. It was odd for two issues of that magnitude to show up and neither my mom nor Brock seemed even the least bit concerned about them. Considering the amount of items I had on my plate, I couldn't really worry about it. I was lost in my own drama, but even so, I knew that I would have handled things differently if it were my wedding, but it wasn't my wedding, it was theirs and I couldn't make them care any more or apparently any less.

"Do you know what time you're coming back? I wanted to see if you could maybe take me to get my car," I asked.

"Where's Bianca? I thought she was helping you today," my mom asked.

"Long story," I answered.

"It's going to be a while, I'm out shopping, but you're more than welcome to hang out at the house, you know that," she stated.

"Thanks, I guess I'll be here for a while then," I said.

"Alright baby, I'll see you when I get home. Love you," she responded.

"Okay mom, I'll see you then. I love you too" I said. After hanging up the phone I lied back down on the couch. I was still feeling pretty weak from the combination of the medicine and the walk and I wanted to sleep, but every time I closed my eyes, my fight with Bianca replayed in my head. I didn't know how I was going to correct things or how I was ever going to make it better. I didn't really know that I could. It's hard to apologize when you don't really feel like you are in the wrong for anything. Even so if there was anything I had ever learned, it was that pride and love are like oil and water. They could never mix. As much as I didn't want to, I picked up my phone and called Bianca. The call went straight to voicemail, which was about what I expected, but I was secretly hopeful that she would have answered. I knew it wouldn't be that easy. I laid back and stared at the ceiling while I tried to figure out what to do. After what felt like an hour I felt strong enough to make the walk to Kymera's house and to my car. I went into the fridge and grabbed a bottle of water and then headed out of the door.

A twenty minute walk when everything is fine is a nice way to get out and enjoy the day. A twenty minute walk when you are going through something is torment. I thought about life without Bianca, life with Kymera, my mother's wedding issue, my deal with Maclayne, Brian and his assorted nonsense. I couldn't quell the storm that was raging in my mind. I felt like the world was on my shoulders, there was so much that I had to do. So many things that required my direct involvement, and yet I felt powerless. I hadn't felt this low since I walked in on Amina.

I was finally turning on to Labrinyth, Kymera's street, when a car raced past me. I thought it was Brock's car, but I couldn't make out the license plate. Even though the windows were tinted just like his, I could tell that that there was a female inside the vehicle. I walked the remaining quarter mile to my car, and just as I was about to get in, Bryan came bounding out of the door, dressed for work.

"Ay was up Uncle Jay?" he asked. I wasn't really feeling very talkative, but I decided to humor him.

"Nothing, I'm about to head back to my house," I answered.

"Do you think you can give me a ride over to Quiggley's? I don't want to be late. They got this thing where if I'm on time or early for thirty days in a row, I get an extra fifty dollars on my check. Today is day number twenty nine, and Wednesday will be day number thirty," he said excitedly. I couldn't explain the change, but I was glad it had taken place.

"Sure I can, get in," I answered. He complied and we were off to Quiggley's. About half way through the ride, Bryan asked:

"Uncle Jay, what went down with you and Kymera last night? I know you come over to help her study, but when I got home from work, papers were everywhere and the ambulence was here." I was too embarrassed to tell the truth. How do you tell someone "Your mother may have raped me?"

"I had a bad reaction to some food she made, and she called the hospital," I answered.

"It was those nachos wan't it? I heard her call those her 'boxer droppers'. Anytime she wants something, she makes those for who ever she wants it fron and she gets it. She either makes that or this spaghetti. She'll sing about how she's going to take this man's money, or be some man's honey, so she can take his money. I mean think about it, how do you think she got that Beemer? Do you know what she does for a living? I don't know and I live with her," he surmised. I looked at him in disbelief. I decided to change the subject.

"Do you still have that tie that you used the time you came to work with me?" I asked.

"Yes, I do. It's in my little safe, where I keep important stuff. When I was sellin' for D'easy, I decided to buy a small safe to keep people from taking stuff out of my room. Kymera is normally in there all the time trying to get something, whether it's my clothes for some dude, or my electronic stuff. I got tired of my stuff coming up missing. Plus since Brittany be lettin' D'easy bring people over all the time, I decided that was the best way to go. No point in having all that money if he'll just steal it all back. That joker is locked down too. I'm the only person with the code, and it's up here. Plus I hid that bad boy too! It's in the safest place I could think of," he answered, pointing to his head. We had reached Quiggley's, but I had more questions. Bryan however, didn't have any more time. "Thank you Uncle Jay! I've only got three minutes to get to the back and clock in! I'll see you later!" he yelled as he bolted from the car. I thought Kymera recorded the study session, but did I really want to see what had happened? I wasn't entirely sure. The one thing that I was certain about was that I needed to get home and get some real rest, and that's exactly what I did.

# 15

I had only meant to rest for a few hours, but when I woke up, it was eleven o'clock at night. The first thing on my mind was to see if Bianca had called me. Just like I thought, she hadn't. I knew it was late, but I decided to call just to see if I could get through. I called her cell phone. It rang twice and then it went to voice mail. She was still ignoring me. I decided to call her house.

"You have the audacity to call here?! She doesn't want to talk to you! Period!" It was Quinn. She was the last person I wanted to talk to at this juncture.

"Quinn, please, if Bianca is available, I need to speak with her," I pleaded.

"No," she said flatly. There was no way that I was going to get past her. Just as I was about to relent, I heard someone cut in on the line.

"Quinn, it's okay, honey. You can hang up. I've got it from here." It was Bianca, and I realized that I wasn't quite as ready to talk to her as I thought I was. I knew that this might be the only chance that I had to talk to her.

"Bianca?" I asked. I heard Quinn hang up the phone.

"What?" she asked.

"Look I don't know what happened last night. I really don't. I ate some of your aunt's nachos and the next thing I know, I'm in the hospital. I know that sounds like a lie or whatever, but it's the truth. Have you talked to Kymera yet?" I asked.

"No, she's out of town. That's immaterial. Whether you two slept together or not is important, but it's not the central issue right now. If you say you don't know what happened, then until I talk to her, there's really nothing I can say, because up until now I trusted you. That having been said, I can forgive whatever transgression may have occurred between the two of you, but what I cannot comprehend is how you can say what you said. You set out to be malicious. I don't understand why you would say something so ugly to me. I thought you loved me," she said. I was guilt stricken. She was talking about the fact that I had said she was on par with Amina. I knew that this one was going to be tough to fix.

"I shouldn't have said that stuff, I apologize. I was upset because rather than trust me, or give any credence to what I had to say, you simply assumed that Kymera would be right. You tell her everything. How did she know we haven't had sex? I didn't tell her that? How did she know that my mother was a masseuse? Or that I had helped her study for her exams? You leaked out all kinds of information and that's my priciple problem with you right now. You cannot do stuff like that," I said. I hadn't really given it much thought, but I wasn't one for sharing peresonal buisness.

"Jayson, I didn't tell her all that stuff. Yes I told her we weren't having sex, but I wasn't being derisive, it was a point of discussion. You're asking me to trust you, and I ask the same of you for myself. But even so why would she have to throw herself at you? What could she possibly have to gain from that?" Bianca asked.

"Why shouldn't she throw herself at me? Excuse my arrogance, but what's so wrong about me that another woman couldn't be attracted?" I retorted. I knew I was treading on thin ice, but I wasn't going to just stand there and just take what she was throwing at me. Bianca was silent.

"That's not what I mean. She knows that you and I are together, so why would she throw herself at you? Kymera is married, that just doesn't add up Jayson," she reasoned.

"And I love you. I am completely satisfied with you, and I don't want anyone other than you, yet you stand by your assessment? Why can't you believe that maybe, just maybe, I'm telling the truth? I've never lied to you before, and so now all of a sudden, I'm Pinocchio? Bianca, we've got quite a long ways to go if we are really going to make it to the altar," I said.

"You'll be lucky to have me back in your apartment, let alone in a church somewhere. Regardless of if I believe you or not, there are still some very simple things to remember, not the least of which is you still claim that you don't know if you slept with my cousin or not. That's not something that we can just gloss over Jayson. This problem isn't solved. I'm tired and I have to get up and go to work tomorrow, and I have more to do considering that Father Potter is away right now. I don't want to stress out about this anymore. We'll talk later," she said dismissively. I decided that a stalemate was better than a loss.

"Bianca, if nothing else, know that I love you, and I promise we'll get past this, you'll see," I said.

"I love you too Jayson and I hope you are correct. Good night," she responded. She hung up without allowing me to say anything else. Considering the difference between what I expected and what could have happened, I could only view the conversation positively.

I sat awake for a few hours more. I tried to work through all the possibilities, all the scenarios. I wanted to make this better. More accurately, I wanted to make this right. There was only one answer that I could see. If Kymera wouldn't tell her, then I would find someway to prove what had happened.

# 16

I let myself wake up naturally. What was the point of having time off if you're just going to waste it with rigid structure? I woke up shortly before ten a.m. My last thought of the day prior was my first thought of today. I reached for my PDA so I could call Bryan and try to find a resolution for my little problem, but before I could even get that far, my appointment alarm started to ring. I had completely forgotten that today was the day of my physical exam before I could switch my health insurance over to Maclayne's. I would have to wait until after that was over before I could do anything else. Whether Bianca was with me in the future or not would not effectively stop me from having a future. If I worked quickly, I could prevent this from becoming an all day event; for starters I had to drive nearly fifty miles away to go to one of their approved physicians. I wanted to complain, but if they were going to pay for it, why not? I had to be there by noon, so I got up, quickly showered and headed towards my destination. I figured at most this would take about an hour or so, three if you factored in driving time.

Seven hours, and two bruised veins later, I was back home. The hospital was, in typical fashion overcrowded and understaffed. The nurse that had been assigned to draw my blood was fresh out of nursing school, and I doubt she could put the nozzle of a gas pump into her car without difficulty, much less a needle into a vein. I felt like she was trying to sew a sweater into my skin. I was dragging myself into my apartment when my phone rang.

"Hello?" I asked.

"Hello, this is Aaron Scottle from Advesco Life insurance."

"Okay?" I asked. I had no idea why he was calling me.

"I'm sorry to call so late sir, but I needed to inform you that in order to complete any changes on your policy, we are going to need to see an original copy of your birth certificate," he said.

"But you have a copy of it on file. Why would you need to see the original? I've never seen the original," I said.

"It's a new Identity Theft countermeasure that we are implicating. Because you are adding a person with an unalike last name, and your age, plus the considerable amount of insurance that your company is willing to pay for, you represent a highly desirable target. We are just looking out for you sir," he asserted. I couldn't really argue with his logic.

"Okay, well I'm going to have to see if I can dig it up, or worst case I go to the hall of public records. Can I get it to you by Monday?" I asked.

"Sure Mr. Sullivant, that is not a problem at all. Thank you for your understanding sir. You have a nice night," he said.

"Thanks, you too," I said. Even though he had just given me a new task to complete, he was so friendly about it that I didn't mind. I hung up the phone and went into the kitchen for a glass of apple juice. Looking at the glasses that I owned, one glass wasn't going to be enough, so I just took the whole bottle out of the fridge and went to sit down on the couch. I turned on the television and started watching Man versus Wild.

*He should do an utban show*, I thought. *Man vs. street or man vs.city*. I had started to run through all the possible permutations when Bianca's ring filled the silent air. I hurriedly picked up the phone.

"Hello?" I said, excited.

"Relax, this isn't that type of phone call. I'm still angry and nothing's changed. But I need you to go over to Kymera's house. Bryan and that boy Da'rell are fighting and Brittany is scared. Something to the effect of Da'rell thinks Bryan was stealing from him. Anyway, can you please go over there before someone gets hurt?" she asked.

"Yes I will go. Can we talk?" I asked. It was horrible timing, but with these sorts of things, you've got to take every open chance you get. Considering that you'll never get that many.

"Goodbye Jayson. This is a little more important than that at the moment," she said. The wheels in my head started turning.

"Why can't you go? Your house is closer than mine," I reasoned.

"Because I'm out at dinner right now, and I'm no where near there, that's why," she answered. I wasn't about to play this game.

"So just like that I get sent to check on the kids while you're out at dinner with some other dude? I don't have time for this! Bye!" I yelled as I ended the call. Inwardly, I was seething. I didn't intentionally betray her, but yet she could go and do whatever with whomever, and I was just supposed to be okay with it? Not likely. I grabbed my keys and my bottle of apple juice, went to my car and headed towards Kymera's house.

Turning down Labyrinth, I was still thinking about how I was going to quell this dispute, when three loud bangs disrupted the tranquility of the night. I knew that they had only come from one place, and only invovled two people. I pushed the accerlator and got down the street as quickly as I could. There in the grass of the front yard, Bryan lay, bleeding on his uniform, and just barely conscious. I grabbed my phone and anxiously dialed 911 as I ran towards him.

"911 what is your emergency?" the operator asked.

"There's been a shooting, I'm at 1026 Labyrinth! What should I do?" I yelled frantically.

"Is the person conscious and breathing?" she asked. I looked down at Bryan. He was unconscious and breathing weakly.

"He's breathing, and he looks like he's falling asleep," I answered.

"Okay. Keep him awake! Talk to him, keep him thinking, don't let him fall asleep, and if you can identify where the wounds are, just try and keep pressure on them until help arrives," The operator replied soothingly. I looked around for Brittany. She was sitting on the steps crying.

"Brittany! Go in the house and get some towels." She just sat there, frozen. This was not the time for tears. Inaction now would cause us more tears later.

"BRITTANY! Go and get some towels!" I commanded, instantly thawing her out. She ran into the house and emerged moments later, her arms full of towels. Still moving at the same speed as when she entered the house, she brought the towels to me on the lawn.

"Bryan! What happened pal?" I asked.

"D'easy…D'eeesy…" he stammered.

"I can't believe he shot'eem…Ova nothin," she stammered.

"Who shot him?" I asked. This might be the only time I could get solid answers from her.

"Da'rell…" she sobbed. I was still trying to get to the bottom of what happened.

"What happened? They were fighting, an' I tried ta break it up, but I couldn't, so I called Bianca," she continued. I still needed more information. Bryan was still lying there, veritably motionless. I was beginning to get agitated.

"Bryan, talk to me! How was work? Were you on time today?" I asked.

"Yeah…Ima get dat extra cake…you gotta give it ta Brit.ney, cause D'easy ain't comin' back." he said drearily, I patted him gently on the cheek. Then I looked over at his sister.

"Brittany I need to know what happened here! Your brother's blood is going to be on your hands if you don't start talking!" I yelled.

"D'easy said that he was missing some weight. He asked Bryan if he had been stealing from him. Bryan said he hadn't, and I believed him, he's really changed lately. But when I was helpin' D'easy put it tagether, he was comin' up a little light. He knew I wasn't taking it, and he ain't had nobody ova fo about a week now," she recounted.

"So that's it, Bryan must have been stealing from him?! He's got a job, he was done with this!" I yelled, my emotions were threatening to get the better of me.

"Unkal Jay, don' be mad at her, she didn't know. I been savin ma paycheks, cause I wanted ta open a bank account like da man on da news said. Dey all in my safe an' I wan you ta get them fa Bri-Bri?" he said.

"I don't know the code Bryan! You can get them for her!" I said.

"I'm about to go ta sleep, so Ah caint. Remembuh da game we played dat one night at da restaurant?

The one dat I won? Now you know da code. I can't tell Bri-Bri, cause she'll tell D'easy," he said trailing off. I patted his face heavily. We had played so many games with numbers, that there was no way I could be certain which one he was talking about.

"BRYAN!! BRYAN! You have to stay awake!!" I yelled frantically. I was losing him and I wasn't sure what else to do even though we were doing the best we could to keep pressure on his wounds which looked to be in his abdomen and his leg. I could finally hear the sirens. I placed my hands on either side of his head.

"Hang in there Bryan. Help is on the way." When I pulled my hands back, my right hand glistened in the moonlight, covered in fresh blood. I looked on the side of his head, where I noticed a large gash. It was only going from bad to worse. Finally the ambulence arrived. The EMTs poured out and ran over to Bryan.

"Gunshots? Are you the father?" the lead technician asked me as his cohorts began to attempt to stabilize Bryan.

"I'm the uncle, and yes, and a blow to the head apparently," I answered while trying to stay out of the way.

"The police are going to want to ask some questions. Were there any witnesses?" he asked me as they loaded Bryan into the ambulence. I pointed to Brittany.

"Yes, she was present." Then I turned to Brittany. "You need to ride with him," I directed. She got up and walked somberly to the vehicle, and climbed in. The EMT closed the doors. "Sir we're heading towards Sisters of Mercy North, if you want to notify the family and meet us there," he said as he ran around to the front of the ambulence and drove towards the hospital. I went to the house door to lock it. After completing that task, I got in my car and drove towards the hospital.

I dialed Bianca with my bloodstained hands. It was eerily symbolic; Bryan's blood was literally on my hands. Should I have tried to show him a different way of doing things?

"Is everything okay?" she asked nervously. I decided to pass up the chance at a free shot.

"No. It's not. Bryan's been shot. I'm on the way to the hospital now. If you can find Kymera, you might want to let her know. I don't know how it's going to work out to be honest. I'm praying and I suggest you do the same. They are taking him to Sisters of Mercy North, and that's where I'm going right now. I have to go now dear, I'll see you at the hospital," I answered just before I hung up the phone.

The path to Sisters of Mercy went through the warehouse district, so after a couple minutes of hard driving, I caught up to the ambulence. About five minutes later, we were at the hospital. I parked my car as they took him into the emergency entrance. Securing my vehicle, I ran to the front desk. Apparently the blood on my clothes made it obvious who I was after. The receptionist just pointed towards a set of double doors.

"OR on the second floor," she said. I pushed the button on the elevator. I looked up, where I noticed it was on the seventh floor and it was moving painstakingly slow. I saw the stairs and decided to take the one flight up. I got to the landing and immediately burst through the door. The OR was down the hall. I was moving as fast as I could without running. Doctor Ross was in full operational garb and heading in the same direction that I was going in. I got to the OR door, and realized that I couldn't proceed past it. I went to the waiting room, and walked over to where Brittany was sitting. She was crying softly.

"It's all my fault. I shouldna let D'easy stay there while Kymera was gone. I shouldna let him stay there at all. I can't buhleave dis," she whimpered. I put my arm around her comfortingly. Even if I agreed with her, adding to her guilt wasn't going to help anything. I went to the bathroom to try and scrub some of the blood off of my hands. When I came out of the bathroom, Officers Morian and Grey were moving towards Brittany.

"Andre? Vince? What ya'll doing here?" she said as she walked over to hug them.

"We heard about what happened. D'easy said he ain't mean fa dis to happen, he called us and asked us to come by and make sure that he was okay. He figgahd dat da boys ah be up herre, so he ain't wanna come" Officer Morian said. I knew something was up, but I wanted to see if I was right. I slowly walked up on the trio. The two officers looked shocked.

"Oh, this is my Uncle Jayson. Uncle Jayson, this is Trajan Morian and Vince Grey, they friends wit me an Da'rell," Brittany said, introducing us. I decided to play along. The three of us recognized each other, and they realized that their cover was blown. Vince shot me a look that was pleading for me to play along.

"Wat up fam?" Trajan asked.

"My nephew is sitting here with three bullet holes in him. You tell me," I said sharply.

"I hope he gon be alright," Vince said. I shot him a look as if to say "shut up." Their insincerity was where my problem lied. It wasn't all that long ago that they were about to try and put the same person in prison. They didn't give a damn one way or the other. Da'rell was a mark; Bryan could turn out to be an accessory, or causalty, put him in a cell or a box, it didn't matter, to them, and that was what bothered me. Josh looked out the window.

"Aye, is dat yo whip out dere, da lil' black one?" he asked.

"Yes, it is. Why do you ask?" I inquired.

"Aw, nothin', man, I was watchin' da news and dey sed dat dey was lookin fa somebody in on uh doze. Sum'in bout drug trafficking uh sumtin. You shud be careful," he said omninously.

"Isn't there an attempted murder suspect you should be trying to locate?" I asked aloud. Brittany looked up.

"Dat's fa da police, we jus came to see Bryan," Josh responded while looking at me incredulously, as if to say "I can't believe you just said that." They stayed for about another five minutes, and then they left. Brittany and I sat and waited for some sort of word from the doctors.

Twenty minutes later, Bianca and Kymera showed up. Kymera was hysterical.

"Ah lawd, dey don killed my baby!" she screamed. While I could comprehend her grief, I couldn't feel sorry for her. She was, in my mind, responsible for whatever happened to Bryan. I felt myself getting ready to say something deplorable, so I got up to walk out of the room. Bianca shot me a look as if to say "Please don't leave me here." My sense of decorum forced me to leave the room. Her histrionics were going to provoke me. I got up and walked to the vending machine area. I stood there for a moment attempting to collect myself. A few moments in, Dr. Ross showed up behind me.

"Mr. Sullivant, are you here with the shooting victim?" he asked. I solemnly nodded that I was.

"How is he?" I asked. Dr. Ross took a deep breath. I held up my hand. "Perhaps you should say this in front of everyone, that way it doesn't have to be repeated multiple times," I suggested. He nodded and followed me into the other room. Kymera's antics stopped, and everyone gathered around the doctor. He cleared his throat.

"I'll start with the good news. We've got him stabilized; all of the bullets exited his body. The fact that you were able to keep pressure on the wounds is the only reason we can have this conversation, considering how much blood was lost. He'll survive. However, there was significant damage to both his kidneys and his brain. The brain damage we are going to monitor, because we aren't exactly certain how much damage was actually done. The EMT's did manage to revive him, but now we are going to let him rest. We want to give him time to rest before we try and bring him out of it. If he doesn't wake up on his on, we'll do it in three days. On the other hand the kidney damage is so extensive, that he may need a transplant. Before we put him on any donor lists, we would like to see if there is a possible donor match amongst his blood relatives, preferrably a male. Does he have any male blood relatives? That could be a father, brother, cousin, uncle, anyone at all?" he asked, looking squarely at Kymera. She looked at the ground. "Where's his father? Do you know?" he asked her.

"He…I…We…His daddy left me right after he was born. I don't know where he is! Are you going to penalize me for that?!" she yelled. Something wasn't right. It felt like she was lying. Dr. Ross seemed to be able to ascertain the exact same thing.

"I will not penalize you for anything; however you and your pride are penalizing your son. Keep up this charade if you desire, but I suggest that if you know where his father is, you get him in here immediately for a screening. In the mean time, I'll have a nurse escort the two of you back to the screening area. If neither of you three works, that is you his mother, his sister, or his father, then we'll proceed to more distant relatives before appealing to the community at large. All minds clear?" he asked. We nodded in unison. Momentarily, a nurse walked in and escorted the mother and daughter towards the back Bianca and I sat there silently, looking everywhere in the room but at each other. We hadn't had a silence this uncomfortable ever. I wanted her to just tell me that I was wrong, I could agree, and we could just move on from it. I realized that this wasn't the best forum for a debate, but considering there wasn't anything else we could do, I deemed now as good a time as any.

"Bianca, I know this isn't the best time or place for this, but—"

"Jayson, you don't have to say anything. I understand. You were angry, I was angry. We both said some off the wall stuff. It's okay. I forgive you if you can forgive me," she said soothingly.

"Why the sudden change?" I asked suspiciously. I wasn't complaining, I just wanted to know what made her change her stance.

"Jayson, I went to dinner with Quinn, and I as she and I talked, I realized something. I love you, and if we are going to be a unit, then I have to learn to believe you until you've been disproved. I was trusting Kymera, because she's family, but if you and I were married, then that would be like trusting someone over myself, which makes no sense at all. I still want to spend the rest of my life with you. This whole thing isn't completely over; we've still got to get to the bottom of this, but if you say nothing happened, then nothing happened. Let's get through this, and then we'll figure it out from there, okay?" she said. I smiled as I ran to give her a hug.

"I love you Bianca. Thank you," I said. I held her for as long as I could. It was the most natural feeling in the world. Just standing there with her in my arms was really all I needed. We sat there for another hour or so before Kymera and Brittany reappeared.

"The test takes forty-eight hours," the nurse said as she escorted them out. Then she looked over at Bianca and me. "Would you two like to be considered?" she asked. I looked at Bianca, and without a moment's hesitation, walked towards the nurse. Bianca followed behind me.

Ninety minutes later, the same nurse escorted Bianca and I back to the waiting room. Kymera and Brittany were no where to be found. I turned to the nurse.

"Excuse me miss, but can you can tell me where Bryan Washington is currently?" I asked. She walked back around the desk.

"It looks like he's been moved to room two sixteen. It's down the hall and to the left," she answered.

"Thank you," I replied. I extended my hand to Bianca. She reached for it, and grasping her hand with my own, I started walking down the corridor. We got to the room, and I noticed, much to my dismay, that Brittany was sitting in there by herself. Kymera was completely gone.

"Where is your mother?" Bianca asked.

"She said she had to leave. She just left like five minutes ago," she said, still sniffling. "I can't believe this happened to him. I can't believe I let this happen," she said ruefully. It was important for her to accept responsibility for her part in what had happened, but there's a limit. You can't change the past.

"It's okay. You can't do anything about it. He'll get better. You have to just start thinking positive, okay. Just pray. That's all any of us can do," I said. I patted her on the back. I turned to Bianca.

"Take her home. I'll sit here with him," I instructed. She looked at me with obvious concern.

"Jayson, Kymera needs to be here with him, you don't have to sit here. There's nothing any of us can do now anyway. Come home with me. I'll call Kymera, and have her come back here."she said. I looked at Bryan's motionless body, lying there with all the monitors and tubes hooked up to him. Bryan had become like my own child, and he was lying there helpless. I wanted be there in his place.

"Baby, I can't leave him like this. I'll stay here until she gets back," I said. I sat down in the chair while Bianca dialed Kymera.

"Jayson's going to stay with him—" Then she thought about it. "We are going to stay with him until you get back," she said. We pulled up chairs and sat down, Brittany on his left, Bianca and I on the right, with me closest to the door. I shut the door, and we all sat keeping a silent vigil. We sat there listening to the rhythmic beating of the heart monitor, and eventually, it carried us all off to sleep. Sometime later I heard approaching footsteps. Two sets, one sounded like women's high heeled shoes, the other like men's boots came down the hall. They stopped just in front of the door. I heard it open just a little. I feigned as though I was still sleeping. I could see Kymera at the door, but the door wasn't opened wide enough for me to see the owner of the boots. But I could hear them talking.

"Those are your children. That is your son. Forget whatever I may have told you, he is yours, and he needs you. You have to get screened. His life may depend on it," Kymera said.

"Aww here you go! Didn't we talk about that in the car? You already know what it is. I'm supposed to get married in a couple days, you can't start this stuff now. I thought he was Craig—" the male voice started.

"NO! They are both yours! When I told you that, it was because I knew he was going to the league. You and I were finished. I didn't want to be tied to you any more," Kymera said.

"We weren't finished, I blew out my knee, and you dumped me! C'mon Ky, tell the truth! That ain't my son!" the male asserted in a harsh whisper.

"I cheated, sure, whatever, I was with Craig, but I was having your baby," Kymera said.

"Well if you was with him, how do you know that Bryan is mine?" the male asked.

"I was already pregnant before Craig and I ever slept together. You don't believe me? Take the DNA test. That is your son and he needs you to find out if you can give him a kidney if he needs it."

"Ky, this is nonsense! Why the games, why, why, why?!" the man asked in a firm whisper.

"Look, when I was younger, I was out chasing men to get at their money. I didn't know anything about love, and I damn sure didn't want to be anybody's momma, but that's the only to lock it up. Ain't nobody gonna just take care of you. I was just trying to use what I had to get what I wanted. Now I know better. I'm about to get my degree. I'm going to start handling stuff on my own, no more using men. Besides that I love you, and I'm trying to get my life straightend out, and I need you in it. You are my rock," Kymera said, almost pleading.

"I wish I could believe you, but you said that the last time, and the time before that. I love you too, but Ky, it's too late for that," the male voice said. It was starting to sound familiar as the two of them had begun to abandon their whispers.

"Don't say that. You always come back to me, and I always come back to you. You ain't gonna ever be happy with her! You can't marry your therapist! You belong with me, and I belong with you. You know that!" Kymera pleaded.

"Kymera, that may be true, but it's too late now. My fiancee is going to be home soon," he said.

"But I'm your wife. We never got divorced, and I won't ever sign an anullment. You are mine. I just made some investments for us. Neither one of us is going to have to work, no more construction. You can just stay home with me," she said.

"You know what Ky, I don't want any part of any of your schemes. You just said no more schemes, but now you're saying that neither one of us will have to work? Look I love you, that much is true, but I'm getting too old for this. How would it be different? I've called off two weddings because of you screaming 'things will be different.' Will they? Will they really be different? It won't be. It will be the same as always. You're only here now because you know that I've got money coming. That's the only reason for us kickin' it now. Look, I'm sorry about your son, but I've got to go. I can't do this anymore. I'll see you later," the male said. Then I heard his footsteps go down the hall. Kymera wasn't quite done.

"I don't care if you come back to me or not, but won't you at least find out if you can help him? Even if you don't think he's your son, think of him as just a child, or at least your daughter's brother," she said pleadingly. The boots came back down the hall.

"I only have one confirmed daughter, and she only has one brother, who is older, successful, and the furthest thing from the knucklehead that one is! Even if I've never told him, I'm proud to be associated with him, even if I'm not his father" he said gruffly, and then I heard the boots go back down the hall. Kymera stood at the door quietly for a moment, then came over towards Bianca and me. I closed my eyes as though I had been sleeping the entire time. Kymera gently shook Bianca.

"Bianca! Wake up! I'm here now. You two can go home," she said. Bianca sat up blearily.

"Okay…Jayson!" she said, nudging me. I put on as though I was still sleeping. I sat up as though I was surprised.

"Huh? What?!" I said.

"Come on. Kymera is here, it's time to go," she said as she began to gather her effects. I stood up and walked cautiously past Kymera to the door. Bianca quickly followed me, as if she didn't want Kymera to literally come between us. "Call me if you need me, I'll be at home," Bianca instructed Kymera, who nodded in agreence before sitting down in a vacated chair. Bianca shut the door softly, and we began walking towards the parking lot. Bianca took my hand as we walked. Once we got outside, I let go of Bianca's hand, expecting us to take our cars and go our separate ways. She hurriedly reached for my hand again.

"I'm too tired to drive. Take me home please," she said. I was too tired to drive myself, but considering what we had been through in our recent history, I decided to go ahead and take her to her house. Since my car was closer to the door, we moved in that direction. I unlocked and opened her door for her as she was getting the car, she screamed. "Jayson! What is all this blood?! I thought you said you called the ambulence!" I looked inside. In the heat of trying to make sure that Bryan reached the hospital, I had forgotten to clean my hands and subsequently, the interior of my car was covered in bloody handprints. What was normally a hot button issue barely cracked my radar.

"Baby, it's okay. Look in the glove compartment, and there is some Armor-All, I'll go ahead and clean this up," I said. She followed my directions. As I reached for the container, she swatted my hand away.

"You just drive, I'll get it," she ordered. I put the car in gear, and we drove off towards Rock Canyon Drive. The ride there was silent. Bianca cleaned up the mess and then went to sleep. When we pulled up in the drive way a short while later, Bianca was clearly ready for bed. I left the car running, because I figured I was going to drive myself home.

"Turn the car off," she directed. I complied and followed her to the door. We went inside and she walked to the stairs. "Lock the door," she ordered flatly. I adhered to her request. She extended her hand and I grasped it, and followed her up the stairs and into her room. She shut the door after I walked in. She changed out of her clothes and into pajamas which consisted of a t-shirt, and sweatpants. I took off my bloodstained shirt and pants, and then we both climbed into bed, thoroughly exhausted. She got as close to me as she possibly could, resting her head on my chest. Instinctively, I curled my arm around her, and kissed her softly on the forehead. I wanted to say something, but I felt as though nothing I could say would make that moment any better than it already was. No, everything wasn't okay, and yes things might only get worse, but at least right there, in that moment, everything was okay. We were okay.

I took Bianca back to the hospital to get her vehicle, and then I headed back towards Rock Canyon. I felt like I needed to spend some time with my mother. I had a sneaking suspicion that there was something she needed to know, and besides that, she was about to become Mrs. Brock Randal, and I knew I wouldn't get to see her much after that, at least not for a while anyway. When I got to her house, Father Potter's car was sitting out front. I was almost used to that sentence at this point. I walked in the house. My mother and Father Potter were dancing around to some old music. My arrival prompted them to stop.

"Jayson! What are you doing here?!" my mother asked.

"I called myself coming to ask you for a favor. What are you doing here?" I asked.

"I live here," she replied.

"I know that Jessica, I mean what are you *doing here?* As in, what's going on here?" I asked. Father Potter looked at me almost ruefully.

"Jayson, it's nothing, your mother and I, we are waiting on Mr. Randal to come home for the final session before the wedding on Saturday. I was teaching your mother the Foxtrot for the customary first dance" He explained.

"So then where's Brock?" I asked.

"He got in early this morning and then went over to the Sisters of Mercy," my mom answered.

"How did he know about that?" I asked. I hadn't told anyone, it was just barely twelve hours ago.

"Know about what?" my mom asked.

"That Bryan was at Sisters of Mercy," I replied.

"Why is Bryan there?" Father Potter asked.

"He got shot last night by Brittany's boyfriend. Right now, they are trying to find out if he is going to need a kidney donor, and if there is anyone that can donate one for him before he goes on a national list," I recounted.

"That is horrible!! How are you doing?" Father Potter asked.

"I didn't get shot, so I can't complain about anything," I answered. It didn't seem right for me to complain about anything.

"That's a good outlook on the situation," he asserted.

"Brock said that he was just going for a check up. He didn't mention anything about someone getting shot or anything like that," my mom said. The wheels in my head started turning. Could that have been Brock last night?

"Fat chance he would," I mumbled.

"What?" my mom asked.

"Nothing," I replied.

"What about the guy that shot him?" my mom asked.

"He's still at large, I don't know what they are going to do about him, but hopefully they find him," I answered. I hated not having the answers to any of their questions, but sometimes, you just don't know. The knowledge that I shared was like throwing a wet blanket on a fire. Moments later, Brock walked in the door.

"Looks like I missed the party. How's everyone doing?" he asked.

"How was your check up hon?" my mother asked. Brock smiled nervously, but quickly regained his composure.

"You know me, healthy as an ox!" he said, flexing his enormous arms. If nothing else, the work in construction had kept his body in athletic form. He looked around the room, and after making eye contact with me, moved in my direction. "Jayson, can I talk to you really quick?" he asked. The only thing rarer than that question was Haley's Comet. I nodded my approval, and we walked towards the kitchen.

"Jayson, I know that you don't know me that well, and I don't know you that well as a person, seeing as how I didn't come around until you were on your way to college, but I want you to know that I am proud of you, and I count it an honor to be connected to you in any way, shape, or form," he said solemnly.

"Thank you sir," I responded. I wasn't really sure how to address that comment. Even though the situation was positive, it was still mildly awkward. As we walked back into the front room, we could all hear Samantha coming down the stairs. Father Potter and Brock were each standing near each other, when Samantha burst into the room.

"Daddy!" she yelled, grabbing one of each man's legs. The mood in the room became as uncomfortable as a hot car in the middle of the summer.

"It's Daddy Preacher, and Daddy Daddy!" she said. My mom tried to lessen the impact of the situation.

"No honey, that's Father Potter, and that's your dad," she explained.

"That's what I said; Fathers are daddies right?" Samantha reasoned. My mom was going to have a tough fight on her hands with this one. Brock seemed incensed.

"Baby, daddy's gotta go now," he said as he moved towards the door. Father Potter looked nervously at his watch.

"I suppose that I too should make haste. The Beacon will not prepare itself for the ceremony," he said, and he was right on Brock's heels going out of the door. I didn't know what to say. My mom stood there for a second with her mouth open.

"I can't believe she said that. I don't know how I'm going to clean that one up," she said sounding exasperated. Ordinarily I would have stayed with her and helped her work through the matter, but there wasn't anything that I could do. Nothing to say about that. I remembered what I wanted originally.

"Mom, do you have time to go to the mall with me? I only have today and tomorrow to go make this purchase, and I need a woman's perspective," I asked. She looked at me perplexed, and then the light of realization clicked.

"OHHHHH!!! Okay, sure, I don't mind. Have you talked to Quinn yet? She might be a good help too," she said. I hadn't, but that was my next thought. I hadn't really figured out how I was going to propose, but the words from the orderly a few days prior were resonating in my mind after everything that had happened over the past few days. I decided that I couldn't risk another day without us moving towards something permanent. I was going to take Bianca with me and let her pick out what she wanted, but I had decided that I would do it my way. Surely I knew her well enough to be able to pick out something that she would like. She was going to be my wife, I should at least be able to pick out a ring that she'd like. Then I thought about it, and decided to call Quinn.

Bianca was at work, and after that she was going to the hospital with Kymera, so we had a window of a couple of hours to find the right one. I had a few ideas from my own personal excursions, but I needed the experts to help me narrow the field down to what the right one was. Quinn met my mother and I at the mall., and the three of us walked around and looked at my choices. After about three hours, and several comments about my taste, and in some cases, lack thereof, I had found it. A beautiful princess cut diamond set in a platinum band. It was simple, yet elegant. Perfect for my lady. The jury approved it, and I brought it. Maclayne had given me my signing bonus early, so I had the ten thousand dollars at my disposal.

I took the ring home, and put it in my top drawer. I hadn't thought of how I would propose, I just knew that I would. I was renown for planning and extravagant displays. This seemed like it called for something different. Like spur of the moment different. I would know when the time was just right.

I went to the hospital on Thursday morning to sit with Bryan to see if there was any change. I had a lot of things to prepare for tomorrow, the day of the signing ceremony. A speech to write, and a lot of loose thoughts running rampant gave me plenty to consider in the quiet room. They say if someone is in a coma it's good to talk to them.

"Well Bryan, I decided to propose to your Aunt Bianca," I said, halfway expecting him to come to life and scream "WORD?!" Instead I got no response at all. "Yeah, I did. I don't know how I'm going to propose, but I know that I want to do it, and soon. Your're Aunt B is a special lady. I can't live my life without her. I'm really going to be your uncle now," I said. The monitor beeped, just as it had for the past two hours.

"I'm nervous about this deal with Maclayne. It's a lot of work. I mean I get paid to do what I love, but I have to be honest, I don't know if I can do it," I said. I tried to imagine what he would have said. "Man Uncle Jay, don't even worry about it man. You the smartest cat I know, you can do that with no problem."

"Yeah, you're right. I can do it. They wouldn't have come after me if they didn't think I could.do it. I can do it. I'm at least that capable."

"Beep. Beep," the machine responded to my statement. I sat there silently for a moment then my phone rang. It was Bianca.

"Jayson, I've got some time, do you want to go look at rings today?" she asked me. I had to think of a way to get out of it.

"I'm going to go get things for the wedding, so I can't tonight, and after that I have to get prepared for tomorrow" I said. Truth of the matter was that it was a very simple ceremony, only seventy-five people, no bridesmaids, no groomsmen. It was the perfect union of what they both wanted. My mom got her wedding in a church, Brock got his quiet ceremony. I didn't have to get anything, besides a pair of shoes. Bianca sounded mildly defeated.

"Okay. Well, do you want me to meet you up at the hospital?" she asked. "I just want to spend some time with you before you start the developmental process for Maclayne. I know you won't have as much time for me," she surmised. She was right. There was a lot of travel involved. She didn't know that I had planned to take her with me whenever and where ever I could. I didn't want to tell her that I was going to propose within the next seven days and that there was no way I would leave my future wife anywhere.

"Actually, I've got a pretty busy day tomorrow, you can come by my apartment, if you'd like," I suggested.

"It's okay. I'll just see you tomorrow at the ceremony," she said.

"Alright then sweetheart, call me later?" I asked.

"Yeah," she responded as she hung up the phone. It wasn't that I didn't want to see her, it was just that I knew there was a storm coming. Bianca and I still hadn't completely resolved the issue, we had just buried it. I'd be a fool to just believe that it was just going to just stay buried. There was a lot of uncertainty in front of me. I still didn't know what had happened that night with Kymera. Call it instinct, intuition, Spidey sense, whatever, I just knew that something wasn't right. I couldn't prove it, but I could sense a storm coming. Sometimes all you need to be able to do is smell rain, in order to know it's on the way.

# 17

I had set my alarm an hour earlier than I really needed to be awake. The ceremony wasn't until six o'clock, but considering that the wedding was tomorrow, I was up against a whirlwind forty-eight hours. I started the day the same way I start every day. I had breakfast, and I got everything I needed for the day, and set out to do everything that I needed to do for the wedding tomorrow. At about one o'clock, I drove to the Beacon and picked up Bianca for lunch.

"Are you nervous?" she asked.

"I just sit in front of a bunch of people, and sign some papers saying that Maclayne Studios can pay me an eighth of a million dollars per year, I say some hellos, some thank yous. We kiss, we schmooze, we go home. What's to be nervous about there?" I said, attempting to be as nonchalant as possible. Secretly I was terrified. I didn't have a problem with the people. Rather it was the accepting all the responsibilty that I was about to take on. This was the end of my cozy nine to five, my set vacations and tiny expense account. The only problem with doing what you love for a living is that it is no can only longer be what you escape *to*, but rather what you escape *from*. I wasn't sure that I was ready to trade it all in. I loved the lack of inhibition I felt on the stage, and with my pen and my pad. Sure I was about to make a boat load of money for a soon to be twenty five year old, but was it worth giving up my rights to the one thing that I loved unconditionally? Bianca saw right through my façade.

"Baby, I know this is a big move for you, and for us even. You'll be fine. We'll be fine. Let's go eat," she said.

"Okay, but it's got to be quick, because I want to go check on Bryan. They say he should be waking up any time now," I said. We went and picked up a quick lunch and then we drove to the the hospital. We went up to the room. Bryan was still asleep, and Kymera was sitting there with him, looking distraught.

"He's not covered by anyone's insurance," she said solemnly. I nearly choked.

"What?! How are you going to pay for all this?" I asked.

"I don't know, but I'll think of something. Worst-case scenario, I just take him off the machines, and we hope for the best," she said. I didn't know what to say. Bianca looked like there was something she wanted to say, but she didn't want to say it in front of me.

"Aunt Ky, would you mind taking me to the ceremony tonight? Jayson's gotta go way earlier than I need to be there, plus we still need to talk," she said.

"Sure. I'm going to be here for a little while, but they say if he doesn't wake up on his own by tomorrow, they are going to try and wake him up. Either way there's no point in my spending my whole life here," she said, drying her eyes. Bianca looked at me.

"You can go, I know you've got a lot to do," she said, releasing me. I walked over to the side of the bed and touched Bryan's forehead.

"I'm going back to the Beacon, I can take you," I said. I didn't want to inconvenience anyone.

"It's okay, she and I, we need to talk," she said. I knew that this was the talk, that storm cloud that I felt earlier was about to roll in. I looked down at Bryan. Seeing him helped me keep everything in perspective.

"You can do it Bryan; you've got to wake up," I said, squeezing his hand. I let it go, and it fell lifelessly to his side. I kissed Bianca on the cheek, and walked back out to my car. On my way back downtown, I stopped and back by the Beacon, where my mother and Father Potter were putting up decorations for tomorrow.

"You guys coming down tonight right?" I asked.

"Yeah, of course," my mom said emphatically.

"What about Brock? Isn't it bad luck to see the bride the day before the wedding?" I asked. My mom laughed.

"Honey, if he saw me two days before the wedding, and the day after, what does it matter? We've got a kid already. No mystery here. But seriously, he went to see his insurance agent. He says he's finally going to add me on the insurance, that way we can have one united front," she said.

"You already know I'll be there Jayson," Father Potter said.

"Of course I knew that. This is a big day for your family, too. Maclayne is going to go fix up your brother's club, and let him keep control of it. That's pretty huge. I look forward to seeing you guys down there," I said. It pretty much went without saying that those two were going to be there, I only asked just to hear them say that they would be there. I sat there with them for about an hour before I drove down to Vive. It was about half past three. There was a flurry of activity going on. Camera crews were moving hastilly from place to place, people shouting instructions, tables and chairs moving around, cosmetic repairs. In a little under eight hours, this crew was on pace to correct almost ten years of do-it-yourself workmanship. Uncle Jeremiah was near tears.

"I can't believe it. This was what I always dreamed about. This was how this place looked in my imagination. Thank you so much Jay," he said as he gave me a big bear hug. I gasped.

"I didn't do anything. I need to thank you for letting me perform, and taking the heat from my mom for my being out so late," I said. I had been doing open mic nights since I was sixteen. The club didn't open until nine o'clock at night.

"It was my pleasure. I guess we made it, huh? I guess we really did it nephew," he said proudly. I just sat and watched the crews work while I tried to clear my head.

At about five o'clock, the City Council representatives started pouring in, as well as reps from Maclayne Studios. I started to feel my palms getting sweaty. I went out to my car and got the outfit that I wanted to be photographed in, and came inside to one of the backstage bandrooms to change. After putting on my change of clothes, I grabbed my tie, and I slowly curled it into a a half windsor knot I stood their, admiring my reflection for a short minute.

"Whatever happens, Jay, it's going to be alright. Let's get these papers signed and get this money!" I said to myself. It was about twenty minutes until six. I walked out of the dressing room, and to the stage. Mr. Tanaka was standing there waiting on me. He extended his hand to shake mine.

"Mr. Sullivant! Welcome to the team!" he said boisterously. Then he walked me over to the stage. "We are going to have you sit right here in the middle, and your uncle will sit on the other side. Then the Councilmen and women are going to take seats on either side of you. Now I'll be off to the side, but I'll be able to talk to you with this," he said, handing me a tiny microphone for my ear. "With all the cameras that are going to be here, you'll need to be facing the right one at all times. Consider this a crash course in Showbiz 101." Then he looked at his watch. "Well, I guess it's time I get the ball rolling," he said. Uncle Jerry wanted to turn this simple act into a community event, so the local news stations had each sent a crew down to get footage of the event. I wasn't used to cameras, but it wasn't like it was that big a deal. At about five minutes after six, Mr. Tanaka stood up.

"Good evening, Port Haven!" I'm Elliot Tanaka, head of marketing for Maclayne Studios. I am here today, representing Maclayne Studio's commitment to its urban contemporary core. We are here for you. We want to create quality programming and entertainment with you in mind. So to that end, I have two big announcements. First off all, Café Vive is going to be the new home of Maclayne Studio's new show highlighting the best, newest, and freshest artists, both locally and nationally, and secondly, as a host, we have Port Haven's favorite son, Mr. Jay Azariah as our host!" he said. The crowd, composed largely of Café Vive regulars cheered. There was a lot of talent in that room, and it was time that someone gave them a mic, and let them speak to the world. "We invited you all here to witness the signing of both of these contracts that will not only stimulate ideological growth here, but fiscal growth here in Port Haven. In Café Vive , we find a bastion of creativity, and in Mr. Azariah, we see the best qualities in civic mindedness exemplified. He represents the best that Port Haven has to offer. Before we do that though, there are people who would like to mark such a momentous occasion," he said. Mayor Hasselberg stood up. She looked around the room before she said anything. I saw Bianca slip in the door and scamper to an open seat. She looked angrier than I had ever seen her look before. I didn't know what it could have been, but I was scared to find out. I tried to wave at her discreetly. Instead it looked like I was waving to the the mayor.

"I don't think Mr. Hasselberg would appreciate that" she said. I blushed. "You're already thinking like a star huh?" she said. I couldn't say anything. The crowd laughed at our interaction.

"Mr. Potter and Mr. Sullivant, as your mayor, I couldn't be more proud of any citizens—"

"An' I hope he ready ta come of a seventeen pacent!" a voice yelled from the back. I knew that voice. It was Kymera.

"Security!" Mayor Hasselberg yelled. I frowned. Uncle Jerry had never hired security in the entire time I had known him. With no one to oppose her, Kymera continued her charge to the front. She was holding up a small piece of plastic. I couldn't tell what it was, but I knew that it couldn't be good. Mr. Tanaka looked at me with the more concern than I had ever seen at one time.

"What is going on?" he whispered.

"I have no idea," I answered.

"Jayson, I am pregnant!" Kymera yelled. "And yes, I swear on err'thing iss yo' baby! So you better be ready to come off that cake baby boy!" she yelled. Every head in the room was turned in her direction. I wanted to disappear. I tried to maintain my composure, but I felt myself losing it. Why was she doing this? My contract was predicated on the fact that I didn't have any children; her display was going to cost me everything. Meanwhile, the t.v. cameras kept right on rolling. I had sat quietly long enough. I decided to try and salvage the situation.

"KYMERA! We need to speak about this later!" I said forcefully. She was unfazed.

"Naw Jayson, we finna talk about it now! I want my cake, cause this is yo' baby!" she replied. I looked around for Bianca, who wasn't sitting in the chair that she had been in. Things had just gone from bad to worse.

"Mr. Tanaka, I apologize for what's going on here. The best thing to do may be to cut the television feeds and do this a little more unceremoniously. On second thought, get remarks from the councilmen, but don't get shots of my empty seat. This can all be cleaned up later," I directed. Mayor Hasselberg was nearly finished.

"Jayson, don't act lik you don't hear me! You see this!" she said, referring to the piece of plastic in her hand. "It says I'm pregnant! And guess who's the daddy?! That's right sucka' you are! Sign that contrack so you can pay what you owe! You hear me? You gon pay what you owe!" she yelled. I was ignoring her. My concern was Bianca. I didn't remember seeing her leave, and I didn't know where she was." I stood up and climbed off stage. The mumbles turned into a full on roar. I'd let Uncle Jerry and Mr. Tanaka clean this up. I walked outside. I could hear Kymera yelling behind me. I didn't care, I just had to find Bianca.

"BIANCA!!" I yelled as I ran to the corner. I saw her across the street, sitting at a bus stop. I darted into to traffic, narrowly avoiding cars to make my way to her. She had been crying.

"Why did you leave?!" I asked, fully aware of the answer. She could barely look me in the eye.

"Jayson, Kymera is six weeks pregnant. I don't understand how you could do this to me," she said, sobbing.

"Bianca, there is no way that child is mine, assuming she is pregnant. I told you what happened. It was NON-CONSENSUAL. She drugged me," I said flatly. I respected how she felt, but I was beginning to grow angry with constantly defending myself.

"Six weeks ago, though, Jayson? How do you explain that? She didn't say she just got pregnant, she said she's six weeks pregnant! That's a month and a half! You'd been going over there for at least three months, how do you explain that? I was ready to give you all of me and you kept telling me no, kept making me wait, but the whole time you were givin' it to her. Why Jayson? WHY? Why wasn't I good enough for you? I would have given you anything you wanted, and you go and do this? Why did you have to do this to me?" she screamed.

"Bianca, I know it's tough, but I'm asking you, no begging you, baby please believe me! It's not my child! I promise! Why would you believe anything that comes out of that woman's mouth?!" I looked over my shoulder. The bus to Rock Canyon Drive was approaching.

"Jayson, I tried, okay, I really tried to believe you the last time we talked about this. I tried to just pretend like it had never happened. I can't do that this time, and you can't ask me to. It just isn't fair! Unless you can prove that it's not your child, I don't want to talk to you," she said. The bus pulled up and opened its doors.

"Bianca, I—"

"Goodbye Jayson" she said somberly. She stepped in, and the doors shut. There was a dust cloud as the bus drove up the street. I looked back over a Café Vive . People were pouring out in droves. It was time to go and attempt to clean up that mess. Given my track record so far on the day, it wasn't looking to good for this either. I went back across the street, and fought through the crowd to get back into the club. The news crews were packing up, the Councilpeople had all left. I looked around for Kymera. I didn't see her, but I did see that Uncle Jerry was standing there with Mr. Tanaka. Both of them had disapproving looks on their faces, and I could tell that my day wasn't about to get any better.

"Jayson, what was that?!" Uncle Jerry asked. "Was that the one girl you were here with two months ago?" he asked. That was the one question that I didn't want him to ask.

"Mr. Sullivant, it appears that we have sorely misjudged you. You do understand that this qualifies as a breach of contract, don't you? However because you haven't signed it, consider the offer rescinded. We cannot have crazy ex-girlfriends and baby mommas running around here. That was the whole point of looking for someone that was squeaky clean. Do you know how many channels this is going to show up on? I don't know how you are going to come back from this one. Not just with us at Maclayne, which I can assure you will be virtually impossible, but just in your community at large. How could you do that to that poor girl?" he asked.

"That's not my child, I know it isn't! Please sir, give me a chance to prove it!" I pleaded.

"Mr. Sullivant, every man in your position says that. I wouldn't claim her child either. How are you going to prove this claim? Can you? Perhaps it's best if you just begin the process of cleaning up now, try to save as much face as possible," he said coldly. I didn't know how to address all his charges individually, but I did know that I had one trump card. One way out of all of this mess.

"She raped me," I said.

I didn't know where the safe was, the combination, or if that part was even on the tape, but I had to hope for the best. Mr. Tanaka didn't look convinced.

"That's a very strong accusation to levy at someone, male or female. How do you intend on proving that?"he asked.

I didn't really know how I was going to prove the rape, but I was certain that I could prove I wasn't her child's father. The wheels in my head turned furiously, until I came up with what I thought was the best possible answer.

"She and I, we can do a blood test. That will prove that I'm not the father of her child," I said, clinging to hope.

Mr. Tanaka seemed about ready to wash his hands of everything. "You have five days to procure whatever evidence you can obtain to prove your point. At that point if it is determined that you are in fact innocent, then I will reissue the contract." Then he turned to look at me one more time. "Mr. Sullivant, I was really looking forward to working with you. Please don't let me down," he advised. I at least had a chance, and that was all I needed. Uncle Jerry looked at me.

"Jay, we need this man. I can't pull this off without you. You've got to make it happen man," he said walking away from me. I stood there by myself for about a minute. I didn't know what to do. My world had officially crashed down around my ears.

Café Vive had emptied in a matter of minutes. I stood there looking around at the empty room. The memories of what could have been and what might not be began to assail me. Could I get to the tape? Would it exonerate me? Could I get my job back at Givend and Moss if I couldn't prove my innocence to Mr. Tanaka? Should I press charges against Kymera? Neither Father Potter nor my mother had made it to Café Vive . Even so, I took out my phone and called Father Potter. I just knew that I would get an answer, or at least some form of guidance, just like so many times before. My mind was eagerly anticipating the solace that he would provide. The phone didn't even ring; it just went straight to voicemail. I almost dropped my phone I was so distraught. I wasn't going to speak to him until he called me back. I knew that my mother was getting ready for her wedding, so calling her would be an exercise in futility. I was going to have to figure this one out on my own. I trusted my own ability; it's just that sometimes, it's nice to have someone else look in on your situation from outside of it to help you figure it out. Before I could sink into the sea of self pity that was inviting me in, my phone rang. I pulled it out, expected to see Father Potter's name in the caller id. Seeing that it wasn't, I dejectedly answered the phone.

"Hello?" I answered.

"Mr. Sullivant? This is Dr. Ross. I have been trying to get a hold of Ms. Windsor for quite some time now. You were the next person listed as next of kin for Bryan Washington—" My heart dropped.

"What's the matter? Did something happen?!" I asked fearfully.

"No, nothing happened, but we are about to attempt to revive him, as was the plan on his admittance. I'm calling because we need a parent or acting guardian here before we take him off the machine. Do you think you can get in contact with his mother?" he asked. Given the situation surrounding his mother, I didn't think that decision wise.

"Can I be there instead? I'm not sure where his mother is, but if I can be there in her stead, I will do so," I answered.

"Yes, Mr. Sullivant, your prescence will suffice, in light of the fact that we could not reach his mother. Can you be here inside of one hour?" he asked.

"I'll only need half that time," I responded as I moved towards my car. There's something about people facing life or death situations that helps to put day to day trials in perspective. I realized that I wasn't in an ideal situation, but he was in a much direr predicament. His need for my support trumped my own desire to feel sorry for myself.

At the hospital, I sat in Bryan's room for nearly ten minutes. Dr. Ross walked in and looked at me solemnly. He didn't need to say anything, and I didn't want him to say anything at all. There simply wasn't anything to say. He motioned to the nurse that had accompanied him into the room, and she went to work removing the breathing tube from Bryan's mouth. The heart monitor beeped steadily the entire time. Even though it had only taken a moment, I felt as though she took at least four hours. With the tube removed, I was afraid that it was the end for Bryan. Yet the monitor kept beeping and his chest continued to pump on its own. I breathed a sigh of relief. At least he was still alive. Maybe only in the techincal sense of the word, but that was better than the alternative. Dr. Ross looked moderately pleased.

"I'm going to give him a little while longer to see if he wakes up on his own. If not I'll be back to see if we can't pull him out of this. Does that sound okay to you?" he asked.

"You're the expert. What ever you think is appropriate is what we'll do," I replied. Dr. Ross nodded at me and then both he and the nurse left the room. I sat there with Bryan still as lifeless as ever. For the better part of the last year, I had been advising him, trying to get him on the right track, and it was only now that I realized, in a way, he had been keeping me in line. There were plenty of nights that I wanted to skip helping Father Potter down at the Beacon, but knowing that he was there compelled me to go. Even though I tried to do things by the book, any corner that I might have ordinarily cut, I didn't because he was standing right there, watching me. Knowing that he was watching the example that I set helped me to execute better. My relationship with Bianca was the first one to go past the six month mark in the last five years, and that was partially due to the fact that I wanted Bryan to see how to treat a woman. That and Bianca was the incarnation of what I wanted in a woman. The fact that I was already thinking about marriage at twenty-four was in no small way due to my goal of setting a good example. I looked over at him. Even in his comatose state, his face still seemed to be curved in a mischievious grin. How could someone so well intentioned come from someone so malicious? Kymera's stunt may have very well cost me everything, I just had to figure out how to beat it, how to beat her at this little game that she had forced me into. If there was ever a time I would have traded Bryan's streetsense for my own intellect, now would have been it. I needed to, as Bryan would have put it, "Get some Windsor in my blood." But how? I sat there, half thinking, half waiting on my phone to ring for the better part of an hour.

Dr. Ross showed up with a small vial, a syringe, and a hopeful expression on his face.

"Some people wake up instantly, others it takes a couple of days, it's a case by case sort of deal. We won't know until he wakes up how long it takes him," he said as he pushed the needle point into Bryan's vein. I was secretly praying for him to wake up immediately. After two minutes, I realized he might very well be the couple of days variety. Dr. Ross looked at me soothingly. "You know what Jayson, why don't you go ahead home and get some rest? I'm sure Bryan would want that for you, just like I'm sure he appreciates you being here, but you look like you need to go home. We have a wonderful staff here, and if there is a change, you will be the first person we call," he informed me. I decided to follow the doctor's orders.

I walked slowly down the hall. All the problems that I had left at the door climbed back on me as though I were a city bus. I was waiting for the elevator when a familiar voice called out "could you hold that for me?" I held the door open, and in a few moments Malachi, the orderly appeared.

"Are you going down?" he asked. Then after recognizing me he exclaimed"Hey young fella, how ya' doin?" I tried not to look as morose as I felt, but my face had long since given it away.

"I'm doing fine, sir," I replied.

"Oh really? Then why is your face lying on you? You look like you're carrying the weight of the world on those shoulders," he postulated. He was right, but I didn't want to get into trying to explain what was going on to him.

"It's nothing major. My nephew is here and—"

"You and I both know that God is going to take care of Bryan, now what's really wrong?" he asked. I wanted to know how he knew Bryan's name, but I couldn't ask. Honestly, I was afraid to ask.

"Everything is going wrong, and I don't know where to turn. There isn't anyone that I can call," I answered. He had a look of pure disbelief on his face.

"Son, sometimes, just because the guiding light doesn't illuminate the sky the way we think it will, doesn't mean that it won't get us to the same harbor that we're trying to reach on our own," he said. I was confused, but I thought I was doing a good job of masking it. Apparently I wasn't. "What I mean is that you already know the answers to your questions, even if they don't look like answers. It's never as hard as you think it is. You just have to trust and believe that He'll never put more on you than you can handle," Malachi said solemnly. I understood what he was saying, but I wasn't sure how much I believed him.

"I appreciate the advice sir," I said, attempting to sound grateful without being dismissive, even if I was more the latter than the former.

"Don't think so hard. Just have a little faith, and know that everything will be okay." The elevator stopped. "This is my floor; you have a good night, and remember what ol' Malachi said," he said to me as he exited the elevator.

"Thank you, sir, I will," I replied. I wasn't really sure if I understood what he had said, let alone if I could remember it. I got to the ground floor and went to my car. My mind was awash with questions. How to beat the issue I had with Kymera, could I get Bianca back, would Bryan ever awake? I just couldn't turn my mind off. I got home and decided to go to bed early. Calling Bianca would have been a waste of time, she wasn't going to answer. I expected to see her at the wedding tomorrow. My mom didn't have a gaggle of friends like most women her age, and so Bianca had been drafted as the functioning maid of honor. She would be there, just as a point of honor; my mother had done nothing to her, and their relationship existed outside of me. I took a shower and tried to go to sleep.

Malachi's words haunted me all night. I felt like there was some deeper meaning to what he had said. Everyone says "it'll be okay" I'd almost come to expect such a hackneyed phrase to show up in this little melodrama, but there was something in his words, maybe the conviction with which he spoke, maybe it was how I received it, I didn't know what it was, but the simple conversation we had in the elevator just kept replaying in my mind. Finally, my body would not go one moment further, and I fell asleep under the weight of sheer exhaustion.

# 18

It was the morning of the one of the most important days of my mother's life and I had overslept. The ceremony started at noon, and it was already quarter to eleven. I hastilly showered, and threw on my suit, and ran out of the door to my car. I got to the Beacon at quarter to twelve. There were about forty cars in the parking lot, and much as I expected, I saw Bianca's Armada parked in the corner. After hastily parking my car, I ran inside the building. Father Potter was near the front of the sanctuary. Most of the eighty or so people that had gathered were sitting, although a few were missing. I moved expeditiously to where Father Potter was.

"Jayson! Where have you been?! I've been calling you all morning!" he said, sounding like an angry parent.

"I'm sorry, I overslept. Yesterday was kind of…" I trailed off, not really sure how to describe the past twenty four hours.

"Tumultuous?" Father Potter offered.

"Yeah, sure…Where's my mom?" I asked.

"She's upstairs with Bianca getting ready," he responded.

"Thank you!" I said as I headed towards the stairway. I looked around the sanctuary, it didn't really look like anyone had spent much time decorating anything, much less spent three hours on it. I was a little nonplussed, but I couldn't really think about it. I bounded up the stairs and knocked on the the only closed door I saw.

"Yes?" Bianca's voice answered.

"It's Jayson, I need to talk to my mom," I said. She may have been able to control a lot of things, but the one thing she couldn't control was my relationship with my mother. I heard the sounds of a brief discussion.

"We don't want to see you right now!" my mom said. I was instantly incensed.

"What?!" I yelled. There was no way that was possible.

"I'm kidding, come on in, baby," my mother said. I walked into the room. The tension between Bianca and me palpable, even if she was strong enough to pretend like she didn't feel it.

"Hey," I said nervously.

"Hello, Mr. Sullivant," Bianca said coldly. Obviously she was still angry. I didn't have anything to say to my mother that I couldn't say in front of Bianca, so I just spoke.

"Mom, I love you, and I'm happy for you. I only hope that I can find the same level of happiness for myself one day," I said, looking at Bianca, who turned to look out of the window before our eyes could meet.

"Thank you, Jayson. I love you, too. Now get downstairs so you can give me away!" she yelled, spanking me playfully on the behind. I ran downstairs, and took my position near the back of the church. As the patrons settled down, I whispered softly to the cameraman.

"You make sure you make my mother look good, okay?" I requested. He nodded at me as though he was going to honor my request. Father Potter cued the music, and the patrons all took their seats. Samantha walked up to me with her little flower girl dress on and a basket of pulled rose petals.

"Jaysee, I'm the flower girl but I don't want Mommy to step on the flowers because they are so pretty," she said exhaustively.

"Well Mommy's really pretty. She looks like a flower too. Maybe we could let her walk on them just this once," I responded. Sammie seemed convinced.

"Okay, but can I have the flowers at the end jaysee?" she asked me.

"Sure, Sammie. You can have the flowers at the end," I replied. She smiled and started walking happily down the aisle, spilling more petals than she was effectively dropping on the ground. Moments later, Brock showed up beside me, as jittery as I had ever seen him. "You alright, man?" I asked.

"Never been good at this sort of thing, I just want to get in here and get it over with," he answered. While I could understand his point, I had to admit that it wasn't exactly what I had expected to hear.

"Well, good luck, and I'll see you on the other side of the broom," I said congratulatorily.

"Thank you son," he said, before he turned to walk down the aisle. I was rocked. He had never ever called me son before. I didn't know how to process it. As soon as I saw Bianca and my mother, I didn't need to process it. Bianca smiled weakly at me.

"Thank you for allowing me to be a part of this, Ms. Sullivant." Then she turned to me. "We'll talk later," she said. I nearly jumped out of my skin.

"Okay!" I said, completely losing my composure. Bianca laughed politely and then turned to walk down the aisle. At last it was my mother and I at the back of the church.

"What did you say to her?" I asked.

"Don't worry about it. Just know that she's a smart girl, and you'd better take care of her," she ordered, pinching my arm.

"Yes, ma'am, I will," I affirmed.

"Who would have thought it Jayson? After all this time, here we are. I'm so happy," she said almost flatly. I couldn't help but feel like something just wasn't quite right. I thought maybe I was just off kilter, and so I decided not to delve into it any further.

"Well, Mom, I'm glad for you. I'm glad that you are happy," I said.

"Okay, so why don't we get this old girl down the aisle!" she said to me cheerfully. Something was definitely wrong. She was painting on a smile, and I knew it. Even so, I couldn't stop her now. The organ player belted out "Here Comes the Bride, and my mother and I began the long walk down the aisle. Her steps felt heavy, like there was some unforeseen gravitational pull on her, trying to keep her from the altar.

I matched pace with her as best I could. At long last, we reached the altar where Father Potter stood, along with Brock. I sat down on the front row next to Samantha. Everyone was in place, and Father Potter flashed a decidedly fake smile and took a deep breath, and began the ceremony.

"Never thought these two would make it here," he joked. There was a small wave of laughter from the patrons. My mom blushed, and Brock looked at the ground. "Nevertheless, we are gathered together today to witness the joining in holy matrimony this man, Brock Christian Randal, and this woman Jessica Marie Sullivant." He seemed to pause a little when he said my mother's name. It was something that only I could detect. Then all of a sudden I started to feel something, a sense, inkling, whatever you want to call it, something just wasn't right. "If there are any among you who have any reason why this man and this woman should not be joined in holy matrimony, let him speak now or forever hold his peace."

"Jaysee, I gotta go to the bathroom!" Samantha said.

"Right now?" I asked.

"Yessss!!" she said, kicking her feet anxiously. Father Potter was still pausing to allow for any objectors to speak.

"Come on," I said, standing up. There was a collective gasp from the gathered crowd. I picked Samantha up. "Bathroom," I said, calming their collective nerves. I carried Samantha as I ran out of the side door towards the bathroom. After she finished, I took her hand and we started back towards the sanctuary. I decided to go through the rear entrance. When I opened the door, I nearly fainted. There was a woman in a white wedding gown who had just entered the sanctuary. Her long hair was tied up in a bun, and she was proceeding towards the altar. Most of the patrons were sitting near the front, so no one had seen her yet, save the cameraman. Father Potter was still proceeding with the ceremony. Samantha and I sat down on one of the rear pews as she kept moving towards the the front. I leaned to whisper in the cameraman's ear.

"Make sure you put a copy of this tape in my hand, please," I pleaded. He gave me a thumbs up sign. As more people could see her, heads began to turn and people started mumbling. Father Potter looked up from his book. Before he could speak, the woman spoke.

"Brock you can't do this! What about me? What about us?" she asked. Brock looked like he had died.

"I'm pregnant, and you are trying to marry someone else? We're still married! What about those vows?!" she yelled.

"I can't do this now! I've moved on, can't you see that?! I told you that was just fun. I can't do this now!" he yelled. "You were a mistake that I made when I was a kid!" he continued.

"Was last night a mistake? Or last week? A month ago? Two years ago? Come on Brock, I'm pregnant with your child, when are you going to be a man?" the woman said. I didn't think it was possible for Brock to get any paler, but apparently it was, because he had done just that. "You don't need a new family, you've already got one. Brittany, Bryan, me and the baby, we all need a daddy. We all need you," she said.

"Kymera now is neither the time nor the place! I'm in the middle of trying to get married!" he said, grasping for some degree of control. My mother was having none of it.

"Brock, what's going on?" she asked.

"I'm sorry, baby, I can explain everything," he said. If anything, my mother was strong.

"You know what, don't bother." She took the microphone from Father Potter.

"Ladies and gentlemen, I want to thank you all for coming out today. As you can see, there isn't going to be a wedding, or a marriage, well at least not a marriage that I have any part of today. God bless you all, and have a good day," she said angrily.

"Jessica, wait! What about us, what about Samantha? I love you both! You can't deny me that!" he pleaded.

"Samantha's not your child. You are free to go," she said coldly. At this point, Samantha and I had made our way up one of the side aisles back to the front of the church.

"You're just saying that. If I'm not the father than who is?" he asked. I wasn't sure if it was just a matter of pride, or if he really just wanted to know. My mother reached down, and took Father Potter's hand.

"Both of my children have the same father," she said quietly. There was a collective gasp. I didn't know what to say. This was all news to me. Father Potter was actually my father? I Brock was visibly hurt, but I could see his masculine pride about to take over.

"Well, then I guess that's that." He walked calmly from the pulpit to where Kymera was standing, and took her hand, and together they walked out the back door.

"Thank everyone for coming out today—"

"Can we still have some cake?!" a child's voice asked from the back of the room.

"Yes Jonathan, you may have some cake. It's in the dining hall everyone, go ahead and partake," Father Potter directed. He needed to keep attention off of the bombshell that both he and my mother had just dropped on the congregation. He and my mother were talking inaudibly and most likely privately. I figured I'd come back to that issue. There wasn't going to be a neat fix for that. I had way too many questions to ask, and right now, they had a lot of questions to answer on their own. Plus I saw Bianca slipping out of the side door. I ran after her. I caught up to her just outside the door.

"Bianca! Wait!" I yelled. She stopped where she was standing. I felt vindicated by everything that had just transpired in front of me. Even if I hadn't proved my total innocence, I was at least off the hook for Kymera's pregnancy.

"How do you feel? Father Potter's your dad!" she said. I had to admit that it did make me feel good, but, it really just opened a slew of other boxes that wasn't really ready to deal with, but I knew in time I'd be able to handle it.

"I don't know, but that's not the most important thing right now. How do you feel?" I asked.

"To be honest, I don't really know. I'm pretty confused, Kymera is a trip, and I don't really know what to think any more," she said. We were walking towards my classroom, and Malachi's words slammed into the side of my head. I tried to disregard them in order to maintain the conversation.

"Well Bianca, I'm not confused. I still love you, I still want to marry you, and I hope that we can get past all of this. I'm not expecting a free pass; I should have tried harder to get away from all of this, but even so, I didn't so I understand why you might be mad at me. But baby, with all that said, I still want you, not Kymera, not Aminah, no one but you," I said. She smiled at me and gave me a hug.

"I love you, too, Jayson, but I until I know what happened that night. I'm not going to lie to you. It's going to be extremely tough," she answered. I was trying to pay attention, but I couldn't shake Malachi's words. We had walked to the door of my classroom, the exact spot where I had seen Bianca for the first time.

"This is the place where my life changed forever," I said, pointing to the spot where she was standing. Bianca playfully moved just to the left of the spot that I had pointed at.

"Are you sure it wasn't right here?" she asked. I laughed. I looked around the room. A shaft of light from the window was shining on the lockers. All of a sudden Malachi's words made all the sense in the world. I walked over to my desk, and took out my list of all the combinations, and then walked over to Bryan's locker. Turning the dial apprehenisively, I eventually got the lock to open. I eagerly removed the barrier, and opened the door. Sure enough, Bryan's safe was sitting right there.

"Safest place in the world," I muttered softly. I took it out and looked at it. There was a numerical key pad on it. Now I had to remember what Bryan had told me. Of course, I was drawing a total blank. Bianca looked at me quizzically.

"Jayson what in the world are you doing?" she asked.

"I'm trying to prove to you that you should marry me," I answered. She nodded approvingly.

"I don't know how you're going to do that, but good luck," she said. What was the combination?! I tried to think of all the games Bryan and I had played, all the codes that it might be. Birthdays? Phone numbers? My license plate? I couldn't think of what it could be. Then Bianca went and looked at my desk calendar.

"Aww, you have the anniversary of our first date circled! Do you remember where we went?" she asked me interrogatively.

"Of course, we went to Casa D' Lorenzo," I answered. I put the safe on the floor and tried to remember the bill from when Bryan and I had gone to Casa D'Lorenzo. Every numerical combination except the correct one showed itself to me. It was beyond frustrating. What was that code? Bianca was going through the pile of receipts on my desk. She had gotten near the bottom when I heard the rustling papers stop.

"Jayson, this is the nonsense I'm talking about! Who did you take to OUR restaurant and spend fifty dollars on!" she asked furiously. I got up off the floor and walked over to the desk to see what she was talking about. I looked at the piece of paper.

"Babe, this is from almost a year ago, and to answer your question I've only taken two people there—you and Bryan," I answered.

Then I looked at the receipt. It was dated a full week earlier than the circled date on my calendar. This was the receipt that I needed! I looked down at the total, and it all came back to me. I walked back over to the safe and pushed the numbers. The tiny door popped open. Inside I found two uncashed paychecks, and a small video camera. It looked familiar, but I wasn't sure why it looked familiar. I turned it on and pressed play. Much to my horror, the image of my drugged body audibly refusing Kymera's advances, but unable to fight them off appeared on the screen. I had seen enough right there. I snapped the camera off. I didn't want to watch it just yet. As embarrassing as it was, I had my proof. I didn't want to watch it just yet. It wasn't the right time; it was just good enough to have it in my possession. Beneath all of that, I found the pink and lavender tie that I had let Bryan use the first time that he came to work with me. It was still tied in a perfect Half Windsor knot. I smiled.

"Bianca, can you come here for a second?" I asked as I reached in my pocket for the ring. She came around the desk.

"What is it baby?" she asked. I looked back down at the tie, and smiled. Every thing was going to be alright. It had to be.

Printed in the United States
107641LV00003B/229-231/A

9 781424 197347